The Vatican Target

The Vatican Target

by
BARRY SCHIFF and
HAL FISHMAN

St. Martin's Press · New York

Library of Congress Cataloging in Publication Data

Schiff, Barry J
  The Vatican target.

  I. Fishman, Hal, joint author. II. Title.
PZ4.S3293Vat [PS3569.C486]   813'.5'4
ISBN 0-312-83801-8   78-21421

This book is dedicated to those whose lives have been touched by the threat and reality of international terrorism and to those who have fought this scourge with courageous devotion and ingenuity.

The
Vatican
Target

prologue

The London air traffic controller yawned. It was an expansive, luxurious yawn. He had time to linger over it. He blinked at the clock above the bank of radar scopes. Two more hours of duty, then he was off for three days. He yawned again. The irritating thing was, he was so bloody sleepy now that by the time he signed off, went outside, got his Austin Mini out of the carpark and drove all the way to Ealing, he'd be wide awake. It had happened to him time and time again. In his studied opinion, late shifts were a ruddy bind. He wished there were a few more aircraft to worry about. A bit of traffic would wake him up, delay the sleepiness until he could make use of it.

And these lulls could be deceiving. All too often they were followed by periods of frantic activity with hardly a second to think about anything else.

How would he spend his three days off? He reviewed the possibilities: cricket at Lord's, watching the Aussies; or a spin up to Cambridge to see Fran's mother? A pleasant outing, taking a spin up to Cambridge—it was only having to see Fran's mother that could put a damper on things—

At that moment, the radar screen shocked him back to reality.

Trans American Flight 901's transponder was squawking hijack code 7500.

Christ Almighty! His heart bounded. He cleared his throat, all thoughts of the touring Australian cricket team and Cambridge vanishing in an instant.

"Hullo, Trans Am 901, this is London Radar. We observe your squawk on radar. Is this an intentional transmission? Over."

At once, a voice from thirty-five thousand feet responded.

"Affirmative! We are being hijacked. Armed men are in the cockpit and in the cabin. I repeat: we are being hijacked."

But if the London radar controller could have looked into the flight deck of the Trans Am Boeing 747, he would have been most puzzled.

The only occupants of the cockpit were the two pilots and the flight engineer.

No hijackers, armed or unarmed, could be seen.

chapter 1

The truck squealed to a stop half a mile from the border.

Within its canvas-covered body, there were twenty men, all heavily armed. They took their weapons and jumped out, their rubber spiked boots pounding noiselessly on the road. The men knew what to do; they had practiced for this moment. Ten of them took up positions on the east side of the road, a similar number on the west side. They moved forward. They were young; they moved easily and eagerly, their eyes bright with anticipation.

On their shoulders they carried M58P semiautomatic assault rifles manufactured in Prague, Czechoslovakia, during August and September 1975. The weapons had been shipped aboard the Russian freighter *Volga* that sailed from Leningrad, calling briefly at Beirut before continuing to its destination, Athens.

Each man carried two hundred rounds of 7.62-mm ammunition in pouches clipped to British army webbing belts.

A chilly wind had sprung up, but the men were scarcely aware of it. Their minds, their whole beings, were concentrated upon their goal. Nothing else mattered. They knew they faced dangers, but they accepted them without question. Danger was the price; a man's life mattered little.

They marched in silence for twelve minutes, then they halted. The leader of each platoon spoke briefly. This was the moment. The men nodded, their lips tight.

Now they left the road and made their way across the sand. It was harder work than marching on the road; their boots kept sinking into the shifting sand and had to be pulled free. In spite of the chill, sweat soon darkened shirts and dotted brows.

At last they were close to their objective. They crouched and

1

tugged hand grenades from their belts, nervously fingering the pins, peering ahead into the hostile darkness.

The squad leaders gestured, pointing, emphasizing, cautioning. More nods. Everyone understood what had to be done. Deep breaths of the crisp night air were taken; more than one young man suddenly, and for the first time, observed how fresh and how sweet it was. The luminous hand of a Rolex watch ticked around to the vertical.

The leader raised his arm.

Now!

They sprang to their feet, their hands yanking at grenade pins. It was splendidly executed, precisely as they had practiced it so many times in the Libyan desert. But before the grenades could be thrown, the defenders' guns blazed. Intense, accurate, the 9-mm Uzi submachine gunfire raked the dunes, bullets ripping through sand and flesh. A boy of nineteen was sliced almost in half. Horrified, he saw his intestines writhing out of him like steaming snakes. He started to cry for his mother, but the words were never uttered; his eyes misted and life dissolved within him. Another man was hit as he drew back his arm to hurl the grenade. He fell on the weapon. His wound was minor: a clean hole in the flesh of the left shoulder. But he wasn't able to wriggle free of the grenade. Nestled against his rib cage, it exploded. He felt the collapse of his chest and the cold night air flooding inside. He had time to see his blood splashing into the sand. As he died, he realized that the arm lying six feet away was his.

They attempted to advance and press home the attack, as planned. But the fire was murderous. Wave after wave of bullets came screaming through the night, inches above the sand. It was all a man could do to stay alive a few moments at a time. Damn them! They must have known exactly when and where the attack was to occur.

A squad leader was hit in the center of the forehead. His head snapped back, then forward again as if on a hinge. His body twitched and was still.

On the left, half a dozen of the foolhardy youngsters pushed forward, ignoring the fire. The orders were to advance, and that was precisely what they intended to do, no matter what the cost.

Two fell before they had advanced a yard. Another was cut down an instant later. Then another. The two survivors hurled themselves upon the sand, burrowing to create some sort of cover.

They had no hope of survival. They were dead men. So be it. All that mattered was to destroy the enemy. To kill. To maim. To make their mark. Breathlessly they snapped out a word or two. Go! Now!

One man yelled as he flung himself at the enemy. A kind of exaltation filled him, because every problem had been solved; his existence upon earth had focused upon this moment. He was free. He no longer knew fear or hope. Only these few remaining instants had significance. There was a splendid simplicity about it. He knew a kind of happiness, a kind of pleasure in defying the inevitable. At any fraction of an instant he might be brought down by a fatal bullet. But while life still propelled his body, he would continue. Bounding across the sand. Firing at them. He knew he had been hit. But there was no pain. It was as if the bullets had struck only the mechanical part of him; the essence of him was untouched.

He reached the enemy. He saw their faces. Young, unlined. Faces like his.

He saw a man kill him.

A stocky fellow with curly hair. No cap. Open neck. White, even teeth, clenched as he took steady, careful aim.

All that had ever mattered in all the history of man was to reach that gun.

He almost touched it.

Then the world became a kaleidoscope of color: a final explosion of the senses, a magnificent finale. . . .

"Schmuck," sniffed one of the Israeli soldiers as he turned the body with a contemptuous boot.

* * *

The meeting took place late the following afternoon. The location was a house in a small Lebanese town some forty kilometers east of Beirut on the Muristan Road, Zahlah by name.

From the road, the house looked innocent enough; in truth, it was a fortress. Guards sat behind the windows, patiently, tirelessly scanning the sunbaked terrain outside. They were ready to repel any surprise attack; they would, without question, die to protect the individuals who occupied the house: the senior members of Black September.

On the second floor, in a handsomely furnished conference room replete with teak paneling and modern lithographs, a dozen men sat at a long, highly polished table. A few wore traditional Arab clothing, the rest favored Western apparel. At the head of the table sat a man wearing a double-breasted suit of conservative cut, a white shirt and plain tie. Of middle age, he had spent much of his adult life fighting Israel. In the early days of the PLO he had battled alongside Ahmed Shukairi; in recent years, however, he had become disillusioned with what he considered the conciliatory attitudes of Arafat and his colleagues; the move to Black September had become inevitable.

Anger and impatience were evident in the set of the man's mouth and brows. He spoke in the high-pitched tone of the Palestinian Arab.

"Eleven men dead out of twenty; six wounded, two critically. The God-damned Israelis were sitting there, waiting for them. A massacre. And what, may I ask, did it achieve?" He regarded the somber, thoughtful faces around the table. No one answered. "Was a single casualty inflicted on the enemy? Was anything accomplished other than to reinforce the Jews' belief in their innate superiority?"

"But Arafat believes that border raids serve a useful purpose. . . ."

"He is a fool! He delivers stupid, meaningless pinpricks when crushing, smashing blows are what is needed! Our young men empty their life blood into the sand and for nothing!" He thumped the table with a fist; the veins stood out on his neck. "Gentlemen, we are at a crossroads. Border raids, occasional bombings, attacking tourists . . . they achieve nothing. The time has come for productive and decisive action. Let us review the situation. Israel has rapidly expanded its settlements in the captured territories. If we don't get them out pretty damn soon, we may never get them out; will have lost the battle for all time. The Israeli government has even claimed that they oppose this colonization of the occupied lands. Obviously they lie! Nevertheless, there are powerful forces we can exploit. Virtually the entire world is calling for withdrawal by Israel to the 1967 boundaries. And don't forget, both the United States and the Soviet Union are pressuring Israel to get out of *our* land."

"With little success," someone observed wearily.

"I agree. But consider the delicacy of the situation at the present time. I have concluded that, with the right action, we can tip the balance in our favor and force the Israelis out of the West Bank! Overnight!"

"And how," inquired a heavyset man, "do you propose to perform this miracle?"

The man at the head of the table reached out as if to grasp the air with both hands. "By taking the world," he said. "And shaking it so fiercely that it *must* pay attention!" He regarded the skeptical faces about him. "Let us be realistic. The deaths of a few Olympic athletes and airline passengers has had limited impact upon the world in general. In Paris and New York they read the news over breakfast and say what a shame it all is. But the next day it's all forgotten; the press makes sure of that. So I declare to you that we must approach the problem with a totally different perspective. Ask yourself, Does the world really care about the Palestinian problem? Does it actually matter to the individual man in the street?"

"Only if that man is an Arab or a Jew."

"Correct! That is precisely the point. To the others, the vast majority, life has problems enough. Taxes, wives, jobs, the price of gasoline, of coffee, of scotch. Why should the average man care? The happenings in the Middle East do not involve him directly. The mission, therefore, is to guarantee that he *is* involved and then he will assist us in our fight."

"How?"

"By means of a kidnapping . . . a kidnapping with a ransom: the withdrawal of Israel from the West Bank."

Now the expressions had turned to disappointment. They

had hoped for something better.

"The Israelis wouldn't withdraw from the West Bank if we kidnapped their own prime minister and half their parliament."

"Very true."

"So . . . ?"

"But I believe they would be forced to withdraw if we kidnapped one extraordinary individual and declared that his survival depends entirely on the Jews' compliance with our demands."

"Who do you have in mind," another quipped sarcastically, "the Queen of England?"

"No, I am talking about someone who, if he were harmed because of Israel's intransigence, would inflame world opinion against Israel. Indeed, every shred of support for Israel throughout the world would vanish immediately. At the very least, we would compel the world to pay attention to our people. Gentlemen, I am talking about the man who heads the world's largest multinational organization, an organization that cuts across state boundaries and political ideologies like no other, an organization that has hundreds of millions of members, countless billions of dollars. That organization, gentlemen, is the Catholic Church! And the man I am talking about is the Pope!"

For a moment, no one spoke, no one moved. It was as if the sheer audacity of the notion had stunned everyone at the table.

Then the burly man shook his head. "Impossible! How could we ever get near him? Request an audience?"

"But if it were possible," murmured another, "think of the consequences."

"Exactly," said the man at the head of the table. "We must employ extreme measures to make the world aware of the wrongs that have been done to our people. And I submit to you that our goals will be achieved because not only Catholics but most people in every country will care far more about the safety of the Pope than about Israel and the West Bank of the Jordan. Surely you must see the point. An enormous amount of pressure will be placed upon Israel by the very countries that have been her staunchest allies. I'm referring specifically to the European countries and, of course, America. In the United States alone, my friends, there are some *fifty million* Catholics—but less than four million Jews. In the world as a whole there are more than half a *billion* Catholics, most of them utterly devoted to the Pope. Intriguing figures, are they not?"

"Intriguing, yes," said the burly man. "But valueless. The matter is academic, for the simple reason that we could never kidnap the Pope. It is an impossibility. . . ."

"Don't be so sure. Our intelligence people inform me that the Pope intends to travel to San Francisco in two months' time to attend the World Conference on Population."

"He will travel by air?"

"Undoubtedly."

"So you propose that we hijack the aircraft?"

"Precisely."

"Out of the question. Security would be fantastically tight."

"Nevertheless, I believe it can be accomplished. You may recall when Pope Paul the Sixth flew to New York in 1965 to speak before the United Nations General Assembly. Possibly you believe he traveled aboard a private aircraft. No. The fact is, he and his party flew on Alitalia Airlines. His party occupied the entire first-class section—an arrangement that was, I suppose, considered suitably modest by the Vatican. The return trip was on TWA. In any event, I understand that a similar plan is likely to be followed for this visit. This time, I believe, Trans American Airlines will be chosen, since they fly regularly between Rome and San Francisco. . . ."

chapter 2

THE VATICAN

Against the potential pros had to be weighed the possible cons. Endless conferences considered the likely and unlikely implications; countless questions were asked; consideration was given to every point of view, every deliberation, every statement. It was, after all, an intercontinental journey by an individual who was far more than a mere head of state; this man was truly a world leader. Prime ministers, secretaries of state, presidents and vice-presidents offered their advice. In the end it was agreed: the Pope's journey would take place.

Subordinates set to work on the details.

* * *

To Warren J. Baumgarten, Manager of Special Projects for Trans American Airlines, fell the task of coordinating all aspects of the journey from the instant the papal party stepped aboard the Trans Am boarding stairs in Rome to the moment they deplaned in San Francisco. It was a formidable assignment, but Baumgarten was equal to it. He cleared his desk of all other tasks. This was to be full time. He flew to Rome, to Washington, to New York, to San Francisco, checking, rechecking, consulting, arranging, arguing, demanding. Within days his files had become gargantuan, crammed with letters, reports, telegrams, notes, photographs, sketches. An earnest, meticulous individual who favored gray flannel suits and oxford cloth button-down shirts, Baumgarten regarded each and every detail of the trip with an eye toward catastrophe. He spent uncounted hours considering all the things that could conceivably go wrong; he developed plans of action to deal with every contingency from the jamming of a lavatory door to the possibility of a summer snowstorm's closing Rome's Fiumicino Airport.

He consulted a New York interior designer, a tall man with flowing silver hair, a velvet vest and lengthy fingernails, who roamed the interior of a Trans Am 747, muttering to himself and making sketches on the backs of envelopes. Baumgarten explained that the papal party would take over the entire first-class section; it was most important that the area be separated physically from the rest of the airplane. No requests for private audiences or autographs could be permitted to interfere with the comfort and tranquillity of the Pontiff and his council fathers, cardinals, and others in the party. Nodding, muttering; more sketches on more envelopes. Screens and curtains, rich yet simple, were the answer, the designer announced, looking up as if the inspiration had emanated from above; he saw a system of silken ties to create "*just* the right sort of ecclesiastical integrity" without the necessity of major renovations to the interior of the aircraft. "It will be a veritable masterpiece," he assured Baumgarten with a modest sigh: "superbly effective yet magnificently understated."

He was back within a week with detailed drawings, which had to be approved by the airline, the Vatican and the State Department. Within the first-class section the Pope was to have a private apartment on the right-hand side of the airplane, complete with a queen-size bed. The rest of the section would consist of standard seating for members of the party, the Pope's physician and security agents. Pale blue carpeting would cover the floor; an eggshell white fabric would grace the papal bed with a gold *fleur-de-lis* in the center. (The Vatican had already advised that the Pontiff was fond of color but not an overabundance of decoration.) Blue drapes would hang from the aircraft's sidewalls. "The overall effect," declared the designer, "will be one of serenity, conducive to the most profound contemplation."

Then there was the selection of a captain for the flight. The simplest course would have been to use the flight crew who would be assigned the flight in the normal course of events. But was there a Trans Am captain who had the seniority and also happened to be deeply involved in Catholic matters? If so, it seemed only fair to let such a man have the opportunity of piloting the Pope on his long journey. Baumgarten talked to the director of flight operations. The answer was Walter Ives. He seemed perfect. A twenty-five-thousand-hour man who had been with Trans Am since 1945, a 747 captain since 1973. His crew would be Clifford Jensen, first officer, and Joe Nowakoski, flight engineer. Records provided the names of stewardesses who were fluent in Italian. Fortunately most of them were also Catholics, according to Personnel—although federal law did not permit such personal data to be included in the records.

The aircraft that would make the trip was a Boeing 747SP, a long-range version of the familiar jumbo jet, ideally suited to the 6,461-mile trip from Fiumicino to San Francisco International Airport. The airplane was six months old. Coincidentally, immediately prior to the Pope's trip it underwent a routine periodic inspection. In New York, a team of decorators transformed the first-class section under the personal supervision of Warren Baumgarten, accompanied by the interior designer and a representative from the Vatican, a serious, slightly plump young man in a black suit and white shirt. In the evening, the aircraft flew to Rome on a regularly scheduled flight carrying a normal complement of passengers in coach but none in first class. It touched down in Rome at 8:21 A.M. local time.

The Pope would leave at 3:00 P.M.

For the first time in weeks, Warren Baumgarten began to relax. His job was essentially done. Now it was simply a matter of the principal players' coming on stage to do their thing.

While the aircraft was parked on the ramp at Fiumicino, he examined it once more. He *was* the Pope, and he was seeing it all for the first time. He was impressed. Clearly an individual of perspicacity and exquisite taste had done all this. Everything had been thought of—and had been executed with skill, efficiency and taste. Warren Baumgarten pronounced himself satisfied. He had completed his assignment; he could do no more. He went to relax in his hotel, leaving strict instructions that he was to be alerted in good time for the Pope's arrival. Everything, he felt sure, would now proceed as smoothly as clockwork. He ordered a double martini, extra dry.

* * *

Dave wanted to come in. For a nightcap.

"It's after two," Jane said. Nice touch of firmness.

"The night's young," he said, undeterred.

She told him it had been a fun evening. "But I'm beat."

A nightcap would perk her up, according to Dave.

"Thanks," she said, "but I don't think so."

"Why not?"

"I told you."

The charm machine was thrust into high gear.

"Yeah, but listen, we've had such a great time together tonight; we can't let it end just like *that*."

"You mean," she said, "without your trying to get me into the sack."

"I wouldn't have put it quite so bluntly."

"But you'd have meant the same thing."

"All I asked for was a nightcap. Remember?" Twisted smile—the one he probably rated as irresistible.

"I'm sorry, Dave. There's nothing in the house to drink."

"I'll be happy with a glass of water and an aspirin. That's not asking too much, is it?"

The old keep-'em-talking-by-asking-questions routine. It was all too familiar, and predictable, like a salesman's pitch. She shook her head as if to convince herself that she meant what she was saying. Some other time. Thanks again. It was fun.

"But not a *ball*," he muttered regretfully. He said he would call her later.

"Great," she said. She heard him sigh, irritated and frustrated. Clearly she had spoiled his whole night. Dave was constitutionally incapable of taking a rejection graciously. She thought briefly of telling him that he reminded her too much of Frank. Too glib, too good-looking—and far too conscious of his ability to charm the pants off the opposite sex.

But she spared him that. He spun on his heel and headed for

his Corvette. She closed the front door and stood beside it until she heard him drive away, leaving a trail of screaming rubber half a block long. Later in bed, Jane ruminated sadly that she seemed to be condemned to spend her life attracting men like Frank and Dave. A depressing thought. The Franks and Daves of this world were sexual carpetbaggers. Takers, never givers. It was wrong, she decided, to let anyone get married until that person had demonstrated the capability of comprehending the great truth that living with someone involved one hell of a lot more than rolling around in bed. They should teach the fact in schools, she declared to herself.

"Choosing a mate is unquestionably one of life's most important decisions; why don't the schools provide some advice on the subject?"

She smiled. She had actually asked the question aloud. Already she was talking to herself. First sign, it was said. YOUNG DIVORCÉE BECOMES NUT CASE. . . .

Damn it to hell, it would have been good—*good*—to have talked this all out with her mother. . . .

No! She clenched her fist. She wouldn't think about it. She refused to become maudlin and give in to depression. It had to be fought at all times. It achieved nothing but to salt the wound.

* * *

In the heart of Rome, on the Via dei Fori Imperiali, a printer's assistant by the name of Camenzulli and his wife were arguing heatedly on the sidewalk. Their disagreement concerned Signor Camenzulli's point-blank refusal to travel to Milan to attend the wedding of Signora Camenzulli's cousin, Marcia. Signor Camenzulli pointed out that he didn't know the girl, had never met her and, God willing, never would. Furthermore, his wife hadn't seen her since the two of them were toddlers, when they had done nothing but spit at one another. Thus, if they were to collide on the sidewalk at this moment, neither would recognize the other. For these excellent reasons, Signor Camenzulli could not under any circumstances justify the not-inconsiderable expense of the trip to Milan to attend this perfect stranger's nuptials. The argument seemed unassailable to him. He was therefore astonished when, quite without warning, his wife slapped his face. Hard. Angered, Camenzulli reached out to grab her. But she darted to one side. And in so doing, she stumbled straight into a well-dressed man of middle years. Caught off balance, the man fell awkwardly against the pavement. There was a loud and thoroughly nasty cracking sound.

Camenzulli ran to the man's aid.

"Are you all right, signor? My most profound apologies for the inexcusable stupidity of my cow of a wife. . . ."

To his surprise the man answered in what sounded like English. Camenzulli knew only a few words, but he was able to gather that the man's arm seemed to have been badly hurt.

"My name is Ives," the man said. "I must get in touch with Trans American Airlines. . . ."

* * *

Steven Mallory had spent most of the morning on a bench in Hyde Park. It had been a pleasant morning: a few hours to reflect and ponder, to let the mind go exploring. He kept telling himself he should be moving, but he remained where he was. The time had to be savored. Precious time. Obedient to the laws of supply and demand, it became more valuable the less you had left. What, he wondered, would he be doing this time next year? Sitting on another bench in another park? For "park," he thought, read "pasture." He swore softly. He didn't want to retire, damn it.

He looked younger than the age he resented so bitterly. He was obviously an individual who had made it his business to keep fit. His features were firm, his eyes steady. Tall and lean, he still earned approving glances from women of all ages.

A man in a tweed hacking jacket sat beside him: a spry old fellow in his seventies, by the look of him. A few words were exchanged concerning the fineness of the weather. The man said that Mallory sounded like an American name; Mallory nodded, whereupon the old guy got to his feet and strode away towards Marble Arch. Mallory watched him go. Didn't he like Americans? Perhaps it was just his abrupt English way; he had nothing more to say, therefore he said nothing more. Sensible, when you thought about it. The world was groggy with words; most of them had ceased to have any real meaning. . . .

He smiled to himself. How philosophical he was becoming in his old age.

Old age. End of smile. Incredible—and not very pleasant—to think that he would soon be sixty years old. Somewhere, somehow, the accounting must have gone wrong; surely there was no way that he had actually been alive six decades, less a few priceless months. Again and again he had told himself that he didn't feel sixty; then he had asked himself how you felt sixty. He still had his hair, or most of it, and his body was relatively trim. But the rule-makers had decreed that he would become an ancient at sixty, no longer capable of flying airliners. . . .

He was becoming stiff; he had sat on the bench too long. He realized with a shock that more than an hour had passed since the visit by the old fellow in the hacking jacket. Past lunch time. Didn't he have sense enough to know when it was time to eat? He could almost hear Nan and her all-men-are-dumb-animals voice, accompanied by a wagging forefinger. Odd—and a little frightening—how difficult it had become to conjure up a mental picture of her face. Why? For God's sake, he knew her face better than he knew his own. Yet somehow the details had become elusive. He had to rely on photographs. But they only captured instants, fragments of time, mere billionths of the whole.

He ambled across the grass. On the way along Park Lane he bought an early-edition *Standard*. With a bit of luck there might be something in the entertainment section that interested him, a movie or a play—although he doubted it. Were they intentionally making dull movies and plays, or was he simply becoming dated? Was it all part of being damned-near sixty?

He stopped at the Kensington Hilton desk for his key. There was a message for him. Would he call Mr. Potter. "Urgent," said the message. Messages from Potter were always urgent. The Trans Am station manager in London had a fine sense of his own importance in the workings of the world. Mallory went up to his room, took off his shoes and jacket and loosened his tie before placing the call.

Potter seemed relieved to hear from him. Something thoroughly unforeseen had happened, a problem of the most urgent nature. Captain Mallory would have to take the Rome-to-San Francisco flight this afternoon instead of the London-to-Bahrain flight this evening. There was just enough time for him to get the British Airways flight to Rome. Mallory asked the reason for this sudden crew change. Captain Ives had had an accident, Potter advised breathlessly. A broken arm. He would be out of action for weeks. A replacement captain had to be found before the flight was delayed any further.

"I need hardly tell you," said Potter, "how important it is for the flight to leave as close to the scheduled time as possible."

Mallory nodded, realizing what Potter meant. "Jesus, it was the Pope's flight." *Jesus?* He shook his head and chided himself for selecting that particular expletive. . . .

*   *   *

Thirty-five minutes after Mallory hung up, a telephone rang in a motel room in California, on the outskirts of San Francisco. The sound startled the occupant of the room, a dark-haired young man of powerful build. He had been lying quietly, attempting to coax his body into relaxing. But he was tense, his muscles like tightly wound springs. As he reached for the phone he saw that his hand trembled slightly. He clenched his fist, then released it.

"Yes?"

"Change of plan."

He recognized the voice.

"What?"

"Ives is out. Injured in some stupid accident."

"Out. . . ?"

"Yes, a man named Mallory has replaced him. His address is 203 Welland Way, Walnut Creek. Write it down. Are you doing so?"

"Yes, I've got it. . . ."

"There'll be a departure delay. I don't know how long. I'll advise you. So forget about Ives. He's no longer of any interest to us. Mallory replaces him. Have you got the address? 203 Welland Way, Walnut Creek."

"Yes, yes, I have it; I told you I have it."

"Good."

The line went dead.

The owner of the motel had been listening in; he frequently did when business was slow; there was no telling when an ear in on the right conversation might prove to be very profitable indeed. But the conversation just heard had meant nothing to him; it had been carried on in a language that was completely incomprehensible. The only words that made any sense were Welland Way and Walnut Creek. Frustrating. Still, you win some, you lose some. Thank God the next call was in English. Of a sort. Very precise. Kind of educated, you'd say. Outgoing call, from Number Twelve. This time the guy called Information, wanting to know the number of the party in Walnut Creek. Mallory was the name. Neat place, Walnut Creek, although property prices were daylight robbery there. . . .

Moments later, the same correct-but-accented voice called the number in Walnut Creek.

A woman answered. She sounded sleepy, as if the phone had awakened her.

"Is Captain Mallory there?"

"No. Sorry. He's away until Thursday, sometime in the evening, I think."

Despite the sleepiness in her voice, she spoke well, sounding the ends of her words. The motel man liked people with respect for the language.

"Is this Captain Mallory's wife speaking?"

"No. She's . . . deceased. This is his daughter. Who's calling?"

"A friend. I'll call later. Goodbye."

"I can have him return your—"

But Number Twelve had already hung up. Almost rude. But with foreigners what could you expect? Different folks, different strokes, the motel man reflected; was there ever a truer saying . . . ?

*   *   *

Jane yawned. Damn people who called before eight o'clock in the morning. She thought about going back to bed, then decided against it. She was up now; she might as well stay up. She went into the kitchen and made a bowl of hot oatmeal and instant coffee. The radio offered only acid rock, country-and-western and sticky-sweet Mantovani. Nothing in between. The man on the all-news station talked about a fire in Chicago and the Pope's planned visit to San Francisco. She turned the radio off, listened to the gastric-sounding rumblings of the fridge, wondered if it was about to conk out, then turned the radio back to Mantovani.

The weather was dull. Heavy, sullen-looking clouds hung low in the sky. "A collection of crud" her father might say to describe the day. Like all airmen, he was always looking at the weather, predicting, complaining, talking about fronts and cumulonimbus clouds, squall lines and coastal fog. When she was a little girl, he had been equal only to God. He knew everything; he was handsome and had been a bomber pilot in the war and then flew sleek Constellations for Trans Am. But in a few brief years she discovered that he knew absolutely nothing about the *real* things, the things that *mattered*. Now the pendulum had swung back again. He *was* wise. And wonderful. A graying rock of Gibralter. She missed him; thank God he'd be home again in a few days and would stay for more than a week. It wasn't that she spent such a lot of time with him when he was home; but his was a marvelous presence to have around the place. Would he marry again? It was possible; you had to be realistic about it. He was an attractive man. Did he pursue women when he was away? She wondered. Stewardesses? Female passengers? Or did he patronize prostitutes and massage parlors?

Mind your own business, she told herself. You have a nasty mind. And it's prying into affairs that are none of your business.

It is my business, she replied to herself, if he marries again. I'll have a new mother.

She breathed deeply. No; she wouldn't think about it. And the only way not to think about it was to get up from the breakfast table and get busy.

She showered and dressed. As she was putting the breakfast

things away, she heard the truck in the driveway. Through the kitchen window she saw it pull up in front of the garage. Toby barked.

A Sears truck.

She wasn't expecting anything from Sears. No doubt they had the wrong house. On this street half the house numbers were invisible from the road; delivery men were always getting things screwed up.

Automatically she glanced in the kitchen mirror before going to answer the door. A touch at her short dark hair, a quick check of lips. Her gingham shirt was decently buttoned up.

The driver was a swarthy fellow with a small scar on his chin.

"203 Welland Way? Mallory?"

"That's right. . . ."

"We have a filing cabinet for you."

"A what? There must be some mistake. . . ."

"Filing cabinet. Ordered by. . ." He consulted his clipboard, ". . .an S. Mallory."

He had an accent. Mexican?

"S. Mallory is my father." She shrugged. "Okay, I guess it's all right. He didn't tell me anything about it."

"It's been back-ordered," said the man, as if that explained it all.

"I see."

"Would you please hold the screen door while we bring it in?"

A second man was at the rear of the truck.

"All right," Jane told him. "You'd better carry it into his study. Down there," she added, indicating the stairs at the end of the hall.

As the two men brought in the long carton, she likened it to a coffin.

Toby came bounding around the house from the back yard. She told him to cool it. An obedient creature, he promptly sat down beside her and panted at the unfamiliar men, his long tongue flopping out of the side of his mouth.

"I think we'll just put it down here for a moment," said the first man when they were in the entrance hall.

"Here?" The first twinge of alarm.

It happened so incredibly rapidly. They dropped the box and kicked the door shut.

Toby sprang to his feet, growling, baring his teeth.

One of the men tugged a gun from a pocket. He fired. And blew most of Toby's head off. The white walls were suddenly splattered with red. Toby became an obscene mess that twitched and pumped blood on the tile floor.

The pistol made little noise: a kind of snapping pop; beebee gun sound. But it left the acrid smell of cordite hanging in the air.

An instant of disbelief. This couldn't be happening. It was impossible; it simply wasn't part of her life. . . .

Then fingers clamped on her arm. Fingers like steel strapping.

"No trouble. We don't want trouble. Understand?"

She stared. A scream rose in her throat. But it was never uttered. A hand covered her mouth and pushed her head back against the wall. The man with the scar on his chin was very close.

"Quiet," he said. "Just keep quiet and everything will be all right."

Now the man with the pistol went hurrying along the hall and disappeared down the stairs.

"Are you alone? Tell me the truth."

She nodded. It simply didn't occur to her to lie.

She kept staring at Toby's body. It was true. It had happened.

She felt the tears springing to her eyes. The man's face became blurred. Breathing, she could smell the flesh of his hand. She tried to wriggle free but it was impossible. His grip was unyielding. God, so this was what it was like. Mayhem. Violence. Murder. Behind her, a picture—one of her mother's Bartlett prints—fell off its hook. The glass shattered when it hit the floor.

The sound destroyed the last fragments of her control. Desperately, mindlessly, she struggled. She succeeded in freeing her mouth for an instant. Words and gasps came tumbling out. She attempted to fling herself toward the front door.

The man caught her and slapped her hard, pressed her head back against the wall.

"Don't be foolish! I mean it! We can kill you just as we killed the mutt. But it isn't necessary. Do you understand that? Do you?"

She felt herself nodding. But she could hardly see the man through her tears of terror.

"I haven't any money. . . ." she managed to sputter.

He ignored her. The other man returned and checked the ground-floor rooms. They exchanged some incomprehensible words.

"Get in."

He indicated the box that was supposed to have contained the filing cabinet. The lid had been taken off. It was empty; there was no filing cabinet. And it wasn't a carton but a wooden box, its bottom scattered with shavings and cuttings.

"In there?" Her voice squeaked. Her throat seemed to be contracting.

"Yes. Get in."

"Why? What for?"

The second man reached for her, a roll of wide adhesive tape in his hand. But she twisted to one side. His cap slipped off; he was almost bald. She tried to run. His hand caught her shoulder and slipped away. She skidded on the polished floor. Her left ankle buckled. She tumbled. Her hand fell on Toby's still-warm body.

Desperately she attempted to scramble to her feet. She got up onto one knee; then the fist slammed into her cheek. Something seemed to snap inside her head. For an instant it was no longer connected with the rest of her. Her vision dimmed. Her legs turned to rubber.

As she went over, she caught the pedestal that her mother had bought in Washington, D.C., a year before she died. Plant and pot clattered and broke on the floor.

"Bitch!"

She felt them grabbing her, dragging her.

They flipped her onto her back; her head banged on the tile. She opened her eyes. The tape was pressed tightly over her mouth. More adhesive was used to bind her wrists together.

The bald man was stooping over her, waving his pistol in her face.

"I'm not going to tell you again!" She blinked as his spittle hit her. "I don't want to have to kill you, but we will if you give us any more trouble. Got that? We mean it! Understand?"

Weirdly, he reminded her of the man at the bank who had tried to explain the penalty-for-early-withdrawal system. . . .

"Please . . . don't. . . ." The words were formed but never uttered, choked off by the adhesive gag.

One man took her feet, the other her shoulders.

The first man—the one with the scar on his chin—spoke in a quieter, less violent voice than his companion.

"We're going to put you in the box so that your neighbors won't notice. Understand? Now don't give us any trouble. If you make a fuss we'll have to shoot you. We don't want to, but we will if we have to. You're a good-looking broad, and we'd like you to stay that way. All right?"

It sounded almost reasonable. Pleas for mercy cascaded through her mind. She wanted to live. She would do anything as long as they would let her live.

They lifted her and placed her in the box. Her head thudded against the unyielding wood.

Scarface said, "Now we're going to put the lid on. Just for a minute, till we get back to the truck. When we get it inside, we'll take the lid back off again. I promise you."

And then the world was black. Panic—sheer, blind panic—raced along every nerve and muscle. She pushed against the lid, but it wouldn't budge.

"Christ . . . oh my God . . ." She could hear herself screaming within her head.

Her body seemed momentarily disconnected from herself: an inanimate lump that wobbled against the sides of the box as it was lifted. What if it was all lies about the lid being taken off inside the truck! What if they were deviates! What if they intended to rape her or bury her alive! If only she could scream . . . now. But she couldn't. It was all futile. Screaming would do no good anyway. If Mrs. Levinson or Marg Swann heard it, what would they do? What could they do? No . . . she had to believe the men . . . she had to do what they said. It was her only hope. They were ruthless; they meant business. Look what they did to poor Toby. Killed him in cold blood. But why? What was it all about. . . ?

Bang. The box was stationary again. A moment later there was the sound of an engine starting . . . and then movement.

Jesus, they'd forgotten about her! They'd promised to take the lid off when they got back to the truck! She'd suffocate! There was hardly any air in this tiny box. . . !

She banged her fists against the lid.

To her surprise, it opened at once.

"You don't have to do that. I told you we would open the box."

Scarface.

She lay still, looking at him, conscious of his eyes traveling the length of her body. She sat up. He peeled the tape from her mouth.

"But no screaming or it goes on again. Understand?"

He held on to a stanchion with one hand as the truck rounded a corner. He extended the other to her. She took it. He held her hand longer than was necessary as she got out of the box.

"Are you Mexican?"

He smiled and shook his head.

chapter 3

When Mallory landed at Fiumicino, Warren Baumgarten was waiting at the British Airways gate, pacing in a jerky, oddly mechanical way. His face was drawn with worry.

"Thank God you're here. . . . The flight's four hours late already!"

Mallory smiled to himself; there was always something vaguely satisfying about seeing management in a panic.

"I came on the first available flight."

"Of course you did, Captain. I wasn't suggesting otherwise; it's just that it was all so superbly arranged . . . *everything.*"

"Is Ives going to be all right?"

"Ives?" Baumgarten had to think for a moment. "Yes, yes, a broken arm, I understand. Fell down on the sidewalk. Can you believe it, I mean, can you believe that such a thing could happen on such a day? If it had been an ordinary flight, of course, there'd have been no chance of it; captains don't just fall down on sidewalks and break their arms in the normal course of goddam events!" He sounded resentful of the fate that had befallen him.

They made their way through the terminal.

"Is the Pope here yet?"

Baumgarten wiped his forehead and shook his head; a forlorn lock of hair fell in front of his left eye.

"No, not yet. I had to call the Vatican and explain what happened. Embarrassing as hell. . . . The whole *world* is watching!"

"How about the newspapers and television?"

"Bastards," said Baumgarten with feeling. "They're like locusts; and the PR guys can't handle them. It all falls back on me.

23

I tell you, I've had to look after *every* aspect of everything. We've released the news that the flight is being delayed for technical reasons; we haven't elaborated. And we're not going to," he added stoutly.

In the operations office, Mallory met his flight crew: First Officer Jensen and Flight Engineer Nowakoski. Familiar faces: Jensen, angular features, fair, an intense, serious man in his mid-thirties; Nowakoski, a few years younger, shorter, stocky, beefy face, humorous mouth. Mallory had flown with both men on several occasions, although he knew very little about either of them as individuals. Airline crew scheduling was like that. The teams changed constantly; you could go for years and never fly with a certain engineer or first officer; on the other hand, you might find yourself sitting beside the same man for months at a time.

The pilots exchanged the usual mandatory words. It was nice seeing one another. Wasn't it a shame about Ives. The weather looked pretty good.

"I'd appreciate it," announced Baumgarten, "if you gentlemen would join me in the briefing room in thirty minutes. I've asked the cabin crew to attend also. A little get-together. Important, on a trip like this, a few words, opportunities for questions; I want to be sure everyone has the same picture."

Executive double-talk, thought Mallory. The picture was a simple one: they were going to fly an airplane to San Francisco and on the way feed and take care of a few hundred passengers, including one very famous and important one. The trip itself was just another flight; only the bullshit quotient was different.

"Captain." Baumgarten touched Mallory's arm. "I wonder if you'd be good enough to come along with me for a moment. I'd like you to meet Mr. Cousins."

"Who's he?"

"Secret Service," Baumgarten replied, lowering his voice. "En route security."

Mallory nodded. It was no surprise. When big names traveled by air, Secret Service agents invariably went along for the ride, occupying regular passenger accommodations and doing their best to look like insurance executives—which was just what they were, in a way. Their presence on this flight was to be expected.

Cousins was a burly, capable-looking man with a warm smile and a powerful handshake.

"Pleasure to meet you, Captain."

All very buddy-buddy. But in fact Mr. Cousins was probably on an intensive search of Mallory's face, diligently seeking out suspicious signs. Security people didn't like last-minute changes of personnel. For which they could hardly be blamed. No doubt the Ives-Mallory switch had meant a flurry of top-priority calls and high-speed checking of records. Knowing this, Mallory felt a bit self-conscious. But Cousins kept smiling.

"There'll be five of us. Myself, Maddox, Greene, Josephs and Macdonald. We want to spread ourselves pretty evenly about the airplane. I'd like to fly in the cockpit and sit in the jump seat, if that's okay with you."

"It's okay," said Mallory. He wondered what the consequences of point-blank refusal would be.

"Greene and Maddox will occupy seats in first class; right in the papal group, in other words. We've already cleared this with the Vatican, of course."

"Did you clear it with Mr. Baumgarten too?" Mallory asked innocently.

Deadly serious, Baumgarten assured him that the Secret Service had indeed checked with him.

Cousins continued: "Josephs and Macdonald will be in coach, one up front, one near the tail. And we're equipped with a rather efficient communications system. You may be interested in this." He unfastened his shirt cuff, revealing a tiny microphone taped to his wrist. "The cord travels up the arm to a transmitter-receiver taped to the small of my back. Uncomfortable but useful at times." Next he indicated his right ear. "You may think I'm a little hard of hearing. Actually, I guess you could call it a hearing aid, but it only gives me messages from the other agents. The five of us will be in constant touch with each other throughout the flight. And we're armed, of course."

"With what weapons?"

"Three-fifty-seven Magnums," Cousins told him. "With

hollow head slugs."

Mallory grimaced. Cousins grinned; he had an oddly jovial expression for a law-enforcement officer.

Mallory never felt entirely easy when there were arsenals of handguns on his aircraft. Airplanes made poor sites for shoot-outs, although they were not quite as vulnerable as is popularly believed. There existed a myth that a bullet hole in the side of a pressurized airliner would mean its immediate destruction. Not so. The aircraft's outflow valves could compensate for these changes in pressure. The fact remained, however, that a single bullet *could* hit a vital spot and reduce forty million dollars' worth of airplane to scrap metal.

But world leaders needed special protection.

"I hope you're not anticipating any problems on this flight. Any threats or anything like that?"

Cousins shrugged. "There are always threats. Phone calls. 'I'm gonna get the President or Liz Taylor or whoever.' Ninety-nine percent of them are hot air. Trouble is, there's always that *one*. The world is full of weird people. A nun may have flunked some guy in math back in 1949, so he decides to pay her back by getting the Pope thirty years later. I'm not saying it's going to happen; I'm not saying it's even likely to happen. All I'm saying is, it could happen. We're around to make damn sure it doesn't."

"I'll remember to keep my head down when the shooting starts."

Cousins chuckled. "No, I think it'll be a peaceful trip, Captain. Seems to me the biggest problem is going to be staying awake the whole way across. How long are we going to be in the air?"

"The computer predicts twelve hours, six minutes."

Interested in the jet's operation, Cousins asked how much fuel would be needed.

"We'll be taking off with full tanks," Mallory told him. "That's a little more than forty-seven thousand gallons. But our projected fuel burn is only around thirty-seven thousand, two hundred gallons, give or take a pint or two."

"Shit," said Cousins, impressed. He smiled in his engaging way. "I'm sure as hell glad it isn't going on my credit card. Well,

Captain, we won't take up any more of your time. We'll go aboard and mind our own business just like any other passengers."

"Unless there's trouble."

"There won't be," said Cousins. "I can feel it in my bones. It'll be a nice, peaceful trip. I mean, who would be sick enough to want to harm the Holy Father?"

Mallory had asked himself the same question.

*   *   *

Vernon Squires was furious.

"I insist upon a first-class seat!"

Flustered, embarrassed, the agent could only shake his head. "I'm really sorry, Mr. Squires . . . really sorry. But you see, the entire first-class section has been reserved for the Pope and his party."

In stentorian tones, Mr. Squires informed the man that he had already been so enlightened. "There is no need for you to repeat facts. I am, as a rule, quite capable of absorbing them the first time. Unfortunately, the same cannot, it seems, be said for your airline!"

"Yes, sir, sorry, sir . . . but you see, there's just no way I can help you."

"My producer purchased a first-class ticket from your airline three months ago. I expect it to produce a first-class seat."

"But you see, sir, the papal party . . ."

"I am not in the least interested in the papal party. They have their problems and I have mine. And at the moment, my principal problem seems to be to get your airline to honor its obligations."

"Sir. . ."

"I am," stated Mr. Squires, "a frequent traveler on your airline. While I don't expect special considerations because of this fact, I do expect the basic courtesies, the simple acts of trust that are the backbone of our commercial system. When I purchase a ticket for the first-class section, I expect to obtain a seat in the first-class section."

"Of course, sir, but it was *after* you bought the ticket that the special arrangements for the papal party were made. We tried to contact you, sir. . . ."

"I was on location in the Himalayas."

"Well, sir, I guess that's why we couldn't contact you. It would be a real pleasure to put you in the first-class section of any other flight, sir; it's just this one that's absolutely, completely out of the question."

"Do you know who I am?"

"Yes, sir. You're Vernon Squires. The actor. I've seen you in a lot of movies. . . . In the last one you played that professor with the terrible temper. . . ."

"It was a role," said Mr. Squires, "that came naturally to me. Some actors enjoy traveling. They revel in recognition; they delight in answering the same, inane questions; they adore scribbling autographs for Auntie Dorothy from Madison, Wisconsin. I don't. I detest it. In the main, I find the human race dull and unattractive. I infinitely prefer my own company. That is why, when I am forced, by the demands of my profession, to travel, I do so only first class, where, with luck, some privacy is usually possible. For that reason, first-class travel is a part of every contract I sign. Now, I have a ticket—a first-class ticket purchased some three months ago. In exchange, I demand a first-class seat to San Francisco."

"We'll give you the difference in cash, sir."

"I do not want the difference. I want my first-class seat."

"I am sorry, sir. That's impossible."

"It is not impossible," said Mr. Squires, with a terrible frown. "It is iniquitous."

"Sorry, Mr. Squires, sir," said the agent again.

The actor sighed. Exactly the same sigh the agent remembered from *Assignment in Calcutta,* in which Mr. Squires played a genius-criminal. The sighs, tight and staccato, were emitted every time someone had to be eliminated.

"I suppose the aircraft is full."

"Yes, sir, just about."

"So there's no chance of a row to myself."

"No, sir."

Another sigh.

"Very well, get me something in the smoking section."

The agent winced. "Sir, I'm sorry to have to tell you this too . . . er, you're checking in kind of late."

"Only because I already had my ticket," Mr. Squires pointed out ringingly.

"Yes, sir. Well," the agent replied, "the smoking seats are all taken. Sir, I want to assure you . . ."

"And I want to assure you," said Mr. Squires, "that the president of your company shall hear of this. Don't worry," he added, "I won't blame you personally. It's not your fault. You simply follow orders. That," he said as he picked up his baggage-claim checks and boarding pass, "was the excuse they used at Nuremberg."

"Sir?" said the agent, bewildered. "Trans Am doesn't fly to Nuremberg."

*   *   *

The crowds had been gathering for hours; some groups had even spent the previous night near the airport in order to have a good view of the Holy Father on his way to board the airplane to America. Many had brought small children—some far too young to know the significance of what they were about to see. But, their parents reasoned, it was important for the children even if they didn't understand, for this was a great occasion, a unique event, a memory to be nurtured for years to come. What a pity it was marred by a delay. They kept asking the policemen—the *carabinieri*—what time the papal party would be arriving and at what time the airplane would leave for America. But no one seemed to know.

"For security reasons it cannot be divulged," was the stock answer.

"But it will be sometime this evening?"

"You may be assured of that."

"And will the Holy Father pass this particular spot?"

"Unquestionably."

Those who knew anything of the airport's layout selected a spot as near as possible to the third turnoff before the freight entrance. It was often used for the reception of VIPs.

*   *   *

In the Trans Am ramp office, six teletype machines clattered in their fitful way, spouting long tongues of yellow paper. Behind them, visible through a window, the Pope's aircraft waited, serene and lovely, her metal skin shimmering in the soft rays of the setting sun. Ground service vehicles darted around the 747 like mechanical parasites. The long red carpet was already in position. The weather was kind; conditions would not force the Pontiff to board the jet by means of the covered entranceway. The photgrahers would get their pictures.

The Trans Am station manager smiled wearily as he handed the dispatch portfolio to Mallory. Normally he liked to spend a few minutes with each captain, exchanging the latest news from around the world. Today he had time only to wish Mallory a good trip; then he hurried back to the vital business of coordinating and overseeing the loading of meals, refreshments, soaps and toilet paper, mail and cargo, and of ensuring that the aircraft was properly fueled and that the cabins were properly prepared for the flight. A journey in a company aircraft by anyone of the Pope's stature created enough problems; to have such a flight delayed was a nightmare.

At the office counter, Mallory and Jensen studied the flight plan. The company's IBM 370-168 computer had prepared it, absorbing the fact that the aircraft was to travel from Rome to San Francisco, passing through almost seven thousand miles of changing winds and temperatures at a constantly decreasing weight. The computer had integrated this information with preprogrammed data pertaining to the performance of the airplane and spent less than a minute calculating the route that would require the minimum flight time—and would therefore be the most economical for the airline. In addition, the computer had rattled off a veritable cornucopia of technical information, literally the story of the flight, before the airplane had left the ground. The lengthy, single sheet of paper told the pilots how much fuel would be remaining in the tanks when they reached their destination, how much the aircraft would weigh when it took off and when it landed, how much fuel it would consume during the trip, precisely how long the journey would take, what effect the winds would have and what average temperature could be expected en route. Then, in orderly columns, the computer divided the entire trip into legs, listing the checkpoints along the way and tirelessly recording the length of each leg in nautical miles, the cumulative total of miles since takeoff, the magnetic course of each leg, the altitude at which each leg should be flown, the temperatures that could be expected en route, the winds, the groundspeeds, the flight time of each leg, the cumulative times, the amount of fuel each leg would consume and the amount of fuel that should remain at the end of each leg. Navigators no longer had to pore over endless calculations; the computer did it all ahead of time.

Mallory, like most veteran pilots, had distrusted the computer-prepared flight plans when they were first introduced. Before long, however, he had become a convert; the row-upon-row of printout data had, again and again, been proved phenomenally accurate.

He checked the weather folder prepared only minutes before by the *Aeronautica Militare Servizio Meteorologico* at Fiumicino. His lack of Italian was no handicap, for the weather charts used the international symbols that could be read and understood by pilots from every country. Of particular interest were the 200 and 250 Millibar Prognostic Charts. He studied the undulating isobaric contours that created graceful patterns on the charts, looking for potential trouble—thunderstorm activity, jet streams, rapid temperature changes, tropospheric data—any of the clues to turbulence. No; it looked good. There was a band of severe weather, a vigorous cold front extending from Southern Norway, right across his projected route, down almost as far south as the Azores. Fortunately, Flight 901 wouldn't feel the effects of the gale-force winds produced by the front; it would fly far above them. Other fronts—like gigantic tides in the sky—were scattered about the Northern Hemispherical Chart, but none would upset Mallory's plan to provide the Pontiff with a smooth, tranquil journey to the New World.

"Looks good," he murmured approvingly.

Jensen nodded in his serious way. "Right, Steve, I'll file it with ATC."

* * *

Clifford Jensen, first officer on Flight 901, drummed his fingers impatiently on the telephone booth glass. Why couldn't they get the call through? He didn't have all day, for God's sake. All he could hear were clicks and bangs and an incessant ringing in the distance.

At last he heard Ginnie's voice.

"Cliff? Is that you, Cliff?"

"Yes. What's happening?"

"He's back," she said. At least that was what it sounded like. There was a momentary interruption in transmission. He wasn't sure.

"Everything's all right? He's back? Is that what you said?"

"Yes, that's right."

She sounded weak with relief.

Jensen sighed. Thank God. "Where the hell did he go this time?"

"The Seattle police called. . . ."

"What?"

"The Seattle police. He said he was going to Canada."

Jesus. The kid was unbelievable. "Where is he now? Let me talk with him."

"He's in bed, Cliff. Fast asleep. I just looked in on him."

"You'd better chain him to the bed."

"What's that?"

The line became a symphony of crackles and static.

"Never mind," said Jensen. "I'll see you tomorrow. We're leaving pretty soon."

"Okay, dear. I have to go too. There's someone at the door."

He said goodbye and hung up. What a kid. Fantastic wanderlust. Ten years old and determined to see the entire world before he was twelve. Not many kids ten years old would get as far as Seattle. The amazing thing was, he probably wasn't the least bit scared. To him, the world was big and full of interesting places, and he didn't see any reason why he shouldn't start looking at them right now.

A kid to be proud of, when you really thought about it. He would go far.

Jensen smiled; the little bastard already had gone far.

One day, by God, one day Master Craig Jensen would get an accounting of all the long-distance, international telephone calls his wanderings had caused his old man.

When Jensen reached the briefing room, Baumgarten was there waiting. The poor guy looked tired and jittery. Hard to blame him, with the flight already late and the whole world asking questions. All eighteen members of the crew were present: Captain Mallory right on down to the most junior stew, including Hammond, the relief officer, who would spend most of the flight in a coach seat, relaxing until needed.

"I want you all to be aware of the arrangements concerning Flight 901," said Baumgarten, sounding as if he were dictating a memorandum. "It is a privilege for Trans American to be selected as the carrier for the outbound flight. As you probably know, Alitalia will bring the Pope and his group back to Rome at the conclusion of his visit to the West Coast. It is particularly unfortunate that an accident befell Captain Ives just a few hours before the flight; one of those unpredictables that seem to take the greatest delight in thwarting the best-laid plans of mice and men." He smiled thinly. "Anyway," he went on, "those problems are behind us. From now on everything will go perfectly. Captain Mallory is in command of the aircraft, and I am confident that there will be no more surprises." He wiped his brow with a sodden handkerchief.

"Now, it is of the utmost importance that each and every one of you understand what is being done for the Pope's comfort and safety. You are aware that we have reserved first class for the papal party. We have also made certain temporary alterations to the airplane to cut first class off completely from the rest of the cabin. I'm sure it's obvious why we've done this. The Pope and his party must not be subjected to any interference by any of the other passengers. The fact is, there's no need for any of your coach passengers to go near first class. And we expect every member of the cabin crew to make sure that no one does.

"Now, boarding. We will load the coach passengers through the aft cabin door. When the last one is aboard, we will bring on the Pope and his party, through the forward door. Special dishes, napkins and silverware have been brought aboard for the exclusive use of the Pope and his party. I should mention that the Pope is an elderly gentleman—and the Vatican advises us that he's somewhat nervous about flying. Not scared, exactly, but a little on the uncertain side, you might say. So we want to do everything we can to make sure he enjoys the trip. Captain Mallory informs me that no en route turbulence is anticipated. It's our hope, therefore, that the Pontiff will be able to rest comfortably and sleep a good deal during the flight.

"The two senior stewardesses, Pennetti and Sullivan, will look after first class; they will serve the food and refreshments to a papal steward who will personally attend to the Pope. Specially prepared meals are being loaded aboard the aircraft at this moment. These will be for the exclusive use of the Pope and his . . . er, entourage. It is the Pope's personal request that the coach passengers leave the aircraft first upon arrival at San Francisco. He said that after such a long journey, they should not be forced to wait for him. A most thoughtful gentleman, the Pope. So, all coach passengers will exit via the aft door. When they have left the aircraft, and not before, the papal party will disembark. I need hardly tell you how vital it is for every one of you to do your utmost to see that everything goes smoothly. We've had trouble enough already. Any questions?"

"Is any trouble anticipated?" asked Nowakoski, the flight engineer.

"No," replied Baumgarten, shaking his head as if something indecent had been suggested. "Certainly not!"

chapter 4

The blue and silver Boeing 747SP bore colored papal emblems on its fuselage beside the forward entrance. Ground crews had washed the aircraft with meticulous care; a swarm of electric buffers had polished the aluminum surfaces until the machine glistened.

Normally it was the flight engineer's job to examine the airplane externally. From time to time, however, Mallory enjoyed following the engineer during his inspection. He did it this evening, walking beneath the 196-foot-wide wings, studying flap linkages, aileron connections, access doors, hatches, fuel-dump chutes. He peered at the main landing gear with its clusters of wheels, sixteen in all, to spread the 345-ton weight of the 747 over the long-suffering concrete ramps. The tires were almost brand new. How many tires had he kicked on how many airplanes? His first instructor, a grizzled veteran of the Western Front, had declared, "Always take a real close look at your airplane before you get into it. Check the wings. Count 'em. See you've got the right number. And make goddam sure your propeller's stuck on the front end and your tail is on the other end. Hold things. Wiggle 'em. If they come off in your hand, get 'em glued back on right away."

It was best not to think how long ago that had all happened. The Olden Times when the Army Air Corps still flew little P-26s, the Boeing "Peashooters," when Astaire and Rogers were the big box office draws, when you could buy a phone call or a cup of coffee for a single nickel. And *Gone With the Wind* was still just a book. Another time, another world; ancient history to young men like Jensen and Nowakoski.

Mallory had learned to fly in a Stearman biplane, a wondrous contraption of open cockpits and fabric skin. You wore a leather helmet and goggles and you learned to keep your rudder pedals active on landing, because there wasn't a nosewheel to prevent ground loops. On occasion, the Stearman had paralyzed him with terror; he had been convinced that he would never master its vagaries. Wings had dropped moments before touchdown or immediately after takeoff; strange snapping noises had occurred deep within the fuselage—but never when the instructor was aboard, only when Mallory was alone. Again and again it had seemed certain that he was about to be the victim of structural failure at five thousand feet: wings and tail surfaces buckling and breaking away, pinning him in the cockpit . . . plunging into eternity.

But it had never happened. And, gradually, faith had been created. A kinship was established; soon it became a love affair; and now, after more than forty years of flying, Mallory still responded to the thrill of leaving the ground and turning on a wing tip. Fate had beamed on him, permitting him to earn a comfortable living doing precisely what he most wanted to do.

Unfortunately, he wouldn't be permitted to do it much longer. A few more months; then it would be the end of the line. Final approach. Compulsory retirement. From captain of jumbo jet, his status in the aeronautical world would shrivel to almost nothing: to that of lowly pleasure flier, buzzing around the local airport in a rented Piper or Cessna. It was an odd fact that he had never owned an aircraft; for more than four decades he had been flying other people's. Okay, then, he would buy one. A retirement present. The more he thought about it, the more he liked the idea. But not a Piper or Cessna. He would buy a Stearman; there were still some around. He would wear leather helmet and goggles. The circle would be complete. He would be back where he started.

The thought pleased him, and he smiled to himself as he followed Nowakoski through the curtained first-class section, then up the spiral stairway to the flight deck.

The two pilots' seats were situated forward, surrounded and separated by a maze of switches, dials and gauges. The flight engineer's seat faced the starboard wall; his station was said by some to resemble a pinball machine gone mad. The 747's hydraulic, electrical, fuel and environmental control systems were represented by endless circuits punctuated by scores of switches.

Jensen was already in his seat.

Mallory unbuttoned his uniform jacket but didn't take it off. He sat down in the left-hand seat, settling himself comfortably, automatically reaching for the controls and adjusting the rudder pedals to the length of his legs.

Behind, Nowakoski was already busy positioning the maze of switches on his complex panel.

The great machine had to be stirred into life, readied for flight. Each member of the crew had his pre-start chores to perform: gauges to be read, switches to be flipped, indicators to be set, aural warnings to be sounded, valves to be exercised, computers to be programmed, visual warnings to be tested, pressures to be checked.

Jensen leaned towards Mallory.

"Ginnie wanted me to get the Pope's *autograph*. Can you imagine! I told her, 'The Pope's not a movie star; you don't ask him for his autograph.' She said, 'Why not?'" He grinned. "You know what wives are like." He flinched, as if the words had caused him pain. "Sorry, Captain, I didn't mean . . ."

"Forget it," said Mallory. "I understand."

"I met your wife once. Five years ago. She came with us to Paris. Nice lady."

Mallory nodded. He remembered the trip. But he had completely forgotten that Jensen was on the crew. There had been so many faces on so many flight decks; they tended to become one: firm of jaw and steady of eye—with built-in head sets. He could already feel how much he was going to miss it all: the organization, the teamwork, the *professionalism*. A satisfying world, that of the airlines. It had been his life, and soon he would no longer be part of it.

*   *   *

"I know. . . . I know. . . ! For God's sake, I *know*!"

The girl's eyes closed tightly; fists clenched, she bounced up and down in a frenzy of frustration.

"Lee J. Cobb . . . no . . . E. G. Marshall . . . yes! That's who you are!"

Mr. Squires shook his head. Once. Good grief, would this line never move?

"No?" The girl looked pained. She had bright red hair. "Not E. G. Marshall?"

"I assure you. . ."

"Are you *sure?* I've seen you. I know you."

"You must be mistaken," muttered Mr. Squires. "I'm in machine tools."

"Jesus," said the girl, disappointed.

The uniformed security man thrust a large and hairy hand into Mr. Squires' briefcase. Then he peered into it as a housewife might peer into a shopping bag from which suspicious odors were emanating.

"Satisfied?" inquired Mr. Squires, his voice heavy with sarcasm.

Now the security man peered at Mr. Squires himself. His brows darkened. He called another man to his side and said something, his eyes never leaving Mr. Squires. More words. The brows lifted.

"Ah, you the actor, yes?" The security man nodded, as if answering his own question. "I think at first I know your face. It worries me." He beamed. "Now I understand why! You are actor! Very good! Boom, boom!" He pointed a pudgy finger. "You go through there now, please. Thank you."

A grim-faced individual passed a metal detector about Mr. Squires' body. He was then directed into a small booth where a tall, lanky official pawed Squires' anatomy and dug into his pockets. Why, Squires wondered, didn't I go by ship? Slower, but by George they didn't put people through this kind of indignity. There was still a modicum of respect left for passengers on the high seas.

Now a Trans Am agent, a pretty brunette, was reaching for his boarding pass. Mechanical, thousand-times-a-day smile. And how was Mr. Squires today?

"Irritated," replied Mr. Squires. "Irritated by the fact that one is never told what is going on. Irritated by the fact the airlines seem to consider all passengers as gibbering idiots quite incapable of making rational decisions. Since you ask, young lady, I might add that it should have been made clear right at the beginning that, by chance, I was booked to travel on the same aircraft that was taking the Pope to San Francisco. I should then have been told that this fact would mean that I couldn't have my first-class seat, and a delay in departure of several hours, plus a revoltingly intimate search of my person and belongings. This intelligence would have given me the opportunity to say, 'No, thank you, I prefer not to travel with the Pope.' As far as I know, he's pleasant enough. But I'm not so sure about his office. I've long held the view that the world in general would be a rather better place if there were no religions. All in all, I tend to believe that, over the generations, they have caused considerably more harm than good. The extraordinary thing is that they survive at all. Think about it, young lady. The human species is remarkably adept at drawing intelligent conclusions from sets of facts. A good example is the fact that the world is round. The evidence was identified, considered and weighed, and the conclusions drawn. And yet when it comes to considering the existence of God, people are quite irrational. It should be obvious to anyone but a complete moron that if there is a God, He doesn't give a tinker's damn for the human race or what happens to it. Look about you; the evidence is there. If there is a divine hand guiding all that, it is a remarkably inefficient hand. Thank goodness it was not involved in the planning of D-Day! Does that answer your question?"

The girl's mouth had dropped open. Speechless, she nodded.

Mr. Squires strode into the departure lounge. It was almost full. He avoided his fellow passengers' eyes, but it did no good.

A man was plucking at his arm.

"Say, mister, you're on TV, huh?"

Mr. Squires shook his head. "I sell drains."

"Son of a gun, I could've sworn I've seen you on TV."

Now his wife joined them. Hard-eyed, she stared.

"Vernon Squires."

"No," said her husband, "he sells drains."

"You're full of shit," she told him.

* * *

Outside, excitement rippled through the crowd. The road had been cleared! In a few moments the Holy Father would arrive! A twenty-two-year-old girl fainted; she had been waiting for fourteen hours and hadn't eaten anything. Two hundred yards away a man of seventy-three died; but, supported by the press of bodies on all sides, he did not fall.

Then the sleek black Mercedes limousines approached, preceded by a phalanx of white-gauntleted motorcyclists. The cars traveled at a steady twenty miles per hour, a slow enough pace to enable the patient spectators a glimpse of the elderly man in the white robes.

As the cars turned into the airport, the *carabinieri* moved into action, sliding steel gates into position to close the lane. It was a neat, well-rehearsed action. The gates were closed and locked before the spectators could flood the access road. They had to be content with what they could see through and over the gates. They gazed with the intense, almost pained look of people who are determined not to miss anything. This was history being made in front of their very eyes; people would talk about this day for years to come. Questions would be asked of those who were there. Every detail must be noted, every action recorded.

A soft gasp went up from the crowd. White hands fluttered in the twilight, making the sign of the cross. There he was, in person. God's representative on earth. White robes enfolding his slight figure, he turned and nodded gently toward the crowd. He smiled, acknowledging their devotion. Then he turned and followed the red carpet toward the aircraft.

* * *

After the last coach passenger was seated, the call came through from the cabin.

"Captain, the Pope is about to board the aircraft."

"Be right down."

Mallory got to his feet. He tugged at his jacket and put on his cap. Jensen nodded approvingly. Nowakoski regarded him with awe; here was someone about to undergo a supernatural experience.

Dee Pennetti was waiting at the forward entrance door. She smiled, nervously, as Mallory joined her.

A moment later two of the Secret Service agents appeared and took up positions on either side of the entrance. Behind them, a company agent whispered:

"He's coming!"

Warren Baumgarten walked just ahead of the Pontiff, indicating the way with a slightly uncertain hand.

Mallory found himself bowing as he was introduced to a slim man of modest stature.

"It is a pleasure to meet you, Captain," the Pontiff said in excellent English. "I am looking forward to the journey. I hope it will be a smooth one."

"I certainly think so, Your Eminence." Mallory found it easier to use the title than he had anticipated. "The weather is reasonably stable over the Atlantic and the North American continent. It should be quite comfortable."

The Pope nodded and smiled gently. "I know that I am in the most capable of hands."

Mallory felt his cheeks burn. "Thank you."

"I am told, Captain, that you recently lost your wife. My condolences. I know that this cannot be an easy time for you."

"You are very kind, Your Eminence."

"I wonder if I might ask you a favor, Captain."

"A favor? Yes, of course. . . ."

"I hope you will permit me to enter the cockpit during the flight. I would be most interested to see the workings of your machine, if it will not inconvenience you, of course."

Mallory grinned, pleased. "It will be a privilege, Your Eminence; and I know that the other members of the flight crew will be delighted to meet you. Perhaps you will be good enough to let Miss Pennetti know when you would like to visit the flight deck. She will be pleased to make the necessary arrangements."

Blushing, Dee assured the Pontiff that it would be a pleasure.

When Mallory returned to the flight deck, Jensen and Nowakoski turned expectantly.

"What was it like? Did you actually meet him?"

Mallory told them the Pope was a very pleasant old gentleman.

They looked disappointed. They had apparently expected a more graphic description.

"He's going to visit the cockpit later on," he told them.

Nowakoski's mouth dropped open.

"Honest? *Here*?"

"Here. In this very spot."

"Chri—" He swallowed. "Gee."

*   *   *

"INS mode set to NAV."

"Flight control power switches on."

"Stall warning checked."

"Window heat on."

"Mach warning checked."

"Emergency lights armed."

"Start levers to cutoff."

"Gear pins removed."

Rapidly they checked oxygen, brakes, flight instruments and fuel load.

"Before-Starting-Engines Checklist is complete, sir."

Jensen called Air Traffic Control for the route clearance.

"Clearance Delivery, this is Trans Am Flight nine-zero-one, IFR to San Francisco, standing by with Information Uniform. Over."

The controller answered at once, in English. "Roger, nine-zero-one. You are cleared to the San Francisco airport via flight-planned route. Maintain flight level two-zero-zero. Expect flight level three-five-zero at Elbe. After takeoff, turn left heading two-eight-zero degrees for radar vectors to Upper Amber One.

Jensen repeated the clearance to ensure that he had copied it correctly. Then he and Mallory adjusted the navigation equipment to conform to the initial routing instructions. The path of Flight 901 had been ordained.

Now there was a moment of relaxation for the crew.

Mallory stifled a yawn.

"I still can't believe it," said Nowakoski. "The *Pope* . . . here in this airplane."

"Been to confession lately?" Mallory asked with a smile.

Nowakoski shook his head. "And he knows, I swear to God he knows."

"You should ask him to hear yours."

"Impossible," Jensen put in. "The flight's only twelve hours long. No way there would be enough time for him to tell it all."

"Gee, *thanks*. . ."

The voice of a ground crewman came through the interphone from outside.

"We're all buttoned up down here, Captain. Ready to start when you are."

"Roger."

Jensen called the tower again.

"Fiumicino Ground Control, this is Trans Am nine-zero-one requesting start-up clearance."

The response was uncommonly prompt and brisk.

"Roger, Trans Am nine-zero-one, you are cleared to start engines. Expect runway three-four left."

They started number three engine first, then number four, followed by two and one. They kept wary eyes on the exhaust gas temperature gauges because the enormously powerful JT9D-7F turbofan engines had a tendency to overheat during the starting sequence. Despite their awesome power, however, only a faint rumble was audible in the flight deck. With engines running smoothly, there were the after-start checks to perform: aileron and rudder trim zeroed; electrical power, hydraulic power, doors, ground equipment cleared . . .

"Fiume Ground, this is Trans Am nine-zero-one, ready to taxi. Over."

"Trans Am nine-zero-one, taxi to the holding position, runway three-four left. Wind is three-two-zero degrees at six knots, QNH one-one-nine."

Jensen acknowledged as Mallory nudged the thrust levers gently with his right hand. He positioned his left hand on the tiller controlling the nosewheel for ground maneuvering.

"Flaps twenty."

Jensen moved the handle to the appropriate detent; outside, the massive trailing-edge flaps extended, drooping behind the rear of the wing; simultaneously, eight leading-edge flaps stepped forward, helping to create a different shape for the wing, one that would be better suited to the business of lifting almost 700,000 pounds off the runway.

The parallel blue lights on either side of the taxiway seemed to stretch away to eternity.

"Okay, Nowakoski," said Mallory, "let's have a little responsive reading, shall we?"

"Okay, Captain." Seconds later, he began to read aloud. "Nacelle anti-ice—off. Flight instruments—checked. Flaps—twenty degrees and green light. Flight controls—checked. Stabilizer trim—set. Takeoff data and airspeed bugs—set and cross-checked. Transponder—on. . . . Taxi Checklist complete, Captain."

Mallory nodded. Time to get the show on the road. Hours late but better late, et cetera, et cetera . . .

The entire population of Rome seemed to have turned out to see the departure of Trans Am Flight 901. A forest of arms waved in farewell as the big jet moved ponderously away from the terminal building trundling along on its multiwheel gear, its broad, swept-back wings swaying regally over the edges of the taxiway. A hundred thousand cameras clicked; bones were broken as people pushed frantically to catch a glimpse of the Holy Father's airplane before it disappeared into the night. They scrambled, they tore, so they might see. He was up there, his head at one of those tiny windows. But which one? No one seemed to know. At this very moment he was undoubtedly looking upon the faithful who had journeyed out to witness his departure for the

New World; and no doubt he was smiling in his gentle, avuncular way . . . if only one knew at which window to direct one's gaze. . . .

Mallory taxied with his usual care, constantly reminding himself that the height of the flight deck made the pace seem slower than it really was. It was too easy to let the speed build up when taxiing 747s; the result could be overheated brakes or even a nosewheel tire pulled off its rim. At all times a wary eye had to be kept on the groundspeed indication of the inertial navigation system.

It was slightly after 9:00 P.M., local time, when Flight 901 began its takeoff roll. Three hundred and forty-five tons of airplane, fuel, passengers and cargo, propelled by the raw power of air. The four great turbine engines that swayed beneath the wings sucked it in, compressed it, expanded it by combustion, then blasted it out in a screaming, lethal torrent to the rear.

Over the airplane's shapely nose, Mallory watched the runway's white centerline stripes. Like slow-moving bullets they ran into the plane, vanishing one by one. The pace quickened. Soon the stripes became a single, wavering line. The great machine hurled itself down the runway, its wings flexing as if readying themselves for flight.

The rumble of the wheels ceased. At 197 m.p.h., the 747 was in its element at last, free of the tiresome bonds of Earth.

At fifteen degrees to the horizontal, the big craft soared upward toward the filmy overcast. The lights of Rome were spread below, like jewels on display.

Inside the airport terminal, a man placed an overseas telephone call to a motel in California.

chapter 5

The trembling kept coming back.

She had to clench her fists and brace every muscle to fight it, to smother it. God, it was hard work, but eventually, inevitably, it would fade. She could sigh and breathe again normally. And think. And try to figure some way to get out of this place, this bare, chilly room with its table and the wooden chairs pushed untidily against one wall. Battered, ancient things. Everything was old and rotten. Boards covered the windows. A single, unshaded bulb provided light for the place. The room must have been pleasant in its day; it had a big fireplace, and the wood floor was of good quality. But it was obvious that the room hadn't been used for years, perhaps decades. Dampness had permeated the walls. They looked as if they would ooze if pressed.

The two guys who had brought her here were in the next room, talking in that damned language of theirs. In vain, she had tried to identify it. At first she was convinced they were Greek; then she realized it was only because one of the men reminded her of a local supermarket manager named Constandinidas. She had asked the men where they were from, but they told her not to ask questions.

She listened, trying desperately to make sense of the sounds she heard: intermittent traffic some distance away, a couple of airplanes, the creaking of the house.

Crazy. It made no sense. There was nothing to be *gained* by kidnapping her . . . *kidnapping.* The word sent a dart of fear through her. She thought of the Lindbergh baby, of bodies found buried in leaves. . . .

Her head ached; her lips were dry. She had asked for a cup of coffee, but they had paid no attention. . . .

Poor Toby. How could anyone be so goddam callous as to slaughter a sweet creature like Toby? Would his body still be there in the hall when her father got home? What a hell of a shock for him. What would he think? What would he do? Were the creeps going to call him and demand a ransom?

Madness. He wasn't rich. Surely, then, this must be a monstrous foul-up. *Sorry, kid, we got the wrong girl. No hard feelings. But you've seen us, so* . . . No, she couldn't waste time thinking of such things. What mattered was to organize and prepare, out-think the enemy, confound them.

But how?

God, I'm scared. I might die here; this might be the end of everything . . . finis, blank eternity. . . .

The trembling attacked her again. It swept over her with a kind of willful deliberation. A maddening rhythm. It was exhausting, fighting it. But she knew she couldn't give in. She had to keep up the battle.

She made herself think of revenge, of kicking the bastards in their goddam balls, of hurting *them,* of seeing *them* cringe. . . .

The thoughts calmed her. Timorously, gingerly, she permitted her muscles to relax. No trembling. Another attack repulsed.

She got up and walked about the room. Her footsteps sounded loud on the bare floor. She tapped her foot. She wished she could tap dance. That would bewilder them. And keep her warm.

How long had they traveled in the truck? An hour? She wasn't sure. About an hour. So, forty or fifty miles. Where could that be? She sighed. Only about ten thousand places. In stories, people always heard freight trains or rushing water that enabled them to pinpoint their locations. But what could you do with a few vague traffic noises and a plane or two? What did they tell you except that cars were traveling and airplanes were flying? You only knew that you were somewhere in the civilized world.

Civilized?

She started humming, loudly.

Morale boosting. For some weird reason the tune that

emerged was "And the Angels Sing." She hadn't heard the thing for years, and yet she could remember it all. Her father had once owned the 78 record. Benny Goodman orchestra, with Ziggy Elman playing the trumpet solo. She could hear it, note for note, even the interjections by the band. And the words, sung by Martha Tilton of the sexy voice. Scared? Yes, she told herself, she was scared shitless. And yet . . . how could she define it? There was an undercurrent of excitement, a sort of thrill deep inside, an almost sexual thing, mingling, merging with the fright. A key had turned in the lock.

The door opened. Scarface.

"I brought you some coffee."

She took the cup from him.

"Your generosity is overwhelming."

"Drink it," he said. "And don't talk so much."

"Why have you brought me here?"

"Drink your coffee."

He spoke English well, but his accent was strong.

"Where are you from?"

"What?" He frowned. "I told you not to ask questions."

"I can't identify your accent. I'm just curious," she said. "It's not so terrible, is it, wanting to know where you're from?"

"I advise you to drop the subject."

She sipped the coffee. It was too sweet but it didn't matter. Rarely had a cup tasted so good.

"My father is an airline pilot. . . ."

"Yes, we know."

". . . so he isn't rich. He can't pay any fancy ransom, if that's what you have in mind."

"That is not what we have in mind."

"What is?"

"You'll find out."

He was about twenty-five. Broad-shouldered under a blue denim shirt. Dark, curly hair. Regular features. Not a bad-looking guy in an elemental sort of way. Was he the one who had killed Toby? She couldn't remember. The whole thing had a strange dreamlike quality about it, as if it hadn't really happened at all. But it had. And this was happening. Now.

The peculiar thing was, only part of her was scared. The other part was merely curious. The recording secretary part.

"It was a lousy thing to do, to kill my dog."

He nodded, agreeing. "It was a pity. But necessary."

"Why necessary?"

"The dog was in the way. It might have caused delay. We couldn't afford any delay."

"So you killed him."

"We had to." He shrugged. "I'm sorry," he added.

Her eyes filled with tears as she remembered Toby. She turned away from him.

"You . . . bastard!"

He didn't say anything. When at last she turned back, he was standing with arms folded, feet well apart, like a soldier on guard.

"Son of a bitch," she snarled, her voice husky.

He gazed at her.

She finished the coffee, holding the cup with both hands to keep it steady. She wouldn't give the bastard the satisfaction of seeing her hand tremble.

"How long are you going to keep me here?"

"Not long. I assure you."

"And what goddam good is your assurance?"

He flushed. "You won't be kept long."

"They put assholes like you in the gas chamber."

"So I have heard."

"What'll you do if I make a run for it?"

"It would be the last thing you'd do."

"I'm no use to you dead," she declared.

He shrugged. "It makes no difference to me whether you're dead or alive, but I don't have to *kill* you," he said as he pointed to her legs. "I could shoot you there. Or I could shoot you there," he said, unfolding his arms and touching her shoulder. "Or possibly there." He squeezed a breast in his hand.

She pulled away instinctively, until the wall was at her back. She could feel its dampness through the material of her shirt.

Rape! Christ, the bastard wants to *rape* me!

She was defenseless and terrified. Must stay calm.

"I guess you need a gun to get a piece of ass."

She tried to make it as crude as she could, but her voice didn't cooperate; tension made it crack and squeak.

He shook his head, slowly, thoughtfully.

She could feel her heart pounding.

He advanced, methodically, with the measured movements of someone acting out a practiced routine.

She pressed back against the wall. There was nowhere to go. He kept coming until he was almost touching her. She could feel the warmth of him. The scar on his chin was moon-shaped, outlined in pale, almost colorless skin.

Don't react. Ignore the bastard; maybe it'll lose interest and go away. . . . No fun assaulting an inanimate object. Someone all-wise had once said that . . . someone who had most likely never been obliged to put the maxim to the test.

Now both of his hands were on her breasts.

"Fuck off," she said.

That was better. Good and crude.

The color had risen in his face. His lips were very slightly parted; she could see the tip of his tongue. With one hand he tried to unfasten the buttons of her shirt. But he couldn't manage it. He released her other breast and used both hands on the buttons.

Jane clenched her teeth, for fear they would chatter. Knee him? Suddenly? Brutally? Yes, she could do it. She would, too. But she would choose just the right moment. Not yet. Not quite yet.

He got one button undone but he was having trouble with the second.

"Clumsy asshole, aren't you?"

He looked at her, his brow creasing momentarily.

Good, she thought, he didn't like the language. Nice little girls weren't supposed to say such things.

Be repelled! Please be repelled!

"You undo the buttons," he said.

"No. . . ."

"I insist." He took hold of one side of her collar. "If you don't, I will simply rip it off. And that would spoil a nice blouse, wouldn't it?"

She swallowed.

"It . . . it's too cold," she said.

She could hear the near-panic in her own voice.

"We'll be warm, I think."

She shook her head. "Hell . . . no, this is a crummy place to get laid. Haven't . . . you got anywhere better?"

"This will do."

"I'll scream my head off."

"No one will hear."

"Your friend."

"He won't care. He isn't interested in women."

Petrified, she slowly undid each of the buttons.

"Good," he said. "That's better."

His hands slid the blouse off her shoulders.

She pretended to shiver. He ignored her, tugging at one of her bra straps; then he reached in and dragged the breast half-free as if it were a trophy. It was misshapen by the still-fastened bra. For a lunatic instant she found herself wanting to show that her breasts were well formed; she unclipped the hook and her breasts fell free. She watched his eyes. Evidently he approved. She could feel his breath dancing lightly on her flesh.

"Take off your pants."

His voice was harsh with desire.

"But . . . "

"Take them *off,* I said."

His white, even teeth were clenched, as if in pain.

"I can't."

"Why?"

"My . . . period."

"What? Oh . . . well, let's find out for sure. Now take off your pants before I rip them off."

One hand was pulling at the belt of her jeans, the other squeezed and fondled her breast. He leaned against her, hard and insistent.

Christ, the time for delay was damn-near over. The guy meant business. But still, he didn't seem to be a totally mindless rapist; it was possible to communicate with him, in a way.

"Very impressive," she managed to say.

"Huh?"

"Don't I get a look at the merchandise? We're not going to have much fun if you keep your pants on."

A moment's pause, as if he was trying to make up his mind whether she was serious. Then he unzipped his pants.

"Jesus Christ," she said. "You'll kill me with that thing. . . ."

"You'll love it."

He stopped. A car outside. Gravel crunching, brakes squealing.

He swore in that foreign language of his; as he dragged the pistol from his pocket.

In spite of herself, Jane wanted to laugh. He was ludicrous: gun in hand, erect penis jutting from unzipped pants; his organ hadn't yet received the message to relax; it didn't know that other matters had just superseded sex in immediate importance.

He made for the door.

She said, "Better zip your pants up."

"What?" He looked down. He seemed about to say something else, then he shook his head quickly as he zipped his fly. One last glance at her, then he was gone. The door banged behind him.

Hastily, Jane dressed as a door slammed outside. Voices.

Help? Was the U.S. Cavalry arriving in the nick of time, saving the heroine's honor before the dastardly villain could have his way with her? And was the heroine vaguely disappointed about it? Jesus, she told herself, you're *weird*, you know that? You've always been weird. A goddam rebel. She rubbed her forehead. Thoughts cascaded in her mind like pennies in a drum. She couldn't control them. *Ordeal Proves Too Much For Kidnapped Divorcée; Mind Disintegrates*. She listened. Footsteps and voices bounced around the empty hallway. An angry voice demanded silence. Someone spoke: a child, by the sound of it.

What the hell is this all about?

Nothing made sense. Was this some all-too-realistic nightmare? Would she wake up soon?

The door burst open.

Another swarthy man in a Sears uniform came in, carrying

an automatic rifle. He glanced at her without interest.

"In here!"

A young woman entered: tear-streaked face, hair awry. Then there were two children, a boy about ten and a girl who was little more than a toddler. Finally, an elderly man with pale, bewildered eyes. He wore slippers.

He said something to the Sears man.

"Shut up! Get in the room! Do as I say and you won't be hurt."

"But . . . "

With the barrel of his rifle, the Sears man prodded the old fellow into the room. He stumbled and almost fell. Jane managed to catch him in time. His glasses fell off.

Jane called the Sears man a son of a bitch. He ignored her and went out, locking the door behind him.

The little girl started to cry.

The boy assumed an inquisitive expression and went off to explore the room.

The adults looked at each other.

Jane said, "I've been here an hour or so. I have no idea why. How about you?"

They shook their heads. Tears welled in the mother's eyes.

"It is madness," said the old man. He had a heavy accent. "I was sitting, reading the newspaper. Minding my own business. They say they come from Sears. Then . . . this. . . ."

"Maybe we should start by introducing ourselves," said Jane. "My name's Jane Sutton. Does that mean anything to you? No? Well, how about you, sir, what's your name?"

"Nowakoski," said the old man. "Nothing like this has ever happened to me since I came to America in 1926. . . ."

"I'm Virginia Jensen," said the mother. "And these are my children, Craig and Karen."

"Where do you live?"

"Near Monterey," said the Jensen woman.

"Oakland," said the man.

"We're all pretty close," said Jane. "I was living in New York, but a little while ago I moved in with my father. He's a captain with Trans Am," she added.

They looked up, their eyes widening. Suddenly, there was a connection, the beginning of an explanation.

chapter 6

Mallory always felt a little self-conscious, chatting away on the public address system like some aerial disc jockey. But the company encouraged the practice—almost to the point of insistence. It was good for the passengers, The PR guy declared. Since FAA regulations no longer permitted captains to stroll among their passengers during flight, friendly, informative PA announcements were the next best thing.

He pressed the interphone button. First step in the formula: make 'em feel at home.

"Good evening, ladies and gentlemen, this is your captain speaking. On behalf of the entire crew I'd like to welcome you aboard Trans American's Flight 901 to San Francisco. I must apologize for our late departure . . . circumstances beyond our control, as they say."

Next step: tell 'em where they are and where they're going.

"We've just leveled off at our assigned altitude of thirty-five thousand feet, just about seven miles above the Ligurian Sea. Presently, we're north of Corsica on a direct course to Torino, Italy. Our route will then take us to the northeast of Geneva, across Northeastern France and the English Channel, abeam London and then to Glasgow, Scotland, where we'll begin our North Atlantic crossing. After passing to the south of Iceland, we'll fly over Southern Greenland and across the Davis Strait to Baffin Island in Canada's Northwest Territories. From there, we'll head across Hudson Bay, over the northwest corner of Manitoba, across Saskatchewan Province and Southwest Alberta. After crossing the Idaho border into the United States, we'll fly directly toward Spokane, Washington, and then make a beeline for San Francisco." Pause. Stage three: the weather. Everyone's interested in the weather. "According to the forecast, the weather for our San Francisco arrival will consist of clear skies and unlimited visibility, and it should be a warm evening. The temperature at eleven this morning—about an hour and a half ago—was eighty-one degrees Fahrenheit." Stage four: the technical stuff. The things they can ooh and ahh about. "Our estimated flying time to San Francisco is twelve hours and six minutes. There is, of course, a nine-hour time zone change between Rome and California, which means that our estimated time of arrival is fifteen minutes past midnight, Pacific daylight saving time.

"We're presently cruising at an airspeed of five hundred sixty-one miles per hour—or, if you prefer, slightly faster than the muzzle velocity of a forty-five-caliber bullet, which is equivalent to eighty-five percent of the speed of sound—almost nine and one-half miles a minute. The temperature outside the aircraft is sixty-five degrees Fahrenheit—below zero. That's minus fifty-four degrees Centigrade. Your cabin has been pressurized to just about five thousand feet above sea level. This means that the atmospheric pressure in the cabin is the same as you'd normally experience on the ground at Denver, Colorado. If you have any other questions regarding the aircraft or the route of the flight, don't hesitate to pass a note to the cockpit. In the meantime, and on behalf of our cabin attendants, I'd like to invite you all to settle back, relax and enjoy the flight. We anticipate a smooth ride all the way to San Francisco."

* * *

The Boeing seemed to hang motionless, suspended from an infinitely distant ceiling bright with stars. Far below, the ground lay wreathed in blackness beneath a mantle of cloud. A man's senses could deceive him under such conditions. He was denied the familiar earthbound references that, since birth, had told him whether he was standing upright or leaning at an angle. He had to rely totally upon indicators and needles on the dimly lit instrument panel. They told the story: that the large swept-back wings were parallel with the invisible horizon and that the nose was pointed in the right direction. Mallory's eyes automatically scanned the gauges; these were his only reference. There was nothing earthly to be seen through the windshield.

He yawned. This was the sleepy time of every trip. It was the time of reaction following the bustle and concentration of flight planning, of preparing the aircraft for the trip, of the takeoff and departure through a system of complex, busy airways. Now the aircraft was at cruising altitude, its airspace cleared by the controller monitoring its progress on radar. Now the autopilot was doing all the work, the gyroscopes and accelerometers, tirelessly adjusting the controls to compensate for every nudge by the wind, every tiny dip and sway. After a surfeit of work and responsibility, there was little for the captain to do but go along for the ride . . . unless something went wrong. And so eyelids tended to become heavy as muscles unwound and nerves settled down.

He took a deep breath and braced his shoulder muscles. Look alive, he told himself. You've got the Pope on board. And a Secret Service agent sitting right behind you. Imagine if Mr. Cousins saw you dozing and then chose to tell everyone about it. The newspapers might get hold of the story. . . .

It was better not to contemplate how the company brass might react.

He glanced across at Jensen.

A serious young man, Mr. Jensen. No doubt he had already calculated how Mallory's retirement would affect his own fortunes. In every airline, everyone kept up to date on the all-important question of seniority. A pilot's seniority number was the key to his earnings, his vacations, his hours of duty, sometimes even his place of residence. To watch your number climb up the pilots' list was to watch the progress of your career.

One of the stewardesses brought in coffee. She was a pretty girl with a generous figure. When she left, Nowakoski said, "I think I just fell in love."

"That's the third time this week," said Jensen.

"Maybe the Pope can marry us," said Nowakoski.

"Can I be a witness?" interjected Cousins.

"Sure," said Nowakoski, "as long as you leave your gun behind. Always been fearful of a shotgun wedding."

"It must be a great life," Cousins mused. "Traveling the world with beautiful girls at your beck and call."

"Yeah, but it's tiring as hell," leered Nowakoski. "I tell you, Mr. Cousins, that's the only reason I got into flying. Hate airplanes, really. Much sooner stay on the ground. Except for the broads. Fantastic broads—and there's something about airports and uniforms and hotels that brings the best out in 'em, gives 'em that 'there's-no-tomorrow' feeling. On second thought, tell the Pope not to bother with the wedding. I'll stay single."

"One day you'll settle down," growled Jensen.

"One day I'll die," said Nowakoski with a shrug.

Mallory grinned at Jensen. Statistically, the young engineer was almost certain to be married within two years. Crew members were the marrying kind. Possibly it had something to do with the job. The constant traveling seemed to create the need for stability: a home, roots. Perhaps it was simply the contrary way of man: whatever state he is in, he wants something different.

Mallory wondered about himself. Could he ever call another woman his wife? After eighteen months, it still seemed inconceivable. Maybe there would be a time when it wouldn't, but so far that time hadn't come.

Why was fate so damned cruel? What purpose did it serve? Nan had been counting the days until he quit flying. That, she said, was when they would really start living. End of worries, of separations; a normal life at long, long last. But she had died and he had survived. If it was part of the Great Plan, it was a lousy plan. Nan had enjoyed life so much. And she was dead. He still found it hard to believe it had really happened. He kept expecting to see her walk into the house . . . that house. He would have to sell it soon. (Why did even the thought of selling seem disloyal to Nan?) It was a drag maintaining the place; half the time it was empty. Jane would soon want to pick up her own life again; he kept telling her that he didn't need a housekeeper. She would meet someone else. A pity that things didn't work out with Frank. He didn't know why. Jane never went into the details. Just as well, probably. These days, kids didn't mess around; if the marriage didn't work, it was summarily executed.

Jane would be okay. A very level-headed young lady. A realist, like her mother.

She would undoubtedly meet another Mr. Right in due course. This time, presumably, she would make a better choice; she would have learned from her mistakes. Second marriages were supposed to be more successful than first marriages, weren't they? Some cynic once said that everybody needs a first marriage for practice. . . .

This particular trip would have been a source of great pleasure for Nan. There would have been a scrapbook of newspaper clippings and volumes of letters to uncles in Georgia and aunts in Michigan, as well as long-lost girlfriends in Scotland and France. A great correspondent, Nancy; she should have been a journalist. She kept saying she was going to write stories for the local paper; and she did; but somehow they were never mailed. They lay in drawers and collected dust. He should have helped her. He could have called the editor . . . too late now; everything was too damned late. Hard as hell not to feel bitter about it.

"Hullo there," said Nowakoski.

"Hi." A girl's voice.

Mallory turned. Dee Pennetti this time. She carried an envelope.

"For you, Captain."

Mallory took it. His name had been neatly printed with a felt-tip pen.

"Wish you'd write to me," said Nowakoski.

"I would if you could read," said Dee in her flat, no-nonsense way. Dee had been a stew for ten years; she knew every line known to man.

Mallory asked her who the envelope was from.

"One of the coach passengers found it in a john."

"A john?"

"That's right, Captain. Taped to a mirror. "

Mallory shrugged. Probably a complaint about the late departure or his lengthy PA, or possibly there was another joker from the Eighth Air Force on board; that had happened once on a trip from Denver to New York; a man named Tolliver had introduced himself that way. Did Captain Mallory remember him? He had been a turret gunner on Dave Webster's crew. Mallory said yes, but didn't have the faintest idea who the man was.

He opened the envelope; the message was typed. It read:

CAPTAIN MALLORY, FIRST OFFICER JENSEN, FLIGHT ENGINEER NOWAKOSKI. THIS MESSAGE IS DIRECTED TO YOU ALL. IT COMES FROM THE BLACK SEPTEMBER ORGANIZATION. WE REGRET TO IN-FORM YOU THAT IT HAS BEEN FOUND NECESSARY TO TAKE PRISONER THE FOLLOWING: JANE SUTTON, VIRGINIA JENSEN, CRAIG JENSEN, KAREN JENSEN AND JOSEF NOWAKOSKI, SR. WE HAVE NO QUARREL WITH YOU OR WITH YOUR LOVED ONES AND WE DO NOT WANT TO HARM THEM. BUT WE MUST MAKE IT CLEAR THAT THEIR SURVIVAL DEPENDS UPON YOUR COMPLIANCE WITH THE FOLLOWING INSTRUC-TIONS. UPON REACHING LONGITUDE 45° W, YOU ARE TO REVERSE COURSE AND PROCEED VIA A DIRECT ROUTE TO EL MAHGREB AIRFIELD IN JORDAN. A CHART OF THAT AREA IS ENCLOSED. UNDER NO CIRCUMSTANCES WILL YOU DEVIATE FROM THE DIRECT ROUTE. YOU WILL INFORM AIR TRAFFIC CONTROL THAT YOU HAVE BEEN HIJACKED AND THAT ARMED MEMBERS OF OUR ORGANIZATION ARE IN YOUR COCKPIT AND IN THE CABIN. BE ADVIS-ED THAT WE ARE NOT BLUFFING. WE ASSURE YOU THAT IF OUR INSTRUCTIONS ARE CARRIED OUT TO THE LETTER, NO ONE WILL BE HARMED, HOWEVER, ANY RESISTANCE, ANY REFUSAL TO OBEY OUR ORDERS, WILL RESULT IN THE EXECUTION OF YOUR LOVED ONES AND THE DESTRUCTION OF YOUR AIR-CRAFT AND *EVERYONE ON BOARD.* WE ARE EQUIP-PED WITH THE NECESSARY EXPLOSIVES. CAPTAIN MALLORY, THIRTY MINUTES AFTER CHANGING COURSE, PROCEED ALONE TO THE REAR OF THE AIR-CRAFT. YOU WILL RECEIVE FURTHER INSTRUC-TIONS THERE. ONE LAST WORD: IF YOU DOUBT OUR

INTENTIONS, CONTACT YOUR COMPANY AS TO THE WHEREABOUTS OF YOUR FAMILIES.

Mallory blinked and read the message again.

My God! A gag in the worst possible taste. . . . It had to be. . . . He looked at the instruments, as if for a reminder of reality. Everything still functioned normally; the control column still moved in gentle response to the instructions of the little black boxes; the needles still pointed to the right numbers, as if nothing had interposed on the flight's tranquillity. Calm, he told himself, be calm. . . .

He glanced at Dee.

"Wait a minute, will you?" No doubt the Secret Service would want to know which passenger found the envelope in which john.

He handed the note to Cousins and announced, "Trouble."

He watched Cousins' brow crease as he absorbed the note's contents.

"*Shit!*" The Secret Service agent sounded angry. "Where did you get this?" he asked Dee.

"One of the girls in coach gave it to me. It was found in one of the aft johns."

Cousins looked as if he were biting through something.

"Hijack message," Mallory told Jensen and Nowakoski.

"Oh, for Christ's sake," muttered Nowakoski. He looked behind as if expecting to find an armed hijacker standing over him.

Jensen glared at the instrument panel.

"That's not all," Mallory told them. No point in pulling punches. "Our families are involved. They're got your wife and kids," he told Jensen, "and your father," he told Nowakoski. "And Jane . . . or so they say."

"*What?*" Jensen didn't believe him.

Cousins passed the note to the flight engineer and tugged the tiny microphone from his sleeve.

"Cousins. We've got a problem. Greene and Maddox, meet me in the upstairs lounge behind the flight deck. I'll brief you; then you can advise the others." He nodded to Dee. "Come with me. And Captain—" he turned to Mallory. "Please don't do anything till I get back." They hurried out of the cockpit and into the lounge.

Suddenly the atmosphere in the flight deck was electric.

Jensen's mouth dropped open. "Sons of bitches." He looked at Mallory. "No, Jesus, this can't be for real. Can it?" Suddenly his face darkened, as if the true significance of the message had finally struck home. "But they know our names . . . and Ginnie and Craig . . . and Karen. . . . They *must* have . . . It *is* for real!"

Nowakoski was shaking his head with a curiously resolute manner. "No, it's got to be a joke. Hell, my father's over seventy . . . and his heart's been giving him all kinds of trouble for the last three, four years. . . . He can't take this kind of crap."

It's no gag, Mallory thought. It's for real.

Jensen punched the palm of his hand. "Jesus! Who the hell do those bastards think they are, grabbing women and kids. . . !"

"Let's cool it," Mallory said. "We're not going to solve anything by losing control. I understand how you feel. I feel just the same. They've got my daughter, Jane, according to the note. We're all in the same boat. And so are our families. But let's stay calm!"

It had all happened too quickly; now he had to sort things out. "It's the Pope, of course. It has to be. He's the one they're after."

"Bastards," breathed Nowakoski. "The Holy Father. . . ."

Mallory nodded to himself. "That's got to be it. They don't really *want* our families, but they figure we're a hell of a lot more likely to do what we're told if our families are being held hostage. You see the point? Nice, huh? Maximum leverage to help the plan along."

Jensen shrugged, frowning. "But I don't get it. What the hell do they want with the Pope? An old man like him; he's not doing those bastards any harm."

"Hell, maybe it *is* a joke," said Nowakoski uncertainly. "A sick, sick joke."

"If it's a joke," Jensen retorted, "it sure as hell isn't funny."

Mallory looked back at the flight deck door. What was Cousins doing? What could he do? Jesus Christ, nothing was so maddening as being faced with a crisis and being able to do nothing but sit and wait.

"What are they going to do with the Pope—demand a ransom?"

Mallory nodded. "God knows. They can demand just about anything they want for him. . . ."

"They ought to lynch those lice."

"They're got to catch them first," said Nowakoski.

Mallory found himself wondering what might be demanded for the Pope's release. A million dollars? Ten million? A hundred million? Who would pay? The Church? Hell, they could ruin the Catholic Church, soak them for every penny they had. . . . Was there a sum the Church would balk at and say, sorry, he isn't worth that much? But would Black September be doing this for money? Somehow it seemed doubtful. Mallory knew that *this* organization never used terrorism for monetary gain.

"And the sons of bitches are on board right now?"

"You saw the letter."

"Armed?"

"Right."

"No. There's no way they could have smuggled guns aboard this aircraft." Jensen's hand was extended as if to grasp one of the hijackers. "Jesus, security was foolproof for this trip. Extra police metal detectors, x-ray equipment, body searches, the whole bit."

"Well, I guess we'll find out soon enough," Mallory muttered.

He set Jensen to work computing the flight time from longitude 45° W to Jordan; he gave Nowakoski the task of calculating the fuel burn and reserves.

Mallory glanced at his watch. In four hours and five minutes it would be time to turn and head for the Middle East instead of North America. What if he defied the hijackers? What proof did he have that anything would happen? Did they really have Jane and the others in captivity?

Cousins returned, ashen-faced, solemn.

"Everything's just goddam normal back there. Nothing."

"Any idea who left the note?"

Cousins shook his head. "My guess is, it's been there since shortly after takeoff. A woman passenger found it. Ada Bronsky, fifty-three. A nurse. Seems she was the first passenger to use that john." Cousins tapped his fingers nervously on the back of Mallory's seat, frustrated.

"What did you tell the Bronsky woman?"

"Said it was an obscene note."

"What did she say?"

"Nothing. Just shrugged."

"What now?" Mallory asked.

Cousins said, "I'd like you to call your company and have them try to make contact with your families. No use sending out a hijack alarm until we find out if this is for real."

Mallory nodded, thankful to have something positive to do. He tuned to the Airinc frequency.

"Airinc, this is Trans Am Flight nine-zero-one. Over."

The Airinc operator sounded sleepy. "Trans Am nine-zero-one, this is Airinc. Go ahead."

"Roger, Airinc. Request a patch with New York Dispatch, over."

"Roger, Trans Am. Stand by."

The crew exchanged glances, but there was nothing to say, there were just thoughts to think.

Three hours fifty-seven minutes to 45 degrees west longitude.

Then a familiar voice came crackling through the ether.

"Trans American Flight nine-zero-one. This is New York Dispatch. Myers speaking. Over."

"Harry, this is Steve Mallory on nine-zero-one. It's imperative that I talk to Henderson right away. Over."

Myers tried to maintain his casual, business-as-usual tone. "Okay, Steve. Stand by, I'll try to reach him. Got a problem?"

"I'm not sure."

"Okay. We'll get back to you. New York Dispatch clear."

Mallory sat back, grimly conscious of the concern his message was undoubtedly causing in New York. Myers, knowing only too well that something big was in the wind, would be on the phone to Henderson, vice-president of operations. In turn,

Henderson would suffer a momentary cardiac arrest, knowing that Mallory had the Pope as a passenger. A corporation man, Henderson. An ex-line pilot. Tough, but capable. About now he would be calling the Airinc office in New York requesting a direct phone patch with Flight 901.

It didn't take long. The SELCAL unit in the aircraft flashed a yellow light and sounded a chime, announcing that Airinc was calling Flight 901.

Mallory depressed the flashing light, silencing the chime. He turned up the volume on his high-frequency receiver.

"Trans Am nine-zero-one, answering SELCAL, over."

"Roger, nine-zero-one. This is New York Airinc. Stand by for a phone patch with Mr. Henderson. Over."

"Roger, Airinc."

A few seconds later, Henderson's direct, rather abrasive tones filled the cockpit.

"Mallory? This is Henderson. What's up?"

Mallory told him.

There was a pause. Henderson's heavy breathing was clearly audible.

"Okay," he said. Typically, there were no outbursts. "I'll get on it right away with the local authorities. And I'll notify the federal authorities, too. How long have you got until you're supposed to reverse course?"

"Three hours and forty-five minutes."

"All right. Anything else we can do for you?"

"Negative. It's quiet here. I suppose the whole thing could be some sort of stinking joke . . . but I doubt it."

"I understand. I'll be in touch as soon as I have word for you."

Mallory returned the mike to its hook. Now it was a question of waiting. Waiting and hoping. He turned to Cousins.

"I don't see any point in telling the Pope about this. Not yet."

"I agree."

Nowakoski said, "Hell, if there really are armed hijackers aboard, surely to God there's some way of identifying them."

"Is there?" said Cousins with a note of apprehension. "If there is, I'd sure as hell like to know what it is. I'd also like to know how the bastards got arms on board." He shook his head in the petulant manner of a man who can see no solution to the problem that faces him; already he was imagining a confrontation over which he would have absolutely no control. "According to the note, and assuming it's accurate, we'll find out who we're dealing with thirty minutes after we reverse course. That's when Captain Mallory goes aft to meet them."

What then? Mallory wondered. A shoot-out? Good guys versus bad guys at 35,000 feet? Someone had planned this thing well. But it had such an unreal quality. Every other hijacking he had ever heard of had involved gunmen, pistols and grenades, screaming passengers and white-faced stewardesses. But on this trip everything was normal . . . so far. Back in the passenger cabin they were enjoying filet with a choice of wine.

Black September claimed to be behind the whole thing. The very name was frightening. Black September: fanatics dedicated to the complete and final destruction of the State of Israel, the same madmen who slaughtered innocent passengers in airports and who had murdered Olympic athletes at Munich. They didn't care about their own lives or anyone else's.

It had to be a gag. Please make it a gag.

And yet they knew the names. Jane. Mrs. Jensen, Nowakoski's father. . . .

* * *

For the first half-hour of the flight, the woman had paid no attention to Mr. Squires. But then someone had stopped by and asked for his autograph. (Not for himself, of course; autographs were always for Auntie Flo or a retarded nephew.) The damage was done. His peace was irrevocably shattered for the duration of the trip.

"Of *course* . . . of *course*." She twisted herself, managing to confront him face to face, despite the fact that they were sitting side by side. "Well, you just sitting like that—how could I tell it was *you?*"

She managed to sound as if it were somehow his fault.

The woman's voice had a maddeningly mechanical quality to

it. She started each verbal barrage quite slowly, but she picked up speed, passing, it seemed, through a series of gears until she reached maximum velocity. She talked incessantly about her cat Willy, her canary, Marmaduke, her ranch-style house in Fresno, her son, Roger, who had his own boutique selling unisex clothes in Los Angeles, and her husband, Manville, who was apparently incapable of making a correct decision about anything.

Mr. Squires felt his sanity was being stretched to its limits. Would it snap soon? Would he be reduced to a babbling idiot by the sadistic forces of fate that put him on this damned airplane next to this damned woman?

And on the other side of the aisle was a scruffy man who had refreshed himself far too liberally before boarding the plane, and who seemed to fancy his chances with a dark-haired stewardess. . . .

What other irritations could the trip possibly have in store?

chapter 7

Officer Gilvenney slowed the car to a walking pace. He peered, squinting. It was tough to see the numbers; the damned houses were set so far back from the street.

"That's it," said his partner, Stafford. "Number 203."

Young eyes.

Gilvenney stopped the car.

"We'll approach the house on foot," he told Stafford.

"Right."

Gilvenney put his cap on and nodded toward the side gate. "You take a look around back."

"You bet."

He was out of the car in a flash. Gilvenney sighed. Not a bad kid, but a little too gung-ho for his own good.

Gilvenney loosened his gun and glanced at the windows. No moving drapes. He swallowed. He hated approaching suspect houses. Bad as hell for his nervous system.

He pressed the doorbell. The chimes sounded like the anvil chorus echoing through the house.

He cleared his throat.

"Anybody home?"

No answer. He tried the door. Unlocked.

Deep breath.

Gun in hand, he stepped inside.

For an instant he thought the corpse was human. He made himself look again. A beautiful dog, once. Who the hell would do that to such an animal?

"Gilvenney?"

Stafford came thumping through the house.

"The back door was open."

His pink face wrinkled in distaste as he saw the body of the dog and the spattered walls.

"There's been some kind of a struggle," he observed.

"Fantastic," said Gilvenney heavily. "They sure teach you great stuff at the academy these days. We'd better look around and see what else has been going on around here."

Stafford was back in a moment.

"Why," he asked, "would anyone write 'BLACK SEPTEMBER' on a dining room wall with a can of spray paint?"

"That," said Gilvenney, "is for us to report and some other son of a bitch to figure out."

* * *

The director of the Secret Service was furious.

"We might as well have saved ourselves the goddam trouble of sending agents to Rome. I mean, they're just sitting on their butts and playing passengers on the airplane. The hijackers are apparently doing just what they please. We're the patsies. That airplane is going to change course in a while. Not because some hijacker is holding a gun at the captain's head. Shit, no! There's no need for them to do anything as crude as that! They just send a nice little note to the captain and tell him to do as he's told. And if he doesn't, the threat is that the flight crew's families will get it. Nice. Neat as hell. And it's making us look like a bunch of goddam amateurs!"

"It's . . . a different approach, sir, one that we . . . well, frankly weren't prepared for." The assistant director felt the prickle of sweat inside his shirt.

"That," thundered the director, "is goddam well obvious! Who's our man on the airplane?"

"Cousins, sir."

"And what the hell is he doing?"

"At the moment, sir . . . he's . . . well, we can only assume he's awaiting developments. We must bear in mind that so far there has been no overt action. Mr. Cousins and his men—four of them—are ready in the event of a physical attempt to take over the airplane."

"Don't kid yourself," snapped the director. "We've been outmaneuvered . . . so far. There may very well be no attempt to take that airplane by force. No, this has been well thought out. And the next move is going to be just as unpredictable as the first, in my opinion. Is there any news on the flight crew's families?"

"Not yet, sir. The authorities are investigating. We're expecting reports momentarily."

The director worked his lower lip. The implications of all this were appalling.

"The sons of bitches have got us over a barrel. That's the fact of the matter. Jesus Christ . . . the Pope, of all people! And traveling on a U.S. flag carrier . . . God Almighty. If they'd set out to make us look like goddam dummies they couldn't possibly have done a better job! The *Pope*." He shook his head. Then he took a deep breath, reached for the telephone, pushed a red button and said, "Get me the White House."

* * *

Mallory found himself remembering the days on B-17s: the massive daylight raids, flying out of the cramped little English bases with their quaint names, scores of heavily loaded airplanes, piloted by kids, wheeling about in the sky trying to sort themselves out into formations, then striking out towards the Continent, everyone steeling himself for the moment when *Luftwaffe* fighters would come sliding, skidding in from every point of the compass, banging away with cannons and machine guns, anything to knock you out of the sky. He could still evoke the feeling—and the smell of cordite from the point-fifties in the turrets as they revolved like spiked eyes glaring at the fighters; and the bits of airplanes and men tumbling, spinning by on their long journeys to earth. You quickly convinced yourself that there was no way you could possibly survive the slaughter. You would soon be dead. Therefore there was no point in hoping any more. You made your peace. And you watched it all happen, almost like a spectator.

It was like that now.

He unlatched his seat belt.

"I'm going to take a look around," he said.

Cousins shook his head. "I think it's better if you stay here, Captain."

Mallory said, "This is my airplane, Mr. Cousins. I'm the captain, and I'll make that decision."

For a moment Cousins looked like a man about to argue a point. Then he shrugged.

"I just don't think we should precipitate anything," he said. "Not yet, not until we know the situation with regard to your families."

"I don't intend to precipitate anything," Mallory told him, as he slipped on his jacket and cap.

He made his way past the pair of worried-looking Secret Service agents in the lounge area, down the spiral staircase into the curtained-off first-class section. The Pontiff was inside his compartment; the other members of his party were enjoying their desserts.

A rosy-cheeked man in clerical garb inquired whether the airplane was making good time. He spoke English with precision and a lilt.

Mallory assured him that the flight was proceeding according to flight plan; a few minutes ahead, actually.

"This is the first time I have ever traveled by air," the priest said. "Odd, isn't it, in this day and age. But I must be honest. I believe I have avoided the experience." He smiled. "Discreetly, I like to think. When I learned that I was to come on this journey, I decided to learn a little about the subject. I therefore consulted the library and found a book that explained the elements of aeronautics. I learned what it is that makes this gigantic airplane leave the ground. A simple matter of increased air velocity creating a decrease in static pressure; the fluid pressure on the upper surface of the wing is lower than the pressure acting against the under surface, the net result being lift."

Mallory smiled in spite of himself. The man's manner was engaging. "I guess all this knowledge made you feel much better when we took off, sir."

"No, Captain, no! Quite the reverse in fact. The truth of the matter is, I wish I hadn't found out! I keep wishing there was more to rely on!" The priest laughed uproariously at himself.

Mallory went into the main passenger cabin. Rows of faces confronted him. Jaws chewed rhythmically.

He tried to avoid their eyes as he strode along the aisle. He had to pass one of the stews. She looked at him in surprise.

"Something we can do for you, sir?"

"No, thanks. Just felt like a stroll. Circulation needs a boost."

Further aft, a man stopped him.

"Bring me a bourbon, will you?"

"I'm not a steward, sir."

"So send me a steward."

Mallory told the man to push the stewardess call button if he needed something. Every flight seemed to have its drunks. Often they were a nuisance; sometimes they had to be restrained physically; occasionally it was necessary to request a police reception on landing. But on this trip a mouthy drunk was the least of his problems.

Everyone and everything looked so damned *normal.*

A man in a dark suit caught his sleeve as he passed. He looked familiar.

"You must be one of the pilots."

"That's right, sir."

"Why are you walking about?"

"Sir?"

"FAA regulations state that crews will remain on the flight deck while en route, unless there's an emergency. Is there an emergency?"

"No, sir; everything's just fine. Say, aren't you an actor? I seem to know your face."

A woman spoke up from the next seat.

"This is Vernon Squires," she announced, as if she were personally responsible for the fact.

Mallory said he was glad to have Mr. Squires on board.

Mr Squires possessed an unblinking glance of singular penetration. Mallory remembered how effective it was in that movie about D-Day. Vernon Squires had played a German colonel.

An astute guy, Mallory thought, as he went on. An elderly lady wanted to know if the Pope was enjoying the trip; a man and his wife were arguing about the time zone change between Rome and San Francisco.

Who was a terrorist? The swarthy man in the red shirt? The tall man wearing the gray suit? Everyone looked so damned innocent and unconcerned.

Surely no one would be sick enough to destroy this airplane and kill all these people. . . . No? Since when had terrorists started worrying about who they killed?

Cousins looked up inquiringly when Mallory returned to the flight deck.

"Anything?"

Mallory shook his head. "Couldn't be more normal."

"Bastards," Cousins muttered.

Mallory told Jensen to call Airinc and find out if there was any more news.

"They've got to make their move eventually," said Cousins. "That's when we'll have our chance."

Mallory said, "Then what happens to our families?"

Cousins looked away, uncomfortable.

Mallory settled himself back in the left seat. Everything mechanical was in order; everything human wasn't.

"They're still awaiting word," Jensen announced.

"Okay."

Jensen turned to Cousins, "If we fly to Jordan and land, and they take the Pope away, then I guess they'll let Ginnie and the kids and everyone else go free, huh? Just like that? Is that the way these things usually work?"

"Sure," said Cousins. "Something like that."

He didn't sound convincing.

"You're full of shit," snapped Jensen. "Our families are about number ten on your goddam priority list. They're the expendables, aren't they? Unimportant people. Hell of a shame about them but when you weigh the safety of the Pope and national prestige and international relations and the fucking Dow Jones average against a few citizens, there's no goddam contest, is there? Is there? Tell me!"

"Take it easy," said Mallory, "For all we know, this is a hoax."

"I doubt that," snapped Jensen. He shook his head and turned away, pale and angry.

Cousins said, "Look, I'm real sorry about your families. But what the hell can I do about them here? This airplane and the Pope are my responsibilities . . . and I've got to do everything I can for them."

"Sure," said Mallory. "We understand. You're in a tough spot, Cousins. So are we, and so are our families. We understand your position. Try to understand ours."

"I do," said Cousins. "I really do."

The cockpit was silent except for radio static and snatches of a Morse code identifier sent by the Benbecula VORTAC station in northwestern Scotland.

Relax, Mallory told himself; just play it cool. They want you to get steamed up about Jane. So don't get steamed up. Never do what the enemy wants you to do. Who said that? He couldn't remember.

"Jesus Christ," snapped Jensen, "how fucking long does it take to find out if a woman's been kidnapped?"

He was chewing gum with furious deliberation.

"It takes a little while," said Cousins. "They'll be in touch. Soon."

"My father's heart is in bad shape," said Nowakoski. "Real bad. He just can't take this kind of crap." He turned to the others, as if appealing to their sense of justice. "I mean, what the hell are they doing, messing around with an old man, for God's sake? Something like this could kill him. They wouldn't have to lay a hand on him, but he could die just the same."

Mallory nodded. He tried to look sympathetic but what he wanted to say was, What the hell do you think I can do about it? Get him released because of his age and his poor state of health?

Mallory looked at his watch. Two hours and seven minutes before reaching 45 degrees west longitude over southern Greenland. The fact of the matter was, he had no choice but to comply. The Pope's life was in jeopardy and everything had to be done to protect it. Jane and the others were the added incentive to ensure that he did precisely what they wanted. Not to mention 277 other lives and a $40 million airplane. Jesus Christ, was there anything in this whole rotten, stinking world quite as despicable as using innocent people's lives as currency?

"But why the Arabs?" wondered Nowakoski aloud. "What the hell have we got to do with them, for Pete's sake? Hell, my old man was always saying he feels kind of sorry for them, the way they got kicked off their own land when the State of Israel was created. I mean, he had a point too. He always used to say, How would the people who live on Long Island like it if some guy in the United Nations suddenly got up and said that from now on Long Island is the official home of the aborigines or some damned things or other? Christ, there are two sides to everything, and my old man always saw those two sides. A fair man. And he's the one the sons of bitches pick!"

Suddenly they were alert. The yellow light was flashing.

"Trans Am nine-zero-one, answering SELCAL. Over."

"Roger nine-zero-one. Stand by for a phone patch with Mr. Henderson. Over."

"Roger."

Henderson didn't mince words.

"Mallory, looks like we've got a problem; your note was accurate. Here's the deal. Local authorities report that the individuals in question are missing. Steve, they went to your house. Your daughter wasn't there, although her car is still parked in the garage. First Officer Jensen's wife's car was found in the parking lot of a local supermarket. Keys in the ignition, bags of groceries in the back seat. No sign of Mrs. Jensen or the two children. Mr. Nowakoski is missing too. Mrs. Nowakoski went out to visit a friend, but when she got back, he wasn't there. A neighbor said something about a Sears truck. The authorities are looking into that. However, there was a message written on a wall in each house: 'Black September'. That's all we've got so far. It certainly doesn't look good. The local police and the FBI are on top of this, and they're doing everything they can at this end.

What are your intentions?"

"I don't see that we have much choice, do you?"

"I suppose not. Do the passengers know?"

"Negative. No point telling them anything yet."

"Okay, Steve. Air Traffic Control is working on your new clearance. They'll be in touch with you soon. Have you had any further contact from the . . . people aboard your aircraft?"

"Negative," Mallory responded. "That's what makes it so weird."

"I understand."

I wonder if you do, Mallory thought. "We'll be turning in a couple of hours."

"Okay, Steve. We'll stay in touch."

We'll stay in touch too, Mallory thought: we'll send you a postcard from the Middle East. He turned to the others.

"If anyone's got any bright ideas, I'd like to hear them."

Nowakoski said, "Maybe they're just . . . you know, all temporarily away from home for some simple reason. Maybe they're not kidnapped at all."

"Did they also decide to decorate their walls with Black September signs?"

Nowakoski didn't answer.

There would be nothing to be gained by going into a steep turn and making the passengers aware that the airplane was changing course. Better to let everyone relax as long as possible. Chances were good that no one would even be aware of a very gradual turn, using a shallow bank angle. The black night sky would conceal the 180-degree turn.

Mallory asked Nowakoski to check on the latest weather and get a forecast for the El Maghreb area.

Everything will be okay, he told Jane silently. Somehow we'll get ourselves out of this stinking mess. We'll make things work out.

Jensen was gazing down at his clenched fists, as if imagining that he was choking the life out of one of the fanatics responsible for all of this.

"Holy Christ," said Nowakoski as he passed Mallory a note with the cryptic weather data. A severe *simoom* was in progress over southern Israel, southern Jordan and the Sinai.

Mallory shook his head and sighed. On top of everything else, a goddam sandstorm!

chapter 8

The Prime Minister of Israel read the message for the tenth time. Then he sat back, folding his arms across his chest. He regarded the men sitting before him, around the long conference table. Their eyes were on him, filled with anxiety. Poor fellows, they know only too well what it means to be summoned at such a late hour and driven at high speed to the Knesset: another crisis.

"I apologize for disturbing your evening. Obviously, it is because of a matter of the most urgent nature." He unfolded his arms and placed his hands on the conference table: a characteristic pose, a favorite of cartoonists. "We have received a communiqué from Black September," he said. "They claim to have hijacked the plane carrying the Pope from Rome to San Francisco. It will land in Jordan in less than ten hours. The Pope will be taken off the aircraft and held for a maximum of twenty-four hours, according to their note. If, within that time, we have not withdrawn our forces from the West Bank, he will be executed. If we refuse to withdraw, they say, Israel will be responsible for the violent death of the Pope."

He felt a momentary sympathy as he saw the effect of his words. They hurt, they stung. Another nerve-shattering confrontation. Each man was already deep in thought, regarding the implications, considering the ramifications, weighing the consequences.

The Minister of Defense, a lean individual in military khaki, said, "Can you tell us the position of the aircraft now and where it is headed?"

Intelligence shuffled his notes.

"The aircraft is a Boeing 747SP belonging to Trans

American Airlines. At this moment it is over the North Atlantic and heading toward Greenland. Upon reaching 45 degrees west longitude, it will turn and head toward the Orkney Islands of northern Scotland on a great-circle course to El Maghreb, Jordan. On the way, I understand it will fly across southern Israel."

"And if we simply ignore the whole thing?"

"The Pope is executed, according to the message."

"I doubt it. What possible purpose would be served by such an action? None, except to sicken the world and make most of it loathe the PLO and all its lunatic fringe organizations."

The speaker was a man of sixty with wiry, grizzled hair. A veteran of the 1948 War, he had no patience for discussions about dealing with Black September. To him, it was simple: all terrorists were bloodthirsty fanatics. You ignored them and went about your business, but if they came at you, you killed them before they killed you. "We are not responsible for this action," he declared. "Therefore no one can hold us responsible for the Pope's death, if it comes to that, which personally I doubt. But if Black September chooses to commit such an atrocity, then the blood is on their hands, not ours."

"But will the world see it that way?" asked the Prime Minister.

"Does it matter?"

"Unfortunately, it does."

"We didn't precipitate this action. . . ."

"No, we didn't. But the terrorists will claim that we did by our continued occupation of their homeland."

"The occupation is defensive. . . !"

"I know that, my friend, and so do you. But does the rest of the world see it this way? Let us suppose for a moment that we comply with the demand. We withdraw our forces and the Pope is released. Everyone breathes a sigh of relief. Another crisis settled. Then what? Presumably Arab military forces will immediately occupy the West Bank."

"We would be back to precisely where we were before the Six-Day War."

"Correct. And if we moved to recapture the West Bank, it

would necessitate a major military expedition. The result could be full-scale war with Jordan and Syria; it could in fact lead to another—and perhaps final—Middle East conflict, one that we might not win, gentlemen."

Defense snapped, "We have never negotiated with terrorists—and I say that it would be a disastrous error to start now!" He pointed at each of the men at the table. "We all know how difficult—agonizing, even—these decisions have been in the past. At times we have been sorely tempted. We have all thought, give in; just this once; there's no other course. But we haven't given in. And we were right, gentlemen! We were right because any tendency toward discussions with these . . . *maniacs* would be taken as a sign of weakness, and God only knows what further demands would have been generated. There is only one language that is understood by terrorists: force. There is no use talking to them in rational terms, because they are not rational individuals. Nothing matters to them but their cause. They don't care who they hurt, who they kill. Now they have taken an elderly man who is on an innocent mission, a man who has no quarrel with them, who wants only peace in the world. And they are threatening to kill this man if we do not meet their demands. It is a monstrous act perpetrated by subhumans, and I declare that to give in to them would desecrate the memories of the men and women who died creating and defending this state!"

There were murmurs of approval.

The Prime Minister sighed. "I understand your feelings, my friends. The fact remains, however, that this is no ordinary kidnapping or hijacking. Black September has captured one of the world's most influential figures. He is revered by millions of the faithful in countries all over the world. To them, he is next to God. I put this to you: It has taken us thousands of years to create Israel and to be recognized as a legitimate sovereign state; and for all those thousands of years we as a people have been regarded as the killers of the Son of God, Jesus Christ. The historians agree that the facts tell a different story: that the Romans killed him. Very well, but I have yet to see any Italian called a Christ-killer. Now we have a sort of ghastly parallel being created. Gentlemen, if we were to stand back and let this execution take place for the sake of a few kilometers of territory. . . ."

"A few kilometers of territory! My God, thousands of men and women gave their *lives* for that territory, and it is our security. . . ."

"I don't have to be reminded of that fact," declared the Prime Minister, his cheeks reddening. "A brother and a cousin are buried on the West Bank. What I am saying is that we are being thrust into a position of great delicacy. While most of the peoples of the world deplore these terrorist tactics, we must recognize the sympathy that exists for their cause. They can hardly be blamed for saying to themselves, The Arabs are only demanding that Israel pull back to the territorial lines that existed before the Six-Day War; and it can't be denied that the West Bank was their territory prior to 1967."

"People who talk that way don't know the facts."

"True. You are correct. But we must look at the world as it is; we must consider how people see this situation, not how we wish they would see it."

A general declared, "To hell with what the rest of the world says! There is only one thing that's important, and that is the survival of Israel. Individuals and their words are soon forgotten. I may sound callous, but we must face facts. The State of Israel is our charge; it is our sacred duty to do everything we can to ensure its survival."

The Prime Minister nodded soberly. "I respect your view. But there is a very real danger of a kind of transfer of guilt. People will, I think, tend to reason this way: The Arabs are guilty of kidnapping the Pope; the Israelis are equally guilty if they let the Pope die instead of acceding to what may be inevitable. We must consider our position among the nations of the world. Our primary goal has always been security through recognition of Israel's existence as a sovereign nation-state. That recognition has been long in coming—indeed, it still remains to be achieved from the Arab bloc. The people who planned this incident obviously realize that most of the countries friendly to Israel have large Catholic populations. And these Catholics would unquestionably create a great tidal wave of resentment against Israel if we failed to do anything to protect the life of the Pope. And who could blame them? As far as they are concerned, the first priority will, of course, be the safety of the Pope; to them, the territorial question will be of secondary importance—something to be discussed once the Pope is out of danger."

A man in his late thirties, wearing glasses, spoke for the first time. "Mr. Prime Minister, we might consider the possibility of agreeing to the terrorists' demands in exchange for diplomatic recognition by the Arab states. After all, if such recognition were to be granted, our need for the West Bank territory would be largely eliminated. Psychologically, the action would return the ball to the Arab court, and it would surely refocus the blame if any deaths do occur."

Angry comments greeted the suggestion. The Prime Minister had to call for order. He asked what steps might be taken to rescue the Pope and the others by force.

Defense said, "I have been giving the matter some thought. We know the destination of the aircraft. It's an abandoned military airfield a few kilometers inside the Jordanian border. My guess is that, with Entebbe in mind, Black September won't be taking any chances. I suspect they will surround the aircraft the moment it lands, and I should think that the passengers will all be under armed surveillance from that moment on. There are a couple of empty hangars on the field. Presumably they will be used as temporary quarters. While there is no question that an assault could be mounted on the airfield, I doubt very much that it could be successful without causing the deaths of the Pope and all, or some, of the passengers. We cannot compare this situation with the one that prevailed at Entebbe. It would be impossible to guarantee the safety of a specific individual. And what of the Jordanians? Would they stand by and permit us to invade their territory? Surely they too would be prepared for a military incursion."

The Prime Minister said, "I wonder if we would have mounted the assault if the Pope had been held at Entebbe. I doubt it."

An elder cabinet member banged the conference table with his fist.

"Mr. Prime Minister, I respect your judgment and I understand the political pressures you have to face. But I declare to you unequivocally that the West Bank is far more important to us than any one individual's life, no matter who that individual may be!"

* * *

The President of the United States lit his pipe, angrily shaking the match until it was extinguished.

"Damn it," he said, "what's the matter with our security? Are we incapable of flying an airliner from one continent to another without this kind of thing happening? My understanding was that security was going to be impregnable!"

The Secret Service chief was clearly embarrassed and angry. "Mr. President, their modus operandi has not been fully revealed. It's difficult to say just what went wrong. I can assure you, however, that it's being fully investigated . . . and we're doing everything we can to protect that flight; there are five agents aboard the aircraft. . . ."

"I don't want details. The point is, we are the host country for the conference to which the Pope has been invited, and he is flying aboard a United States flag carrier. His safety is our responsibility and we've dropped the goddam ball!"

The Secretary of State wanted to know the position of the aircraft at that moment. One of the air force generals had the information at hand.

"They're presently south-southeast of Iceland, Mr. Secretary. The pilot has been ordered to reverse course upon reaching south-central Greenland. The turn will actually take place to the south of Sob Story, one of our radar sites on the ice cap."

"Why in the hell do the hijackers want to fly so far west before turning toward their destination?"

"We wondered about that too, sir. In the end, we came to the conclusion that we are dealing with hijackers who are well informed about the 747SP aircraft. For example, it occurred to us that your average hijacker might have taken over the airplane as soon as it took off from Rome and immediately ordered the pilot to fly to Jordan. After all, it's a much shorter journey from Rome to Jordan, than from Greenland to Jordan. All of which made us believe that our hijackers know airplanes. They know, for example, that a Boeing 747 fully loaded with enough fuel to take it from Rome to San Francisco is far too heavy to land until most of that fuel has been consumed. So, if the aircraft flies all the way from Rome to Greenland, and *then* changes course, by the time it reaches Jordan it will be light enough to make a landing on a fairly short and probably soft runway such as there is at El Maghreb. However, they could have dumped the fuel in flight. But they probably need the additional time to put their plans into effect. At least, that's our current hypothesis, sir. Technically speaking, someone in Black September has done his homework."

The President thanked the general in his gravely courteous way. "On the face of it," he said, "serious consideration must be given to the terrorists' demands; after all, it is unthinkable that the Pope's life could be lost in such a manner."

The Secretary of State pointed out that the action had to be taken by Israel, not the United States. "And in the past, Mr. President, Israel has consistently refused to negotiate with terrorists."

"The rest of the world," said the Secretary of Defense, "doesn't have the guts to follow their example."

The President nodded; decisions were sometimes simpler for countries in a state of war, or even semiwar. "We cannot possibly permit the Pope's life to be further jeopardized," he declared. He was only too aware of the appalling political consequences should it be felt that the United States was responsible, either directly or indirectly, for the murder of the Pope.

A four-star army general with bone-white hair said, "Do you mean, sir, that we should attempt to persuade Israel to give up the West Bank?"

"We can't *persuade* Israel to do anything."

"No, but we can make it goddam awkward for them if they don't." He lit a cigar and clenched it between his teeth; the action twisted his mouth into a fiendish grin. "Anyway," he went on, "in my opinion, Mr. President, we would be well advised to take no action at all."

"No action?"

"Precisely. In my opinion, the Palestinian radicals have gone too far this time. What the fanatics are suggesting is so goddam evil that I believe they should be permitted to proceed . . . because they'll destroy themselves in the process!"

"Are you suggesting that we sit back and do nothing?"

"More or less. We tell the world that we are shocked and saddened by the acts of these criminals; we state categorically that if the Pope is executed, his blood is on the heads of his killers, not on those who had nothing to do with it. The act will be so disgusting that it will be a fatal blow—and self-inflicted, at that— to left-wing terrorism all over the world. It could be a blow from which it might never recover."

"And I doubt, General, that we could ever recover any of the prestige we would have lost by taking no action to prevent this slaughter." The President shook his head. "No, I'm afraid I can't agree with you."

The Secretary of Defense declared, "I would be ashamed to call myself an American if we stood by and did nothing."

The general shrugged. "I suggest, Mr. Secretary, that it would be one hell of a lot more effective to let Black September destroy itself rather than to negotiate with them."

"An innocent man's life is at stake. A very powerful innocent man."

"By dying this way he might make his biggest contribution to mankind."

"Your attitude is disgusting."

The general shrugged in reply.

The President drummed his fingers on the table and called for an end to that particular line of discussion. He turned to the Secretary of State.

"Mr. Secretary, I would appreciate hearing your views on the situation."

Heads turned toward the intense, scholarly-looking individual at the President's side.

"In my opinion," he said slowly, deliberately, "we face the very real possibility of a . . . major confrontation with the Soviet Union." He looked at the faces around him. "We are, I believe, facing one of the most serious crises in recent times."

The President interrupted, "Mr. Secretary, I must say I am not convinced that the crisis we face is likely to result in such a confrontation. No hijacking has ever escalated into a mass mobilization of armed forces or, indeed, any real increase in tensions between ourselves and the Communist bloc. Admittedly, the present case is unique, and surely the Soviet Union *will* condemn this act. How could they support it? And how could they support the terrorists? On the other hand, if you are proposing that any overt action on the part of the United States could lead to. . . ."

"Sir!" the Secretary interjected, "I am only cautioning that our actions in response to this situation could conceivably lead to a nuclear confrontation . . . because of the fundamentally unstable and explosive state of affairs in the Middle East."

"Anything's possible." The President was clearly irritated. His fingers were intertwined; they worked as if one were trying to overcome the other.

"Mr. President, I think one factor has been overlooked." The Undersecretary for Security Affairs was the youngest member of the Security Council—and widely known as an intensely ambitious individual. "The Jordanian army could surely be the factor that makes the big difference."

One of the President's personal advisors on national security nodded in agreement. "We have already had direct contact with the Jordanian government," he said in his precise, academic way. "I can state with some confidence that the Jordanians will do nothing to prevent the Pope's aircraft from landing at El Maghreb. It seems likely that the Jordanian army will surround the airfield—and probably prevent the Pope from being taken away to some unknown destination. The Jordanians seem to believe that the Pope will be handed over to them after the Israelis accede to Black September's demands. Whether this is fact or supposition, we have no way of knowing. The Jordanians say they are powerless to interfere in any other way, without jeopardizing the Pope's safety."

An army general asked, "Are the Jordanians aware of the possibility of an Israeli strike across the border: an attempt to rescue the hostages?"

"Of course. They have already told us that they will not tolerate any Israeli incursion on Jordanian soil; they will repulse any such attempt with every means at their disposal. Gentlemen, in my view, any hope of receiving assistance from the Jordanians is remote indeed. We must face the simple fact that the Jordanians have not the slightest objection to Israel being forced out of the West Bank—particularly if they are not directly implicated. Why should they object? They can stand back and watch others achieve what they themselves have been unable to do. What did the Jordanians do when the PLO hijacked four civilian airliners and forced them to land in the desert near Amman? Nothing. They will do nothing in this case. I tell you frankly that I can think of no worthwhile action on our part. We must be practical. We are talking in terms of a matter of hours about an event that is taking place thousands of miles from here on foreign territory involving armed bands of terrorists with whom we have no formal relations!"

"I am only too aware of that," the President murmured unhappily. "But we can't for a moment lose sight of the fact that we are talking about an American aircraft flown by an American crew, with American passengers on board, as well as the Pope and many others to whom we owe a direct responsibility. We have failed to prevent the seizure of this airplane. We must not fail again. We must do something."

"Mr. President, there is one obvious course of action." An air force general had spoken. He stood up, his lanky frame dominating the conference table and the men who sat around it. "Sir, whenever the Israelis have used force to free hostages or remove hijackers from aircraft, they have won the admiration and respect of peoples around the world. Now, sir, if the Jews can fly all the way to Entebbe in East Africa to rescue their people, I say it is time for us to employ force to rescue ours! And the Pope and the other passengers who are traveling under the so-called protection of the American flag! We can, in one blow, regain one hell of a lot of the prestige we have lost around the world!"

"And what if some of the hostages are killed as they were at Entebbe?" asked the President. "And what if one of those casualties happens to be the Pope?"

"At least we would have tried."

"An 'A' for effort!"

"Maybe an 'A' for doing something positive. Damn it all, he's liable to be killed anyway!"

"But not by us, General!"

"Israel will never negotiate with those terrorists!" The general was almost shouting, venting a frustration created out of the defeat and retreat from all the principles and practices he had once learned at the Academy. Was there never to be a victory again? There was no victory in Korea, none in Vietnam; now, not even against a lunatic bunch of radicals. "If Israel refuses to give in to the demands, then the head of the Catholic Church will be executed and we will have done nothing!"

The President sighed. "I am in agreement with much of what you say, General. But I cannot, in the framework of the current Middle East situation, order United States military forces to invade the territory of a friendly state, violating its sovereignty, endangering the lives of God only knows how many soldiers and civilians." He folded his arms and glared around the table. "I simply cannot do that!"

The Secretary of State nodded soberly. "That, sir, is precisely how I believe we could run a terrible risk of great power involvement, of nuclear confrontation, in fact. If we use American military forces, there is certain to be an armed battle between them and the regular Jordanian army. We would, in effect, be aiding the Israelis, thus prolonging their occupation of the West Bank. Do we really believe the Soviet Union would not intervene? Surely the Kremlin would seize the opportunity to come to the aid of a weak Arab state under attack by the United States. What a logical excuse for them to vastly enhance their power in the Middle East. Gentlemen, we could be immersed in a global conflict in a matter of hours!"

The air force general threw up his hands. "For God's sake, don't we fight for what is right anymore? Don't we have the guts to risk anything for our national interests? I declare that every country has the right to pursue and destroy pirates! And that's what these bastards are, Mr. Secretary! Pirates! Christ, we wouldn't be invading Jordan; we'd be helping to destroy international terrorism. And if the Russians are that anxious to get involved, then let's call their bluff just as we did during the Cuban missile crisis."

The President seemed to be contemplating the enormity of the problem and its ramifications. "There has to be a middle ground between impotence and nuclear cataclysm. There is an answer. There has to be. And it's up to us to find it. That airplane will be landing in a matter of hours!"

*   *   *

The President and the Israeli Prime Minister were well acquainted. They met back in the early sixties when the one was a congressman visiting the world's trouble spots and the other an Israeli Air Force general who still flew combat missions in *Mystere* jets. Since then they had met on numerous occasions. They liked and respected each other, generally sharing a common view of world politics. Even so, the telephone conversation between them quickly assumed a kind of stiltedness; both men were conscious of the fact that they spoke not for themselves as individuals but as heads of state and the decisions to be made this day could haunt them forever.

The President said, "I must tell you how very deeply we regret that this has happened while the Pope was traveling aboard a United States carrier."

"There's no need for apologies, Mr. President. I am quite confident that everything possible was done to ensure the Pope's safety. The immediate question is what can be done now."

"I think you will agree that the Pope's life is the most important single factor to be considered, but we must not forget for a moment the crew and nearly three hundred civilian passengers."

The Prime Minister said, "But I must tell you that we view the West Bank as vitally important. It is essential to our security, you understand. In light of our recent history, it is inconceivable to us that we should unconditionally withdraw from the West Bank in order to save one man's life—no matter who that man is."

"But, Mr. Prime Minister, you must be aware that there would be a veritable tidal wave of indignation—directed at both Israel and the United States—if we stood back and let this outrageous act of murder take place."

"Neither of us would be responsible for it. Any indignation should be directed at the Arabs; they are the perpetrators, not us."

"I agree, of course, Mr. Prime Minister. But we in the United States are deeply disturbed about this situation. It is explosive; the murder of the Pope could be as shattering to world peace as was the death of the Archduke at Sarajevo; it could well be the event that upsets the delicate balance in the Middle East once and for all."

"I agree with your interpretation of the situation. It is indeed an extremely dangerous one. We, however, do not feel that we should be the ones to suffer. We feel that another solution must be found."

"An Entebbe?"

"An appealing thought. But not, I'm afraid, very practical. The fact of the matter is that we simply do not have time to mount an operation of that magnitude. Neither do we have a similar set of circumstances. There, of course, we were familiar with the layout of the airfield; furthermore, we were aware that there was likely to be some confusion and laxity on the part of the Ugandan authorities. This time I doubt that such an operation would succeed. The terrorists would be only too aware of the possibility; they will, I am positive, mount a very strong and alert guard on this one man as soon as the aircraft lands."

"I am sure you are correct, Mr. Prime Minister. I should tell you that the State Department is approaching the PLO via the United Nations. It is possible that Mr. Arafat might be as horrified by this operation as we are. Perhaps he can exert some tempering influence on Black September, but frankly, Arafat may not want or may not be able to do a damned thing at this point."

"It is good to know that the approach is being made. I am not, however, very hopeful of results. Arafat seems to have very little control over the more radical elements of the PLO, and while he may publicly and personally repudiate such actions as the one we are discussing, I doubt that he will take overt action—even if such action would have any chance of success."

"May I ask your intentions then, Mr. Prime Minister?"

A sigh. "At the moment, I just don't know."

chapter 9

The bald one seemed to be the leader. Jane called him Telly. The name stuck. It was easier to remember than Abou Youssef, which was the name the others used when they addressed him.

There were four of them. Telly, Scarface, Icy Eyes and a very young one they named Billy the Kid. Dark-eyed and sturdy, all of them, with an arsenal of weapons.

Scarface and Telly came in. Scarface stood beside the door, looking at each captive in turn, Jane last.

Telly announced:

"You will be held here for a few hours. It will not be long." His English was almost perfect; only a rolling of some letters gave him away. "When the necessary formalities have been successfully concluded, you will be released."

Jane asked what sort of formalities were involved.

"That is none of your business."

"Why not?"

He ignored the question. "You must understand," he told them all, "that your lives are of no importance when measured against our mission."

"And what is that?" Jane asked persistently.

Again he ignored her. "It is imperative that you understand this: any trouble from you will result in the most severe action. We have no wish to kill you, but we will if it becomes necessary."

"Kill?" Virginia Jensen seemed incapable of believing her ears. "But . . . my children."

Telly sniffed. He regarded her with disdain. "I do not care about you or your children. I do not care about any of you. Understand that you do not *matter* to us."

Jane said, "We're not too crazy about you, either."

The words sounded braver than she felt. If he hit her, wouldn't she be crying, pleading for mercy? Her courage was a brittle thing.

Telly sighed, as if bored by the proceedings. "By now," he said, "I imagine you have had time to realize that you share a common bond. Each of you has a close relative flying as a member of the flight crew of a Trans American airliner which at this moment is supposed to be flying from Rome to San Francisco, carrying the Pope and other passengers."

The captives looked at one another.

Jane said, "My father was supposed to be flying to Bahrain from London. . . ."

"Correct," said Telly. "But he was assigned to the Pope's flight at the last minute."

"And you're going to hijack the aircraft? Is that right?"

"It has already been done," Telly told them. "You should be relieved to know that our instructions have been obeyed without question."

"You will be punished," said Mr. Nowakoski, pointing an accusing finger.

Telly smiled frostily, as if the old man's statement was a mild joke. He said, "I repeat to all of you: You will be released in due course. We won't harm you unless we have to."

Virginia Jensen sounded bewildered.

"But . . . what good does it do, holding us here?"

Telly shrugged. "Certainly the pilots will obey instructions if they know that their families are being held hostage and that those dear to them will die if the instructions are not obeyed."

"Die. . . ?" The old man coughed.

Jane said, "Has anyone been . . . hurt so far?"

"I don't think so. Soon you will be allowed to return to your homes."

"How soon?"

"You will find out at the appropriate time."

"And our . . . the flight crew?"

"They will be released also."

"And the Pope?" Jane asked. "What happens to him?"

"Nothing. He will be free to go on to San Francisco or to return to Rome . . . once our demands have been met."

"You are evil," declared the old man, his cheeks quivering with indignation. "How dare you do this to His Holiness!"

Telly paid no attention to him and turned toward the door.

Jane said, "What's your price, for releasing the Pope?"

"That is not your concern."

"I think it is. We're involved, aren't we?"

"I am not prepared to say anything more." Telly folded his arms.

"You guys are Palestinians, right?"

Telly regarded her for a moment; he nodded.

Jane said, "So you're trying to coerce Israel in some way . . . using the Pope as hostage. Correct?"

"I told you, I am not prepared to discuss the matter further. Don't try my patience. Like most women, you talk too much. If you wish to survive the next several hours, I suggest you do your best to keep your mouth shut."

"If I do," Jane said, "will you keep your gorillas away from me? One of them tried to rape me," she added, noting the Jensen woman's startled look.

Telly said, "Did the rape succeed?"

"No."

"Then you have no reason to complain." He rubbed his eyes, apparently weary of the conversation. "You will be fed shortly. In the meantime, I suggest you sit quietly or sleep. The time will go quickly. Soon it will all be over and you will be able to go home."

He turned and headed for the door, a short but powerful figure in jeans and a leather jacket. "I will not say anything more at this time," he added, as if a television reporter's microphone were being thrust at him.

Both men left; the door slammed; a key turned.

Mr. Nowakoski shrugged, bewildered. What a world, where the Pope himself could be plucked from an airplane and become the prisoner of such men. . . .

A thin voice piped, "He'd just better bring some food soon."

Jane smiled at the sight of Craig Jensen, ten years old, standing in the middle of the bare floor, hands on hips, a pint-sized David facing a tribe of Goliaths. Our Hero. Unafraid.

"He will, dear, he will." Virginia Jensen held his shoulders as if to restrain him.

"I have some Life Savers," Jane told Craig. "Want some?"

"Sure do."

"Say thank you," his mother reminded him.

"Thanks."

"You're welcome," said Jane as she fished in her pocket. She had bought them the previous day, at the market while waiting for her dry cleaning. Toby had been sitting in the back seat of the car, panting, misting up the window.

Toby. Poor Toby. The casualty. The first of how many?

"Are you going to fly an airliner when you grow up?"

Craig thought about it for a moment.

"Could be," he said. "Flying's neat. But I have my eye on electronics too."

"Good field," Jane nodded with due gravity.

Craig said, "You weren't scared of that man, were you?"

"A bit," she admitted.

"But you didn't show it. That's the important thing."

"Is it?"

"Sure. They said that on a TV show," he told her. "So I guess it's true."

Mr. Nowakoski muttered, "I think everything will be all right, ladies. Look, they capture an important man like the Pope . . . well, you bet the world isn't going to let anything happen to him. It'll be all right."

"Of course it will," said Virginia Jensen, almost curtly, as if she wouldn't permit the slightest hint of doubt to enter her mind.

Jane wondered what the ransom could be.

Something fantastic. Something to make the world sit up and take notice. Was the world already doing that? It was impossible to know, stuck here in this room, without radio or television. . . .

But the truth was, things might go wrong; things could very easily go wrong; indeed things were almost *likely* to go wrong. So what would happen? Would the door suddenly burst open, and would Telly and Scarface and the others come storming into the room with their guns and start shooting, and would they keep on shooting until all the quivering and crying and whimpering was done, and would the police or whoever stumble on this place days or weeks or months later and find their rotting bodies, like Toby's, spread all over the floor like bloody sacks?

These guys are *terrorists,* she thought. They don't give a damn about anyone or anything; they just keep shooting; killing is their business. . . .

Was this the way her all-important life would end?

Finis for Jane, because someone somewhere didn't do something that someone else wanted them to do, or perhaps did something that wasn't wanted. In any event, the net result is that things didn't go according to plan; but then nothing in her life had gone according to plan. "Incorrigible," the nuns had called her. Two days after they had expelled her, she had been comfortably ensconced in a commune in Mendocino County . . . then the almighty effort to conform . . . and the numbing boredom, exploding into six months in the North Beach drug scene. Conformity was impossible. The fascination with rebellion was irresistible.

I hope they kill me before they kill the Jensen woman and her kids. I couldn't stand seeing the children die. . . .

Couldn't stand it? In a ghoulish sort of way, that was funny.

Wryly she thought about the time she had braked too violently while riding her bike down a hill after a rain shower. She had skidded. She remembered floating through the air, seeing the handlebars hitting the road. In a strange way, everything slowed down; her flight seemed leisurely. She had no recollection of falling. But afterwards she was told that the hand of God had unquestionably protected her that day. According to witnesses, she had landed in front of a truck. Providentially, however, she had rolled—just enough to clear the massive speeding tires. For years she had been comforted by the thought that God had protected her because she was required for some grander purpose later on.

Was the purpose to act as target practice for some bloodthirsty Arab? A bit unkind, God. The truck would have been a quick, painless death; messy but painless. Would her life flash before her eyes as the bullets were fired? High school. Two years of college. A dull job in a publishing firm watching obtuse young men getting the few interesting jobs that became available. She had thought seriously of following in her father's footsteps. A splendid ambition: she would take flying lessons; she would, with his expert assistance, obtain her commercial license; she would be one of the very first woman airline pilots (pilotesses?). Flying, she discovered, became more difficult the more you found out about it. It had its own peculiar fascination, however; no wonder the small charter companies had tousle-headed young men only too happy to fly for next to nothing just to get more and more precious hours recorded in their log books. Then Frank entered the picture. Flying was forgotten. All that mattered was being with Frank: Frank of the curly hair and the Paul Newman smile. He sold business machines; he was a Success; he had a Future. Life became horniness. Clutching, clinging, reeling from one orgasm to another. Counting the hours—*literally*—until the next encounter.

She took a job as a clerk with an accounting firm because it occupied office space in the same building as did Frank's company. Six months later they were married. They gorged themselves upon each other. They wondered at the miracle they were living; surely no two human beings had ever experienced such happiness. But gradually, insidiously, the truth emerged. Nature had played a dirty trick on them, had smothered each of them with some chemical irresistible to the other; but when it had all worn off, there was nothing between them. Frank, perfect, divine Frank, turned out to be something of a pain in the ass; there was little conversation; he never read books; his idea of a big Sunday afternoon was sitting with a six-pack of Schlitz, watching football on TV. She was appalled to realize that the thought of a lifetime with Frank was a drag.

Inevitably, the relationship began to disintegrate; the brittle structure was unable to survive the disappointment. When it went, it went fast. Frank began to schedule sales meetings late into the evening two and three times a week. He would return with a hint of perfume clinging to his clothes. Jane accused him of screwing around; he denied it; he lied well, like most salesmen.

Jane met a young TWA captain who had just been divorced; she spent a weekend in New York with him. When she returned, Frank didn't mention her absence; a day later she found a strange earring under the bed. Apparently the apartment had been put to good use while she was away. And in the middle of it all, her mother died. For some weeks she had been complaining of headaches and fatigue. Migraines, she called them. One Wednesday she lay down for a nap after lunch. And died. Cerebral hemorrhage, they said. She was alone at the time. Jane had telephoned at two o'clock. No answer. She tried again an hour later. Then a neighbor called. For that first numbing day all she could think of was her mother lying dead while the telephone rang incessantly over her body. Later she wondered whether it was her mother's death that finally fractured the marriage. Soon she even stopped wondering; the marriage was simply of no importance anymore; Frank was nothing more than a phase, an error in judgment, to be quickly forgotten. And so Jane had moved to her father's house. At first the idea was simply to be there to help out with the arranging of her mother's things and the gradual sorting and packing. But somehow none of that ever got done. The weeks rolled by. Soon it was six months. A year. Now this.

Christ, she was thinking only of herself. Fear stabbed her somewhere in the middle when she considered her father's situation. He might be in even more danger than she was. Perhaps he was already . . . No; she wouldn't allow herself to think that. She refused. She kept thinking she would wake up. Arab terrorists? They weren't part of her life; they belonged on the TV news and in *Time* or *Newsweek*. What were they doing aboard that plane? And how was her father reacting? No doubt his reactions were calm and professional; he always seemed to know just the right thing to do at just the right time.

"I've been wondering," said Craig. He wrinkled his face as if in distaste at having to admit the fact. "Who is the Pope? I mean," he added quickly, "I sort of know who he is . . . but I'm not sure just what he *does*."

"I guess you're not Catholic."

He shook his head. "I know some kids who are, though."

"The Pope is their . . . spiritual leader."

"Oh."

"What I mean is, he is the top man in the Catholic Church. He's very important."

Craig nodded, thinking this over.

"I guess that's why these guys want him."

"Maybe. We don't know yet."

"I bet my dad's really mad about this."

"I bet he is, too."

"He gets real mad at things sometimes. Me sometimes. Your dad is the captain, right?"

"Right."

"My dad ought to be a captain. I guess he will be soon."

"Of course he will."

"He's the best pilot in the world."

She smiled. "I thought my dad was."

Craig shrugged. "I guess they're both just about as good as each other."

"Thank you."

"You're welcome."

He had an oddly formal way of speaking; he reminded her of the young boys in Paris, so grave and courteous.

Virginia Jensen was looking their way.

Jane said, "We're discussing whose dad is the world's greatest pilot."

Virginia nodded vaguely, not smiling.

Jane said, "How long has your husband been with Trans Am?"

"About ten years, I think."

"Does he like it?"

She nodded, her pale blue eyes suddenly filling with tears.

"It'll be all right," Jane told her. "You don't have to worry. They won't let anything happen to that airplane . . . or the crew. I'm sure." She turned to the old man. "Aren't you sure too, Mr. Nowakoski?"

He nodded, shrugging. "Sure, sure." He coughed; he seemed short of breath.

"Were you born in Poland?"

He looked at her, surprised. "Poland? Yes, I was born there."

"Where? Warsaw?"

"No. A place called Bydgoszcz."

"Where's that?"

"Northwest of Warsaw. A hundred miles or so; I forget." He smiled. "It was a long time ago. I was a little boy when we left. His age," he said, pointing to Craig. "We lived in Belgium for some time. Then I came to America. A long time before you were born. My son was born in America. I tell him he should realize how lucky he is. You young people, you don't know how lucky you are."

Then he chuckled. It was, he admitted, a pretty dumb thing to say under the circumstances, but he always said it to young people, because he meant it.

"You have to be born someplace else to know how nice it is to live in America," he said.

Virginia Jensen was still fighting tears.

Jane touched her hand; it was cool and clammy. "Everything will be okay," she said, cursing herself for not being able to conjure up anything more original and more reassuring. "Your husband will be safe . . . and you'll get home again. I feel it in my bones. I'm always right about things like that."

A sniff. "Are you?" Tiny morsels of hope sometimes worked wonders. "I once had a girl friend who was like that. She *felt* things, you know. And sure enough, things always seemed to work out the way she said."

"So don't worry," said Jane.

"I'll try not to." She looked down at the baby, then back at Jane. "Are you married?"

"I was. Just divorced."

"I'm sorry."

"I'm not." Defiantly positive. She laughed. "Sometimes divorce day can be the happiest time in a girl's life." She sighed to herself; she had failed utterly to amuse the other woman; there had been no smile, no riposte. The Virginia Jensens of this world were one-dimensional. What happened to them when the kids grew up and left home? Did life become empty and meaningless? It was the fault of the System. Some girls were brought up to think in terms of babies and diapers. Nobody got around to talking about what they were supposed to do when the babies grew up. All of which, in Jane's opinion, led irresistibly to the conclusion that the trip through life was easier the tougher and more cynical you were. You had to expect life to kick you in the ass; if you were ready for it, you could kick back.

Craig was intently studying the fireplace.

Somewhere within the house voices were raised in anger.

Jane hurried across the room and pressed her ear against the damp wall. She could hear sounds, angry sounds. But she couldn't make out what was being said. Which was hardly surprising, she thought, because the jabbering was being carried on in Arabic or Palestinian or whatever the hell they all spoke.

She shrugged at the others. "I can't make out any of it."

Mr. Nowakoski said, "Does anyone have any idea where they've brought us?"

No one had.

"In TV shows," Mr. Nowakoski said, "people always seem to be able to figure it out; they hear a noise and they know just where they are."

"I tried," said Craig earnestly. "I heard a plane and lots of cars. But that was all."

For some reason Virginia Jensen promptly burst into tears again. Jane had an urgent desire to tell her to can it. Tears were tiresome and totally unproductive.

"It's funny," said Mr. Nowakoski. "When I came to America, some people told me I was crazy; they said it was full of gangsters who would shoot and rob me. When I first arrive, I look for them. By golly, they weren't going to catch me unawares! For years I am on the lookout for gangsters. What happens? Nothing. Ever. Then I retire; I settle down . . . and this!"

The door opened. Scarface came in.

"We're making sandwiches. We've got beef and cheese and tuna. Who wants what?"

Jane sat down on one of the hardwood chairs. That son of a bitch, she thought, was trying to rape me an hour ago. Now he wants to know if I want a beef, cheese or tuna sandwich. It's not real; the whole thing is a crazy, stupid dream. . . .

"Cheese," she said, "and I want to go to the john."

He gazed at her a moment, as if wondering whether she had concealed an insult in those few words.

"Anyone else?"

Everyone decided to go. Mr. Nowakoski explained that his bladder wasn't what it used to be.

Jane said, "What did it used to be, Mr. Nowakoski?"

"Pardon?"

"I'm sorry. I misunderstood you."

Craig grinned secretly at her.

They were permitted across the bare hall to the bathroom, one by one. Jane went first.

"Whose house is this?" she asked when she returned to the room. Scarface was standing guard at the door.

"It's mine . . . for the time being."

He grinned as if genuinely amused.

"I thought you might tell me who really owns it," Jane said.

"You must think I'm very stupid."

"Not *very* stupid."

He grinned again. "Just a little stupid."

Jane asked him where he was from.

"You ask too many questions."

"It passes the time. How much longer are you going to keep us here?"

"A little longer."

"How much longer?"

"You'll find out." His dark eyes explored her face, as if he was attempting to memorize every feature.

Then Craig emerged from the bathroom.

"What kind of a gun is that?"

"Colt automatic . . . forty-five caliber."

"An army gun," Craig informed Jane as he went back into the room.

"Very good," said Scarface. "He is the captain's son?"

"No. The first officer's."

"A bright boy."

"We think so."

Mr. Nowakoski returned. He had decided to change his

order to beef. "All right?" he asked Scarface. "Can I do that?"

"I guess so."

"I don't know why I ordered tuna," Mr. Nowakoski told Jane. "I don't like tuna. But I was upset, I suppose. I don't know."

When all the captives were back in the room and when Scarface had locked the door behind them, they realized something.

Craig was missing.

Jane glanced at the fireplace. Fresh ash had fallen from the chimney.

chapter 10

The Pope entered the cockpit and looked about him with the delighted eyes of the child who is suddenly confronted by a gigantic, complex and staggeringly expensive plaything. He was accompanied by an aide, a fleshy, black-suited man of middle age who regarded everything and everyone as slightly suspicious.

The Pope said, "It is kind of you, Captain, to permit us—" He stopped, puzzled by Mallory's expression. "Something is wrong, Captain?"

Mallory said, "Your Eminence, I'm terribly sorry to have to impart some unpleasant news. I thought it better to tell you in here because there's no point in everyone knowing about it right away."

"Go on, Captain."

"I'm afraid that . . . well, the fact of the matter is, we are being hijacked."

"We are?" Mild surprise. Another glance around, in search of evidence to reinforce the statement. His gaze fell upon Cousins.

Flustered, Cousins, said, "No, your Eminence . . . I'm United States Secret Service."

"Security," said Mallory lamely. "This particular hijacking has so far been accomplished without guns or bombs, although we are told that they are aboard the aircraft and ready for use when necessary. And, believe it or not, we haven't even seen any of the hijackers . . . yet." Briefly, Mallory explained the situation.

The Pope nodded. "I am extremely sorry," he said, "that my presence has resulted in such danger for you and your families. Have any demands been made?"

"Our company has informed us that some sort of demand

has been made directly to the Israeli government. But we don't have any details."

"Ah . . . and we are at present flying towards the Middle East?"

"Yes, your Eminence. We made the turn as gently as possible so that no one would be disturbed."

"You did your job well. I was unaware of it."

"In fifteen minutes," said Mallory, "I have been instructed to go aft . . . to the rear of the coach cabin. I presume that at that time I will meet one or more of the hijackers."

Cousins said, "So far the circumstances of the hijacking haven't given us much room to maneuver."

"I understand your difficulty."

"But we have to assume they are telling us the truth about having explosives and arms aboard the aircraft. And knowing Black September, we've got to face the fact that we're dealing with people who won't hesitate to blow up this airplane—themselves included—if things start going wrong. So we have to feel our way and go along with their instructions, at least for the moment. My men have been alerted."

"I see. Do you wish us to inform our colleagues of this development?"

"We'd prefer that you don't, your Eminence. The fewer people who know about it, the better, we feel. There's nothing to be gained by creating alarm."

"Better that everyone get a good night's sleep," said Cousins. "They may need it."

"Very well, we shall keep the news to ourselves," said the Pope, nodding toward his aide.

Mallory said, "Your Eminence, you'll excuse me for saying this, I hope, but you don't seem very surprised by what we've told you."

The Pontiff smiled. "When you have lived as long as I have, Captain, the world offers very few surprises." He looked at the controls again. "In spite of our little problem, Captain, if it wouldn't be too much trouble, I would like to take this opportunity to inspect the cockpit a little more closely. . . ."

*   *   *

Mallory eased himself out of his seat.

"I guess it's rendezvous time."

Cousins nodded.

"Josephs and Macdonald will be keeping an eye on you," he said.

"Fine," said Mallory, in what he hoped was a confident tone.

"Good luck, Captain." Jensen accorded him a rather formal nod.

"Sure you wouldn't like one of us to come along?" Nowakoski seemed eager to leave his station.

"Thanks anyway; maybe some other time."

Nowakoski smiled automatically.

Cousins accompanied Mallory into the lounge area behind the flight deck.

"Remember," he said, "they're nervous as hell. Bound to be. They don't know what tricks you've got up your sleeve. So the calmer you can be, the better. I know it won't be easy. . . ."

"That's for sure," said Mallory.

"But it could help a lot if they see you're assured and unafraid."

"Okay, I'll try to remember that."

"I wish I could come with you."

"No; it's better that we follow instructions. Besides, let's hope they don't know you guys are on board."

Cousins nodded. He extended his hand. Mallory shook it.

"See you later."

"I assume so," said Mallory.

He descended the spiral stairway into the darkened, curtained-off first-class cabin. Most of the passengers were asleep, but one man in priest's garb was reading beneath a solitary light. Mallory assumed the man was studying his Bible; but the book was a sightseer's guide to San Francisco.

"I am looking forward to seeing the city. It looks beautiful."

"It is," said Mallory.

Unfortunately, however, the airplane is heading the wrong way; you may as well throw your book out the window.

He moved aft into coach. The lights had been dimmed here too; most of the passengers were sprawled in the awkward way of airline passengers all over the world when they try to sleep in their seats.

Mallory stepped with care. Sleeping aisle-seat passengers often stuck their legs out to trip the unwary.

He nodded to Dee. "Stay cool," he told her. Tough for the poor kid, especially when she was under orders to keep quiet about the hijack note.

A hand caught Mallory's sleeve. It was the actor, Vernon Squires.

"You're back again, Captain."

"Nice to see you again, Mr. Squires."

"What's wrong?"

"Nothing. I enjoyed it so much the first time, sir, I had to come again."

"Not very convincing, Captain."

"Nothing to worry about, sir."

"I prefer not to be kept in ignorance. Some people would prefer not to be enlightened, but I'm not one of them."

"Everything's all right, sir."

"I doubt that," declared Mr. Squires.

Mallory pushed on down the aisle, smiling perfunctorily at the few passengers who were still awake. Was one of them a terrorist?

He reached the rear of the cabin. It appeared to be deserted.

"Captain Mallory!"

He turned, startled. A woman. Young and pretty. At first, Mallory took her to be one of the passengers. He started to nod in reply, but then he stopped.

There was an aura of intensity about her.

"I have surprised you, Captain. You didn't expect a woman."

Mallory shook his head. "No, I didn't," he admitted.

"My name is Fadia. You are Captain Steven Mallory. Your age is fifty-nine. You live at 203 Welland Way, Walnut Creek,

California. You have a daughter named Jane."

Mallory's heart pounded. "What about Jane? Is she all right?"

"That depends on you," said Fadia. She spoke evenly; her English was excellent but heavily accented. "You have no need to worry about her as long as you follow instructions."

Mallory bit his lip. A slick professional, this one. She was well dressed in a stylish safari suit; she kept one hand in her pocket, like a model in *Vogue*. She wore a confident smile.

She moved aside as a yawning passenger came by on his way to the lavatory.

"I'm sure you understand that I'm not alone, Captain."

"How many of you. . . ?"

She shook her head impatiently.

"Don't bother, Captain. Do you think I am such a fool as to answer that question?"

"No harm in trying."

"Don't be so sure." The smile was gone. "I want to remind you that we have arms and explosives aboard this aircraft and will not hesitate to use them if necessary. I hope it will not be necessary, however; I would prefer an uneventful flight to El Maghreb."

She removed a small compass from one pocket and said, "I'm glad to see that you changed course as you were instructed."

"We aim to please at Trans Am."

"Very amusing, Captain. It's good that you are able to retain your sense of humor. Now the first thing we must do is take care of Mr. Cousins and his associates."

He swallowed. "Who?"

"Come now, Captain, don't take me for a fool. Mr. Cousins is in charge of a group of four Secret Service agents whose mission is to protect the Pope. Unfortunately for them, they have already failed in that mission. What you and I will do is to stroll quietly to the front of airplane, through the first-class section, then upstairs to the lounge area. You will arrange to have Mr. Cousins meet us there. He will then call his cohorts on his portable transceiver, summoning them to join him in the upper lounge. Where is Mr. Cousins at this moment? It doesn't matter; I won't embarrass you

into creating a lie. The only thing you have to remember, Captain,
is that I have five kilos of *plastique* fastened to my body. If any
attempt is made to interfere with me, the explosive will be
detonated. Immediately. It will blow a very large hole in this
aircraft; in fact I should think it will blow it into two quite distinct
halves. In any event, the complete and utter destruction of the
aircraft would be a certainty, as would the deaths of everyone on
board."

"Including you."

"Of course. That is obvious. Now let's go forward, Captain.
And let's try to do everything as discreetly as possible. We do not
wish to frighten the other passengers, do we?"

She had a pleasant, lilting voice; she should have been
talking about shopping and clothes, not arms and explosives.

Mallory said, "I don't believe you have any arms on board. I
don't believe you could get them past Security."

She shrugged and pulled a German Luger from her pocket.
"Satisfied?"

Mallory was visibly startled. "How did you get *that* on
board?"

"Efficiently. Now, be a good little captain and maybe I'll tell
you later. But right now we're wasting time. Get moving."

"Look," said Mallory, "this airplane is full of innocent
people . . . and the Pope is . . ."

"Save your breath." She shook her head. "It is not a matter
for debate. Understand that. The rights or wrongs, the little
injustices, are not of the slightest concern to us. We care only
about results. You have your instructions and I have mine. You
are to fly to El Maghreb and land there. That is all. After you have
done that, you have nothing more to worry about."

"The safety of my passengers does worry me."

"When we land, the passengers will disembark and they will
no longer be your passengers."

"They're my passengers, lady, until I get them to their
destination, which happens to be San Francisco, California."

"But there has been a slight change of plan, hasn't there?
Your passengers are going to be given an opportunity to see the
Middle East, firsthand, *before* they get to San Francisco. Right

now, let's move. I need hardly remind you that the safety of your families depends on your strict obedience." She motioned with one hand. "Now I want you to use the aircraft interphone to summon Mr. Cousins. Tell him we are going to the upper lounge. I wish to meet him there."

* * * *

Her self-confidence was awesome. She greeted Cousins with a casual nod, as if he were an acquaintance of no great importance.

"Call your men, Mr. Cousins. Tell them to meet you here."

"No," said Cousins, testing her.

"Perhaps you've noticed," she said, "this short chain dangling from the pocket of my jacket. It is connected to an electrical relay. If I give it a little tug, the electrical circuit will be complete, and five kilos of explosives will be detonated instantly."

"I don't believe you." Cousins folded his arms and glared defiantly at her.

She shrugged, shaking her head like a teacher after chiding a slow pupil. "Don't be foolish, Mr. Cousins. I know this is a blow to your professional pride. A shame. My condolences. But it's not the end of everything, is it?" Her lips tightened. "What you must understand, Mr. Cousins, is that it *will* be the end of everything if you don't do as I say."

"Is that a fact?"

Mallory ran his tongue over his lips. He had a sudden desire to clear his throat, but he was reluctant to make the slightest sound.

The girl said, "I thought you might doubt me, Mr. Cousins. For that reason I arranged my clothing so I could conveniently show you that I am not bluffing." Holding the gun with one hand, she undid the buttons of her jacket with the other. Beneath it she wore a loose blouse. She raised it. Around her bare midriff the *plastique* was neatly packed, taped close like some surgical application.

Cousins stared at the stuff. Pale, angry, he nodded. "All right. I agree to your terms . . . for the time being."

"Very sensible, Mr. Cousins. Have your men approach the area slowly and with their hands empty and plainly visible. They are not to interfere with anyone coming up the staircase to the lounge."

Cousins turned away as he spoke into his wrist microphone. It was then that two of Fadia's men appeared, emerging from the spiral staircase, pistols drawn. They were young, dark-haired, wearing sports jackets and open-necked shirts. She said something to them in what Mallory presumed was Arabic. The men nodded briskly and took up positions on either side of the lounge. Evidently Fadia was someone whose instructions were to be obeyed—an experienced leader in the organization? What did she do to earn it? A very tough young lady by all appearances; she wouldn't hesitate to kill—or to blow away the airplane and everyone aboard.

"Who are these characters?" Cousins wanted to know.

"Associates of mine," Fadia replied.

"Aren't you going to introduce us?"

"That won't be necessary."

Now two of the Secret Service men appeared on the stairway.

"Sorry," Cousins told them. "We seem to have struck out."

Fadia beckoned with her Luger.

"You will please come in and sit there."

Cousins nodded, instructing them to obey.

"Go ahead. Do as she says."

Fadia asked the men to identify themselves. Again Cousins nodded his permission.

"Maddox."

"Greene."

She turned to Cousins. "Are there any more of your men aboard?"

Cousins shook his head.

Fadia's mouth hardened. "That is the last lie you will ever tell *me*, Mr. Cousins. Do you understand? Is that clear? Now, summon Josephs and Macdonald. At once!"

Cousins's chest heaved, like a man on the verge of a heart attack. But it was hopeless. He sighed, then flicked his wrist microphone and called the other two men. "Shit," he exclaimed.

"How in the hell do you know our names?"

"We have many friends, Mr. Cousins. There are more people in sympathy with the Palestinian cause than you may realize. Such people keep us well informed. When armed security guards travel aboard U.S. carriers, various documents are required, detailing names, types of weapons, et cetera. It was so for this flight. We were fortunate enough to learn the contents of those documents just before the takeoff. . . ."

Cousins whirled on Mallory. "Some son of a bitch in your company is passing out security information."

The girl prodded him with her pistol.

"All right, Mr. Cousins, no more talk." She looked up as the last two Secret Service men arrived on the upper deck. "Mr. Josephs and Mr. Macdonald, you will join your colleagues in those seats over there."

"Go ahead," muttered Cousins, looking at the floor.

When the men were seated, Fadia said:

"You will now remove your clothes."

They stared at her.

"You've got to be kidding."

"At once, if you please."

"No," snapped Cousins, "absolutely no!"

"There isn't time to discuss this," said Fadia. "Take them off or you will regret it, I promise."

Cousins started to get to his feet, but one of the Arab men thrust him back into his seat and shoved a pistol hard against the side of his head.

"If you don't," she said, "we will be forced to inflict some very intense pain. My associates have knives. And they are skillful . . . surgeons. Now, I want to make it quite clear that we have no personal interest in you. We must be sure, however, that you don't create any problems for us. For that reason, you will remove all your clothing. Naked men tend not to indulge in heroics. Besides, you gentlemen have so many useful little gadgets spread about your bodies. Only by stripping you naked can we be sure that all your little gadgets are found."

She smiled. A sort of joke had been made. She turned to

Mallory. "You'll be happy to know, Captain, that there's no need for this ruling to apply to you and your crew. Somehow I think we will all feel safer knowing that our pilot is fully dressed."

The extraordinary thing was, the girl had a kind of chilling charm.

Cousins, poor outwitted Cousins. He told his men to comply.

"There's not a goddam thing we can do about it."

"Place your guns on the floor, gentlemen, if you please."

"You'll never get away with this," Cousins said.

Fadia smiled. "Why do people always say that? Do you think those words will convince us to immediately abandon our mission? Do you, Mr. Cousins?"

Defeated, Cousins shook his head.

As the Secret Service men stripped, the male hijackers took their guns and the communications equipment taped to their bodies. One of the men shook his head, refusing to drop his underwear in front of the girl. A pistol muzzle pressed against his left ear changed his mind. In a few moments the men were all naked; one of them stood in the awkward, knock-kneed way of unclothed men, hands over genitals.

"Good," said the girl, regarding them without embarrassment. "Now I want you all to occupy those seats. And fasten your seat belts . . . carefully, I suggest." Again that cool humor. "Now you will be handcuffed to your seats and each other in a chain. I hope you won't be too uncomfortable." Now she spoke pleasantly, like a tour guide.

"What a schizophrenic," Mallory thought.

"If you wish to use the washroom," she informed them, "I'm afraid you are out of luck. We are not taking any chances. Make any suspicious gestures and you will be seriously lacking in vital equipment for the rest of your lives."

"Can't we at least have a blanket or something to put on our laps?" Cousins sounded plaintive.

The girl shook her head; her black hair tumbled loosely about her neck. "Sorry, gentlemen, I simply can't oblige. You are all well trained and innovative. I'm afraid the only way to keep an eye on you all the time is to have you in this somewhat revealing condition. Nothing personal, I assure you. Remember now, no talking, no moving. My colleagues will not hesitate."

She nodded at the men, then turned to Mallory.

"All right, Captain, now let's concern ourselves with the rest of the trip, shall we?"

She's Jane's age, he thought. And just as bright and pretty. They have a lot in common. If they ever met under different circumstances they could be friends. It was a strangely disquieting thought.

She nodded toward the cockpit door.

He led the way.

Jensen and Nowakoski turned, eyes wide, as they saw Mallory enter accompanied by the gun-toting girl. She regarded them with no more interest than she bestowed upon the rest of the cockpit.

"This," said Mallory awkwardly, "is Fadia."

"I will be joining you for the rest of the flight," she told them. "You may get on with your work in the usual way. Captain, I suggest you sit down; from now on your only concern is to get this airplane to Jordan. Everything is proceeding according to plan. Your families are quite safe, gentlemen. . . ."

"They'd better be," growled Jensen.

"My father has a heart condition," Nowakoski said. "How could you take an old man like him? He could die, just from the shock of it all."

She said, "I sincerely hope that doesn't happen."

Jensen snapped, "If you do anything to my wife and kids. . ."

"Nothing will happen to them," she told him impatiently, "as long as everyone does as they're told." She dismissed the subject with a toss of her head. "Now, as I have informed Captain Mallory, we have enough explosive aboard this aircraft to sink a battleship. The simple truth of the matter is that if anything goes wrong, if any attempt is made to stop us or interfere in any way, then everything—the airplane, you, me and every passenger—will be summarily destroyed. Is that clearly understood?"

Mallory told the others about the *plastique*.

Jensen asked him, "How did they smuggle arms and explosives aboard? The security was tight as hell."

"It was really quite simple," Fadia volunteered. "As I mentioned to Mr. Cousins, our organization has sympathizers all over the world. Fortunately for us, one of them is a food handler in the commissary at Rome Airport. Obviously, he had access to the containers used to carry and store meal trays aboard the aircraft. He simply substituted handguns for turkey sandwiches and *plastique* for Danish pastries. These items were then wrapped in aluminum foil. Afterwards, our man discreetly marked the appropriate container with a grease pencil. So, you may be a little short of food during the second meal service."

"So that's why you waited so long to reveal yourself," Mallory said.

"Very astute, Captain. Yes, we had to wait until after dinner when the galley would be vacant and the cabin lights had been turned down. Timing is so very important in these matters, don't you agree?"

No answer.

"Breaching your security was not particularly difficult for us."

Jensen snapped, "But is it necessary to kidnap women and children and jeopardize the life of an old man who has never done you any harm . . . ?"

"Unfortunately," she said, "yes."

"You're a goddam bitch."

"I suppose I am," she said, unconcerned. She settled herself in the jump seat behind Mallory and laid the pistol in her lap. "We have a lengthy flight, gentlemen; I suggest we try to make it as pleasant as possible. I should tell you that I have more than a casual knowledge of aviation; I possess a pilot's license and have spent some time as a control tower operator. So please do not attempt to deceive me with your technical knowledge. It's a failing of Americans, you know. You are all under the impression that the rest of us are all a little slow in technical matters. It probably comes as a bit of a shock for you to realize that foreign women can operate electronic calculators and fly airplanes just as well as

Americans. And I can also operate this gun. Very effectively, I might add. And I do want to assure you that I shall not hesitate to use it if necessary. So bear that in mind, gentlemen. You see, the stakes are far, far too high to permit us to have any concern about a life or two. Ours or yours. I will not hesitate to shoot if necessary. And let me assure you, I am quite without mercy or conscience. All right? Everyone got that?"

Mallory sighed. He believed her.

"Now," she said, "I think I will check your inertial navigation system. I would hate to think that you are not heading directly for El Maghreb. . . ."

* * *

The East German general was suspicious. He studied the maps that dominated his office wall. An aide had drawn a line indicating the course that the Trans Am 747 would take on its way to Jordan. It was to fly to the southwest of Hamburg, penetrate East German airspace near Magdeburg, then proceed directly over Dresden before crossing the Czechoslovakian border.

A curious coincidence that the war maneuvers of the Warsaw Pact nations were being conducted northwest of Dresden. A full-scale affair. Some of the most sophisticated Soviet weaponry was being employed under the most realistic battlefield conditions. The exercise was known as Red Shield IV. More than a hundred thousand troops were taking part.

Could this be an elaborate plot on the part of the Americans to obtain unique intelligence data or to perhaps test their defense procedures?

It was possible; anything was possible with the Yankees. They were a devious people, in the general's opinion, always up to something crafty.

The Air Traffic Control people seemed to feel the hijacking was genuine. The trouble is, there wasn't time to confirm the fact through the PLO or the Black September group, even if they had someone in authority, someone who could be believed, which they didn't. . . .

Why, the general wondered, should this hijacking take place

at just this time, and why should the aircraft be forced to fly just such a route? This had to be more than coincidental. And why should the hijackers be so stubborn as not to permit even the slightest route change. . . ?"

He picked up his telephone.

chapter 11

Craig Jensen reached for the top of the chimney. His fingers closed on the old, jagged masonry. He grimaced. It was sharp. It hurt. Kids used to do this for a living, he once read. Poor guys; he didn't envy them. The climb had been a nightmare of stink and dirt, of grazes, cuts and bruises. The remains of the spark arrestor, which had long ago rusted away, cut his left arm as he wriggled upward. Again and again he had been on the point of abandoning the climb. But he had continued because it seemed that clambering down the chimney would probably be even worse than climbing up. Gingerly he pulled at a brick. It felt wobbly and brittle, but it didn't break. The smell was awful; his throat tickled and dust kept drifting up his nose. He fought the desire to sneeze. Much too noisy. Already it seemed to him that he had made a fantastic amount of noise; every inch of the way had been a heart-stopping symphony of scrapings and tumblings of bits of stone. There was, he knew, a very real possibility that his escape attempt had already been discovered. Up there, just a few inches away, the men might be waiting for him, laughing at his foolishness.

He bit his lip. Yes, he supposed, it was pretty dumb . . . but the opportunity had presented itself; he had looked at the fireplace; he had turned around; no one had been paying any attention; they were all too busy with the washroom. And so he had stepped in and looked up. And then started climbing.

And now he was almost there.

Deep breath.

A cool wind played on his face as he pushed his head out of the chimney.

Another deep breath. It tasted marvelous. He turned. First to the left, then to the right. No one. The roof was deserted.

It was perilous enough climbing up the chimney, but it was almost as bad getting out at the other end. He wormed his way up a few more inches until he was half in and half out of the chimney. Cautiously he raised one leg. Tears of fright filled his eyes as the movement shifted his balance and he felt himself wobbling. Okay. One more little twist and his foot would be over the side. He panted and smeared the back of his hand across his eyes. Now. He reached forward and clasped his foot and gently pulled it free of the chimney. He had a crazy desire to shout for joy when his toes touched the roof. He gulped down fresh air as if it were Coca-Cola. Another heave pulled his other leg out. He was able to stand up and look around.

Fields, trees . . . and what looked like a road, over there to the right.

Okay. That was the way to go. Get to the highway. Stop a car, ask for a ride to the nearest police station.

The question was, Would the men inside see him running away from the house? There was no cover. He would have to take a chance on it. Just run like hell and hope for the best.

He shuddered. There was a chance he might be shot in the back. A real chance. He could *die*.

He bit his lower lip, then stopped because his mother had repeatedly told him not to.

You've got to continue, he told himself. There's no one else to do it. So it's up to you.

All right, he answered. I will. I'll move now.

The roof was rocky and apparently about to crumble under his weight. The only place to walk was along the center ridge, and that was kind of scary because the whole thing seemed to sag in the middle like an old horse. But he had to keep going; there was no other way to get help to rescue his mom and the others. He sighed. It was an awesome responsibility. He felt tiny and insignificant. What would those men do to him if they found him trying to escape? He shuddered.

Then he looked at himself. He was incredibly filthy. He shook his head in wonderment; he had no idea chimneys were that messy. Mom would be mad, that was for sure; his jeans were almost new; she'd already chewed him out for wearing them while goofing around in the back yard. Now it was hard to tell what color they used to be.

But now he had to get down from the roof. He didn't know how. It was nuts; he had managed to wriggle all the way up the chimney and cross the roof; now he was stranded aloft, like a dumb cat or something.

On TV, people always seemed to be able to jump from roof to roof without any trouble; there were always convenient pipes and ledges. This roof was nothing but steep angles and rickety tiles.

He lay full length and peered over the edge. A drainpipe. But how to reach it? It was set under the eaves. To get to it you had to turn around and stick a foot out backwards and try to feel for it. And then what? He wasn't sure. The only thing was to try. If he missed, there was a long way to fall, right onto a wooden shed.

The pipe cracked and groaned and seemed to be about to collapse under his weight. He begged it not to. Please, pipe. Just hold a little bit longer.

He took the deepest possible breath. Now he had to let his whole weight shift onto the pipe as he came off the roof. And he would be pulling it away from the house. . . .

In the Saturday morning Laurel and Hardy movies, it had been a big laugh when drainpipes broke and sent the pair of them flying into beds of flowers.

Suddenly it wasn't funny.

He knew his father would approve. He could almost see him, nodding, encouraging him to go ahead, take the chance.

Another big, big breath. He let go of the roof.

A chunk of masonry fell away from one of the pipe connections. But the pipe held firm. He held it so tightly, his knuckles cracked. He heard them.

He scrambled down the pipe, clutching it like a rope. It was painful because there wasn't room for his fingers, and they were cut and bleeding by the time he reached the ground beside the shed.

He was filled with excitement . . . and fear. He wanted to tell someone what he had done. But he stood still for a moment, taking stock of the situation as he had seen countless cowboys and private eyes do.

No sound from the house. He hadn't been missed. Not yet.

All right. Time to run. Crouched, he made his way to the corner of the house and stole a glance. No one in sight. Over that way . . . that was the direction of the highway.

He paused for a long moment, his teeth scraping his lower lip. He clenched his fists, then he ran. The ground sped beneath him. His feet seemed hardly to touch the blurring grass. Every limb, every muscle, was in perfect harmony.

He kept his eyes half closed, and his face was taut with the anticipation of sounds: shouts, shots. . . .

The wind rushed past his face. Ahead, the line of trees bobbed with every step. He felt his jeans slipping. With one hand, he pulled them up. In a few moments he would be out of sight of the house. He mustn't slow down. . .

He imagined he heard voices. At once his mind conjured up a fast-moving sequence of images, like a preview for a new TV show: a man pointing, reaching for a rifle, a lever-action Winchester, snapping the weapon to his shoulder, squinting along the barrel . . . a running boy dead center in the sights.

Gentle, professional squeeze of the trigger.

Bang.

Craig hurled himself into the trees. He gasped, sucking in air. His heart pounded as if it were going to break out of his chest. He turned. No man with a rifle. No shot It had seemed so real.

Now that the run to the trees was over, he wanted to lie there. But he couldn't. He had to find help. And he had to find it fast, because the men would soon realize he was missing. And then they would be after him. He shook his head; he couldn't stand thinking about it.

He was sitting beside a wire mesh fence. All right. He would follow it. It seemed to go in the right direction, toward the highway.

As he ran along the fence he wondered for the umpteenth time why it was all happening, why the men had come in the Sears truck and had taken Mom and Karen and him and brought them here. . .

He tripped and sprawled full length. A rip at one knee. Automatically he found himself phrasing the excuses, pointing out that he certainly hadn't tumbled *on purpose;* it was an accident, something that could happen to anyone, anytime. . . .

He got to his feet and plodded on.

Then he saw the house. Just visible through the trees. He grinned. Help at last! He scrambled between the trees.

But he stopped suddenly. He stared. Disbelieving. He recognized the house. It was all *too* familiar: the very place from which he had just escaped. The fence had led him in a great big circle. He had run all that way for nothing.

He felt tears springing to his eyes. He blinked them away. Bawling wouldn't help. It was dumb. He had an important mission. All he'd done so far was waste valuable time.

He turned again. Okay. Now he would set off in *that* direction.

* * *

George Donato was in a hurry. It was the usual story: trying to pack too much into too few hours. But of course it was to be expected of one of the genuine greats of the selling business, even if he said so himself. Your average run-of-the-mill salesman has too much time on his hands; your exceptional salesman is always trying to squeeze twenty-five hours into every day. Time, as George frequently reminded himself, is money.

Of course, the trouble was, old man Horrocks had insisted on recounting how the hardware business wasn't what it used to be; according to him, it had been a story of dismal decline for the last fifty years. It was an old story that didn't improve with repeated tellings. Besides, who could possibly pay attention to that old goat with Alice Forbes waiting only a lousy twenty-two miles away. Ah, Alice. Bountiful Alice. His error had been to schedule Alice *after* old man Horrocks. He should have done it the other way around. It would have meant a few more miles of travel, but it would have been a small price for Alice's sensual charms.

He had brought her a hot-dog maker, a brand new product,

just the sort of thing she went for. A $22.98 retail item, it cost him a mere $11.49. An incredible bargain when he considered what he would receive in return.

The more he thought about it, the more he regretted having scheduled Horrocks before Alice. He *knew* Horrocks was a garrulous old buzzard. So why? It was a tactical goof, not to be repeated. Ever. Now, the project of the moment was to do justice to Alice and then depart before her husband got home from work. No lingering today. A shame, but a guy couldn't possibly relax and concentrate on the moment when there was the possibility of a two-hundred-pound, six-foot slaughterhouse worker coming in, looking for dinner and finding God knows what else. . . .

A good half hour was the insurance policy.

Lay 'em and leave 'em, he instructed himself; don't linger; live to love later. The alliteration pleased him; charmed by his inventiveness, he repeated the maxim. He hummed something from *Camelot*. You wouldn't call Alice fat. He shook his head emphatically. Yet there was an inherent generosity in the way she was put together. Great proportions but a little more here and a spot more there; all balanced and arranged as only dear old Mother Nature knew how . . . an abundant assortment of pleasures, was Alice. . . .

He was driving too fast and he knew it. It was as if Alice herself was pressing her foot down on his. He tried not to think of her; such thoughts tended to blur his vision and impair his driving judgment.

Ten minutes. Maybe even nine. And he would be in her presence, drinking in the warmth of her, fingering the merchandise, caressing the package.

He glanced at his watch and swore. If he got there in nine minutes he could spend only thirty-one minutes with her. Then he would have to go. Flee.

Thirty-one minutes with Alice. It was a crime.

But it was infinitely better than no time at all.

As he swung around the corner he felt his rear wheels slithering on the slick tarmac road. Easy, baby.

Then he saw the boy.

Dirty, *really* dirty little bastard, standing in the middle of the road, waving his arms.

George hit the brake. The car skidded. Quickly, he recovered and swept past the forlorn little figure.

"Dumb little son of a bitch!"

Kids these days, they seemed to have no sense of danger. . .standing in the middle of the road like that, just on a bend. . . . Some kind of a thrill thing, maybe; they were always cooking up stuff like that. . . .

A glance back as he got the car straightened out.

The kid was still waving frantically. A ride, the little creep wanted a ride. Any other time, kid, but today there are more important things on the agenda. . . .

He shifted his gaze to the rearview mirror.

Jesus, did anyone ever look so goddam *woeful?*

No. There wasn't *time,* for chrissake!

Alice was waiting. Luscious Alice.

Another look in the rearview. The small, pitiful figure receded like a fade-out in a movie.

Any other time, kid.

One more glance.

"Jesus H. Christ!"

Cursing himself for his stupidity, weakness of character and total lack of chivalry, George Donato stomped on the brakes. The car screeched to a halt. George had already thrust the car into reverse. Engine whining, the vehicle lurched backward toward the boy running to meet it.

George jammed his finger on the electric window button.

"I'm in one hell of a hurry, kid."

"Please, mister, they've got my mom and some other people. I've got to tell the police!"

George stared. Just his luck. He had to waste precious Alice-time conversing with a mental retard. "Who's got your mom?"

"Some men."

"What men, for chrissake?"

"I don't know who they are."

"I'll bet you don't. Now, listen, I've got better things to do than play goddam games. . . ." He looked the kid up and down. "Where the hell have you been, up a chimney for chrissake?"

"Yes," said the kid.

"I—" George was on the point of driving away; he didn't have time to listen to jokes; his mission was vital, all-important, all-consuming. But the realization kept growing that the kid wasn't joking. "What do you want me to do?"

"I've got to get to the police, mister."

George shook his head, trying to think. He remembered seeing a highway patrol station. But where? He couldn't remember. "We'll find a phone and call them. Okay?"

"Yes, that'd be all right, I guess. But please hurry, mister, they might be after me."

"After *you?*" George looked about him. A gag, a big put-on? "Are you for real?"

"Honest."

"You mean, these men might be after you?"

"That's right. Please hurry."

"Okay," said George, "you'd better get in." He sighed as the soot-caked figure jumped in and plopped down in the genuine leather bucket seat. Did the owner's manual say you could get soot out with a damp cloth and a mild detergent?

"I'm going to find a phone for you," said George. "Then you're on your own."

The kid seemed weak with relief. If he was acting, he was doing a fantastic job, in George's opinion; and George, as a salesman par excellence, had a very high opinion of his ability to judge people.

"What's your name?"

"Craig Jensen, sir."

"And you don't know why the men have got your mom?"

"I kind of think it has something to do with the Pope."

"The *Pope?*"

"That's right. My dad is flying him to San Francisco."

"You're putting me on, kid."

"No, sir. *Honest.*"

* * *

"You see," he told her, "there was this kid. All alone . . . and dirty. And I stopped."

"The Goddam Good Samaritan." Alice sounded suspicious.

"Yeah, sort of."

"A *female* kid?"

"Hell, no. Of course not. But I had to take him to a phone booth. And then we couldn't find any change. We had nineteen cents between us . . . a nickel and fourteen pennies, for God's sake . . . so we had to find a store to get change to call the cops . . . and they told us to wait until they got there . . . and I think the kid was on the level."

"Which is more than I can say for you," snapped Alice, and hung up.

* * *

The latest weather report showed no improvement. An intense low-pressure system was making its slow but violent way eastward across North Africa. A steep pressure gradient had developed, resulting in a strong counterclockwise flow of air around the center of the low-pressure area. Sandstorm. The Arabs called it a *simoom,* "wind that poisons the atmosphere."

Mallory turned in his seat. "We've got one big problem, young lady. We may not be able to land at El Maghreb."

Fadia stared at him. "You'll land there, Captain."

Mallory shrugged. "Not necessarily. There's a hell of a sandstorm blowing. A bad one. Know anything about sandstorms?"

"Of course."

"Then I don't have to tell you the details. If it's bad enough, we just won't be able to land there. Period."

"You will land there."

Mallory shook his head. "You don't understand. I've got to have certain minimum weather conditions if I'm going to put this airplane down in one piece. Surely you know enough about airplanes to know that. This storm is a screamer—winds in excess of fifty knots, according to the weather report. Sometimes you can't see more than a couple of hundred feet in those things. Now, I don't know if it's going to be that bad at El Maghreb, but I am telling you that there's no conceivable way we can get down safely if the visibility is too low. This isn't a Piper Cub, lady."

"I am aware of that."

"And I may as well point out something else. If this storm keeps up, there's one hell of a good chance that we may not even find your airport, much less land there."

"You'll find it, Captain."

Mallory said, "I hope you realize that I'm telling you the truth."

"I have the greatest confidence in you."

"Glad to hear it. I'm going to tell you something else."

"What is it?"

"We're going to slow this airplane down."

"Slow it? No, I forbid it!"

"I have to."

"Why?"

"Let's suppose the sandstorm is still blowing hard when we get to El Maghreb. The only available navigation aid there is a low-frequency radiobeacon, and it just doesn't offer enough precision to guide us close enough to the airport to find it during low-visibility conditions."

"You'll find the airfield, Captain."

"Maybe. But it might take a few passes. Do you see what I mean?"

"Go on."

"Assume that I can't find the airport during the first approach, or the second, for that matter. In this airplane, each missed approach consumes one hell of a lot of fuel."

The girl considered this . . . suspiciously.

"If this airplane runs out of kerosene, lady, we've all had it. So what I'm suggesting is that we reduce airspeed to long-range, economy cruise. That way we'll reduce our fuel consumption to the most efficient rate, and that'll give us more reserve fuel when we get to Jordan."

The girl's eyes seemed to bore into his, as if she were searching for truth within him. Then she nodded. "I agree."

Mallory heaved a sigh of relief and asked Nowakoski to adjust the power settings. About an hour of precious time had been bought. The question was, What could be done with it?

* * *

The girl named Fadia folded her arms. A hard, unyielding posture. Total dedication to the project. Now was the critical time. A time of ceaseless vigilance, mental as well as physical. Ignore the sweat on the palms and about the neck. Unimportant. An involuntary reaction. Damn the hunk of valves and pipes and flesh that was her body! Sometimes it still persisted in reacting as if it belonged to some whimpering *bourgeois!*

Calm, controlled breathing. By no quivering of limb or voice must she betray the slightest suggestion of weakness to these men. Icy, nerveless: that had to be her image. Her duty was to dominate them every moment from now until the landing at El Maghreb. They hated her. Understandably. And their hatred was the more virulent for their being impotent. Squirming, they were caught in an inextricable trap, and they knew it.

And the fact that she was a woman made it all the more difficult to bear. Low blows to their foolish male pride.

They would never accept the truth that she had no feelings of animosity toward them. She cared nothing about them as individuals; they were simply instruments who happened to be in the wrong place at the wrong time.

The Luger lay in her lap. She could retrieve it, aim and fire in a second. But she doubted that it would be necessary. These men wouldn't risk their aircraft and their passengers' lives in a flight-deck shootout. Safety was their prime concern. They were professionals. Therefore, they were predictable. The captain, Mallory, was obviously a capable man, handling himself well in a difficult situation. No doubt he was seething under the calm, business-as-usual exterior which all airline pilots seem to possess. But he didn't show his anger. Smart man. Never let your enemies know that you are intimidated by them. Who said that? She couldn't remember. Mallory was no youngster. But he still looked interesting—virile, even. He had solid, strong hands. A handsome man with a firm, well-formed jaw, intelligent brow, determined mouth. Yet there was a tenderness, a gentleness in the

eyes. Under other circumstances it might have been interesting —
even enlightening—to get to know him better. . . .

She chided herself for permitting her thoughts to follow such
conventional lines. Here she was, on the biggest assignment of her
life and she was wasting time and energy contemplating intimacy
with a man more than old enough to be her father.

Concentrate, Maria! she commanded herself. "Fadia" was a
cover name. She had been christened Maria Burckhardt in
Dortmund, West Germany, where she was born in 1950. Her
mother died when she was an infant. Her father, a prosperous
insurance salesman, had been an SS officer during the war. He
made no secret of his admiration for Hitler and the Nazi
philosophy. From time to time, old comrades would visit the fine
home in Dortmund; late into the night, drunken and foolish, they
would reminisce about the great days, when the world cowered
before them. As a child she wondered how they could possibly
have lost the war; they were clearly so much stronger, smarter and
infinitely more valiant than their enemies. But why did they keep
repeating the same stories, over and over again? Then, at the
university, she lived with a student activist, a boy with unruly
black hair and wild, almost frightening eyes. He taught her the
truth: about the world, about the struggle for power, about the
maniacal Nazis and how her parents' generation did nothing to
stop them, and how the new state, with its military-industrial
complex, was starting it all over again. He tore the rotten veneer
off it all; she saw the parasites, the exploiters, the victims, the
stupidity, the culpability. Erich, long dead, killed by a police-
man's bullet during a riot in Munich protesting a visit by the
Shah of Iran. To Erich she owed everything. Without him, she
would never have understood; today she might have been a
housewife in some dreary suburb, tending screaming babies, not
a fighter in the greatest revolutionary cause in the history of the
world. . .

chapter 12

They worked in silence, pummeling and puffing the cushions and sweater, then covering them with a blanket. More shaping. They stood back and nodded uncertainly; it wasn't bad—but it certainly wasn't good. Perhaps another push there and another squeeze there. Maybe if you didn't *know* it was only cushions and a sweater. . . .

Five minutes later Icy Eyes and Billy the Kid returned, carrying plates of sandwiches. Scarface stood in the doorway, watching.

"Eat," said Icy Eyes, putting the plates on the table. He glanced at the captives. "I do hope we have your orders right," he added sarcastically.

Jane said, "The boy's sleeping. Can you keep it down a bit?"

Icy Eyes regarded the motionless form without interest. Billy the Kid leaned against the wall and folded his arms. The two of them looked as if they intended to stay awhile.

Don't look at the Jensen woman or the old guy! Don't! Don't!

Jane could almost hear her voice shrilling the order. She dare not look. A meeting of eyes would instantly telegraph mutual guilt to the Arabs.

Diversion. Quickly.

"These sandwiches taste like shit."

"You have a foul mouth, woman."

Jane shrugged. "It's a foul sandwich."

"What is wrong?"

"The butter tastes rancid."

130

Scarface and Billy the Kid exchanged a few unintelligible words.

"The butter is fresh," said Scarface. "He bought it only yesterday."

"Where?"

"The market at—" Scarface glared like a man who discovers he is being mocked. He turned and made for the door. Billy the Kid followed.

Jane tried to look disinterested.

Then Mr. Nowakoski had to ask whether there was any more news about the airplane.

Jesus! Jane wanted to throw the sandwich at him. Silly old bastard! Had he forgotten about Craig already? Didn't he realize that their only hope lay in that kid's getting help before his absence was discovered. . . ?

"There is no more news," said Icy Eyes.

"Where is the airplane now?"

"I cannot say."

The door closed. The key turned.

Jane breathed again. A silent whistle of relief. Incredible, fantastic, that the bundle of cushions and a sweater had deceived them. But it had. Beautiful cushions, delectable sweater. . . .

At this very moment Craig might be telling his story to the police or the FBI.

Please, she thought.

Virginia started to say something. Jane raised a cautioning finger to her lips, nodding toward the door. Ten to one they were still outside, listening.

"Nice sandwich," said Virginia. Her eyes said that she was as worried as hell about her little boy and wanted desperately to talk about it.

"I still think the butter tastes rotten," said Jane.

"You made them mad, talking about it."

"They made me mad, too," said Jane, "so we're even."

She turned to old man Nowakoski and asked him about his sandwich. He shrugged.

"It's okay, but I don't have much appetite."

"Feeling all right?"

"Sure, sure." He half smiled. "Don't worry about me. Worry about—"

Jane interjected in time. "I've been wanting to ask you, Virginia, where did you meet your husband?"

The first officer's wife was flustered, but she managed a reply. "At a party. An office party. I used to work for an insurance broker. I was a secretary. I liked the job. Well, there was this Christmas party, and one of the agents brought Cliff; they'd both been in the air force in Japan. Cliff was all set to join Trans Am the next week, and he was doing all his drinking ahead of time. Both of them were smashed when they got to the party. And Cliff got fresh the moment he was inside. I didn't like him much. He was kind of soppy and silly; you know, the way some guys get when they drink. But he sounded nicer a few days later when he called me for a date."

Jane nodded. "How about you, Mr. Nowakoski? How did you meet your wife?"

"My wife?" The old man smiled, surprised by the question. "It was a long, long time ago. You young girls don't want to know about such things of so long ago."

"Sure we do. Come on, Mr. Nowakoski, no secrets."

He looked up at the ceiling. "I think the year might have been 1927. Very long time ago, many years before either of you girls was born. I worked in a factory then, in a town in New Jersey." He chuckled, remembering. "I was employed in the shipping department, and I used to go to the packing department because they had a lot of pretty girls in there. One day there was a new one. Nice, very nice. I asked someone her name. Pesowski, they tell me. My eyes light up! A Polish name! How very clever of me to pick her! So along I walk to where she is working. I tell her my name and that I am making twenty-six cents an hour and that I was born in Bydgoszcz and that I think she should maybe talk with me after work." He laughed. His cheeks colored. "You know, the funny thing, it took a lot of courage to make myself walk up to this girl and say these things, but I wanted to get everything straight from the very start because I felt that this was something . . . that *mattered,* you understand. But it was strange;

she just stared at me!"

"Stared?"

"That's right. She couldn't speak a word of English! I had to go through the whole thing again in Polish!"

Jane began to relax. Every minute meant a better chance for Craig. But what about her father? What was happening to him? Was he still alive? No, she wouldn't even think of the possibility of his death. He would be all right. He was a survivor. He'd often said that. Anyone, he said, who could come unscratched through twenty-five B-17 missions in mid-1943 earned his skilled survivor's badge.

"I'm sure everything's going to be all right," said Virginia Jensen.

"You bet," said Mr. Nowakoski.

"They'll work something out."

"Sure."

"They won't let the Pope . . . and everyone else, get killed."

"Of course they won't. No way."

The real danger, Jane thought, is that something could go wrong in the air. Someone could lose control and shoot at someone and hit something vital. And God only knows how many lives would be shattered. And the politicians would exchange diplomatic notes, and everyone would say what a hell of a shame it was and how the world should wise up. . . .

"I believe them," said Mr. Nowakoski. "They say they will release us as soon as everything is worked out about the Pope. I believe them. They only want us because of the crew of the airplane. Once it lands someplace, they don't have any more use for us. They'll let us go."

Or get rid of us, Jane thought.

* * *

Craig, we're depending on you.

The highway patrol uniform seemed ill-suited to the man's gray head and porky, spreading body. Craig had never before seen a patrolman who looked so *old*. Over forty, for sure. But he seemed important. The other patrolmen were polite to him and called him sir.

He was rude and direct.

"You're putting us on, kid."

"No, sir."

"Yes you are. Now, admit it. You heard the story on the radio, and you figured you'd have yourself a laugh or two at our expense."

"No. . . ."

"Don't lie to me, kid!"

His voice was terrifying. Like a clap of thunder in the night. Then suddenly it was gentle. . . .

"Aw, c'mon, we're not mad at you. We know you just wanted a little fun, huh?"

Craig shook his head. "No, sir. . . ."

"Sure you did. We understand. Hell, we were kids once."

"No, sir. It's not fun . . . honest." He remembered. His mother had told him again and again. "Honest*ly*." A deep breath. "My father is flying the Pope to San Francisco. That's why they got us."

"Got you?"

"Yes, we were leaving the market. . . ."

The big man chewed his lip.

"What airline does your father fly for?"

"Trans American, sir."

"And what's his name?"

"Jensen, sir, same as mine, I told you. . . ."

The men exchanged glances. A moment's thought; then the big man picked up the telephone. "Get me the FBI. Quickly!"

* * *

Mallory called the cabin on the interphone. Dee Pennetti answered.

"How are the passengers?"

"Pretty good, Captain. No one seems to have any idea what's going on. No suspicions . . . nothing."

"Good," said Mallory. He wondered how the poor bastards

would react when they did find out. "How about you and the girls? Any problems otherwise?"

"No, it's okay so far. Kind of weird in a way; it seems just like any other trip; no one's causing any problems or anything."

"The Pope?"

"He's sleeping, Captain."

"Sleeping?"

"Yes, sir. Most of the other members of his party are wide awake but he's fast asleep. Very cool of him, isn't it?"

"Very cool," Mallory agreed.

"Can we get you something, Captain? Coffee maybe?"

"Sounds good. Bring up three cups."

Fadia tapped him on the shoulder. "Make it four cups."

"Better make it four," said Mallory. "And will you bring another half dozen cups up to the lounge area? And, listen, try not to look too surprised when you get there."

"Sir?"

"There are five naked men there . . . handcuffed."

A momentary pause. "Okay, Captain."

Unflappable Dee.

Mallory shifted his weight. For the first time in fifteen years he felt the need for a cigarette. He could taste the tobacco and feel the peculiar satisfaction of exhaling a stream of gray-blue smoke. Tobacco might spark inspiration, give him an idea, something to fight back with. Anything was better than this damnable compliance with every order. . . .

There's got to be some goddam thing you can do. Think, for Christ's sake!

He sighed. The fact was, the hijackers had done one hell of a good job of planning; they seemed to have thought of everything. But no one ever thought of *everything;* there was always a loophole. . . .

Jensen had turned to Fadia. His voice quivering with anger, he declared, "I want you to know, that if any member of my family is harmed by you or any of your creeps, I'll get you. I swear to God I'll kill you all."

Fadia shrugged, unimpressed. "Very well, Mr. Jensen, now that you've got that off your chest, I hope you feel better."

Jensen was on the brink of rage. "You sons of bitches think you can get away with anything. You think you're above every goddam law there ever was, don't you? You wave your guns, and everyone bows down to you. What gives you the right to kidnap my family? Tell me that, you bitch. . . ."

Flatly, as if uttering the statement for the fiftieth time, she said, "I wish your family no harm, Mr. Jensen. I wish you no harm either, for that matter. But there are certain things that must be done. Unfortunately, it seems to be impossible to do these things without . . . some people getting hurt sometimes. I'm sorry. I wish it wasn't that way, but it is."

Jensen muttered, "I wonder how brave you are without that gun."

"You won't have an opportunity to find out," Fadia replied. To all the crew she proclaimed angrily, "End of discussion!"

"Just remember what I said," Jensen growled.

"Shut your fucking mouth," she shouted.

She turned as the flight deck door opened. One of the men in sports jackets said something. She nodded. Dee was admitted with a tray of coffee cups.

Mallory caught a glimpse of pink bodies huddled in the lounge seats behind the cockpit.

Poor guys.

Dee was surprised to see Fadia. She had expected a man.

"Those guys are getting cold out there. Can I get them blankets?"

Fadia shook her head. "Give us the coffee and then go."

Dee opened her mouth, then seemed to change her mind. Lips set tight, she served the steaming cups.

"One moment."

"Yes?"

Fadia said, "You will exchange my cup of coffee for that given to Captain Mallory."

"There's nothing wrong. . . . "

"In that case there won't be any objection to exchanging them, will there?"

"That's ridiculous. . . ."

"Possibly, but you will still do it. And slowly, so that I can keep an eye on both cups."

Dee sighed. She took Mallory's cup and gave it to the girl.

Mallory glanced at the stewardess. "Okay to drink this stuff?"

"Sure thing, Captain. Best cup I ever made."

"You may go now," said Fadia, "and thanks for the coffee."

"You're goddam welcome," Dee replied as she let herself out.

chapter 13

Stewardess Fran Ludwig was relaxing aboard this smooth, powerful motorboat, reclining on a comfortable chaise lounge, wearing the cutest bikini she had ever seen: pink with darling little spots and stripes. And Robert Redford was sitting in this sort of chair, looking over the back of the boat, holding a fishing rod and wearing nothing but a yachting cap and the most adorable smile. . . .

She fought consciousness. It wasn't fair to drag her back; she wanted to stay a little longer; God only knows what Robert Redford was going to do next; he had this sort of wicked-cute look in his eye. . . .

She sat up. Jesus Christ, she thought—at once she mentally apologized; she had forgotten the Pope's presence. She opened her eyes wide, guilty about thoughts of Robert Redford. . . . Next to her, Lucy Sullivan was dozing, hands upturned in her lap, like someone begging.

Stewardess Ludwig blinked the sleep from her eyes and glanced at her watch. Eight-forty in the evening, San Francisco time. Puzzled, she glanced at the bright sunlight sparkling at the edges of her window shade. She nudged Lucy awake.

"What time have you got?"

"Time? Eight-forty, San Francisco time."

"Strange. How can there be a sunrise during a flight that takes off and lands at night?"

"Oh, it's probably the midnight sun. Nothing unusual about it when you fly north of the Arctic Circle in the summer."

"Yeah . . . I guess you're right. Maybe we should brew some coffee for the passengers. They're likely to be waking up soon."

She peered through a corner of the shade. Bright daylight. Solid layer of cloud a long way down.

On her way back to the galley, Fran was stopped by a passenger's arm.

"My name is Squires."

"Yes sir, Mr. Squires. I know you. . . ."

"Perhaps you can provide me with some information."

"I'll be happy to do that if I can . . . but you see, I'm on my way to the galley. . . ."

"I think this may be important."

"Oh?"

"I am correct, am I not, in assuming that our destination is San Francisco?"

He had a clipped, precise way of speaking, just as he had in the movies and on TV. Stewardess Ludwig nodded; yes indeed, San Francisco was where they were going.

"But are you sure?"

"Sir?"

"If we are headed for San Francisco, how do you account for the sun rising in the west?"

"Well, sir, it's because we're over the Arctic and the midnight sun. . . ."

"Young lady," he interrupted, "that would be plausible if the sun were to our north, but the sun is rising ahead of us. This means that—if you are correct—we are headed for the North Pole. Or, this aircraft has turned around and is heading due east, opposite to our direction of intended travel. Observe." Vernon Squires motioned toward the windows and then folded his arms across his chest in the manner of a magician who has completed a trick.

Stewardess Ludwig started to say something, then stopped. The man made sense. The sun was rising on the nose! She shook her head as if to clear herself of the last vestiges of sleep.

"Possibly," said Mr. Squires, "the Pope has arranged this little miracle to impress us all."

She bit her lip; something was wrong, terribly wrong.

"I'll get back to you, sir."

"I'll look forward to it."

"Please don't mention this . . . you know, to any of the other passengers for the moment."

"If you wish."

"Thanks."

She hurried to the nearest interphone station. Turning to face the wall so that her words couldn't be overheard, she jabbed the cockpit button.

"This is Fran Ludwig in Coach. Will someone please tell me why the sun is rising in the west . . . ?

* * *

The Pope prayed—not for himself, but for the men and women whose lives were in danger because of his presence. He prayed also for the Palestinian hijackers, driven by circumstances to such desperate lengths. Would there ever be a time when people would truly be able to live in peace? Was the human race doomed forever to slaughter one another? Would there ever be a time when men realized that no cause justified the taking of lives? Men could create miraculous machines such as the extraordinary craft presently soaring so smoothly through the sky. Surely such genius could be directed at solving the problems of living together. . . .

He contemplated the immediate future. It was a possibility, a very real possibility, that his sojourn on earth might be concluded in a few hours—or even minutes. So be it. The prospect was not frightening; if it happened, his only duty would be to ensure that he faced death with dignity and forgiveness for those who caused it. . . .

* * *

"I've got to level with the passengers," said Mallory.

Fadia thought for a moment. "This is as good a time as any."

"You're very kind," said Mallory.

"Get on with it, Captain. Spare me the sarcasm."

Jensen reported that the East German border would be

reached in about five minutes. "But we still haven't got clearance to overfly East Germany."

Mallory nodded. Air Traffic Control had advised that overflight clearances had been obtained from all territories over which Flight 901 would have to fly in order to reach El Maghreb: Greenland, Scotland, West Germany, Czechoslovakia, Hungary, Romania, Yugoslavia, Bulgaria, Greece, Turkey, Cyprus, Israel—all but East Germany. He again asked Bremen Control to advise the East Germans of the imminent arrival of Flight 901 and to arrange for an emergency clearance through their airspace. He anticipated no trouble. The whole world must be aware of the progress of this flight. God knows how many people must be monitoring it at this very moment.

What the hell was happening at home? No one seemed to be able to tell them anything meaningful. Everyone was talking, but no one was saying anything. There was still no further word about Jane and the others. But, Henderson said, the feds were working hard on it.

He cleared his throat and picked up the public address handset.

"Ladies and gentlemen, this is Captain Mallory speaking. I know some of you are just waking up, and I'm very sorry to have to start your day with some bad news. Unfortunately, this aircraft is presently headed for Jordan . . . in the Middle East. The reason, I very much regret to tell you, is that we have been hijacked. Now, please do not be alarmed. I know this is distressing news, but I have been assured that the hijackers mean no harm to you. This flight has been chosen because of the presence of the Pope. I imagine that something will be demanded to secure his safe release. We don't have any details. In any event, it is not you who are the target, I want you to understand that clearly. I am led to believe that as soon as we land, you will be able to disembark. Now, in the meantime, the cabin attendants will serve coffee and a snack. I deeply regret that this has happened. I'm sure that everything will turn out all right. Please do not take any action. There is an armed hijacker in the cockpit and there are others in the passenger cabin. We don't know how many. So just sit quietly and try to relax. We'll get you out of this as soon as we can. Thank you."

* * *

"No," said the woman. She thumped her fist on the armrest to emphasize the response. "No, no, no! No way! It's not possible." She grabbed Mr. Squires' sleeve; she had an astonishingly fierce grip. "It is absolutely not possible. Is it? For God's sake, tell me it isn't possible. I mean . . . *Jordan* . . . no, no, no!"

Her face had become slightly twisted; her eyes seemed about to pop out of their sockets. Mr. Squires pried her fingers free one by one.

He told her the flight appeared to be heading east.

"God."

"Irritating, isn't it?"

"*Irritating*? Oh my God." She shook her head as if despairing of the human race. "I don't know what to say. . . . I'm beside myself. I am . . . positively beside myself."

"How uncomfortable for you."

"What are we going to do?" She grabbed his arm. "I mean, what the hell are we going to *do*?"

"We wait," he said. "We wait and see what happens next."

"Wait?"

"Precisely."

"God, no, we've got to *do* something!"

"What do you suggest?"

"I think I'm going to faint," she replied.

"That'll be a great help," sighed Mr. Squires.

* * *

The West German air traffic controller sounded worried.

"Trans Am nine-zero-one, we have again contacted Schonefeld Control in East Germany and explained your situation. But we have not yet been able to obtain a clearance for you to overfly their territory. We suggest, therefore, that you enter a holding pattern prior to reaching the East German border until the necessary clearance has been obtained."

But Fadia was already shaking her head. "No delaying tactics, no tricks, Captain. You will fly a direct route as instructed."

She sounded as calm as if she were declining a second cup of coffee. Mallory tried to explain the danger of the situation. "You heard what the West German controller said. So far, we have been denied permission to overfly East Germany."

"You have my instructions."

"I know, but you've got to understand. This is hostile territory. . . ."

"No diversions, Captain."

"But . . ."

"Do as I say," Fadia insisted.

Mallory shrugged. "Bremen Control, this is Trans Am nine-zero-one. We are not permitted to hold. We have to maintain our present course. Please advise the East Germans that we have no choice in the matter. We have an armed hijacker in the cockpit."

"Very well, Trans Am nine-zero-one. I will convey your message. Suggest you switch now to Schonefeld Radar on frequency one-two-five point eight-five. Good luck."

"Thanks for trying. Changing to one-two-five point eight-five."

Jensen pointed excitedly. "Sonofabitch, we've got company! Look, eleven o'clock position!"

They came skidding across the sky; four sleek shapes with rockets and missiles tucked beneath their swept-back wings.

"MIG 21s," said Jensen.

"Are we over East German territory already?"

"Just crossed the border, Captain."

Mallory glanced at Fadia. Her features were taut. He guessed she hadn't anticipated this problem with the East Germans.

The fighters darted across the airliner's path, as if to demonstrate their agility. Then they disappeared from view. Mallory sighed, his stomach knotting. It was like old times: plowing across German skies, the target for fighters determined to blast you from the sky. Were these the sons of the pilots who had flown the Messerschmitts and Focke-Wulfs? Their grandsons, maybe?

"Where the hell are they?" Jensen was contorting himself, trying to catch a glimpse of the fighters.

Mallory didn't bother looking. They would be back soon enough. He reached for the interphone and told the passengers not to be concerned about the MIGs; they were simply investigating the Boeing because it had not been scheduled to fly across East German territory. Everything would be all right; no problem; no sweat; not a thing to worry about. . . .

Like hell, he thought.

"They're back," Jensen announced, pointing to the nine o'clock position.

The leading MIG had pulled alongside the Boeing; it rose and fell as if suspended on a rubber string. The pilot, wearing a bright orange crash helmet, was gazing at the big airliner with more than casual interest.

"Nosy bastard," said Nowakoski.

Mallory told Jensen to establish contact with the East German controller. "Tell him to have the fighters keep their goddam distance; they could hit us, the way they're maneuvering around."

Now the MIG was forging ahead. Mallory took a deep breath. He had been expecting this. Sure enough, the fighter started rocking its wings. Left wing down, then the right wing, then back to the left. Crisp, unmistakable movements: the international sign language of the air.

Suddenly the MIG veered slowly to the left in a descending turn.

Mallory pointed. "He's telling us that we've been officially intercepted and we're to follow him."

"No," said Fadia. "Maintain your present heading."

Jensen was trying to explain the situation to the East German controller.

"Here he is again," shouted Nowakoski.

The MIG repeated the procedure, a little closer this time as if the pilot wanted to be absolutely sure that he was seen.

"Ignore him" was the order.

"He's going to be goddam difficult to ignore if he starts shooting."

"He won't."

"How do you know?"

Jensen interjected, "Skipper, Schonefeld says he can't do anything about it. We've got to obey the fighter's instructions. He's standing by on number one."

Mallory pressed the transmit button on his microphone.

"Schonefeld Control, this is Trans Am nine-zero-one. Listen carefully. Please. As you must know, we were originally en route from Rome to San Francisco with a full load of civilian passengers. . . plus the Pope and his party. Do you understand that? Please confirm."

"Affirmative, Flight nine-zero-one. I understand your message; we are aware of your situation. But the military commandant has jurisdiction and insists that you obey the instructions of his fighters. . . ."

"Listen, tell the commander that I have an armed hijacker preventing me from altering course."

"If you do not follow these instructions, the fighters have been ordered to commence firing."

"Commence *firing?* Good God, man, this is an unarmed civilian aircraft! The *Pope* is a passenger. The *Pope.* Don't you understand? We have been hijacked and are being forced through your airspace. We must maintain this heading and continue toward Jordan. I cannot alter course because I have a gun at my head."

"He's going through his routine again," Jensen observed, his face drawn.

Mallory asked the East German controller for the air-to-air frequency of the fighters.

"Negative, Trans Am. I am not permitted to provide you with that information. Please obey the instructions."

"That's impossible," Mallory snapped. "There is an armed terrorist in my cockpit, and I'm being forced at gunpoint to overfly East Germany. There is absolutely no way for me to comply with your instructions."

He sat back. Okay, let it happen. He'd said everything that

could be said; if the crazy bastards chose to shoot him down, there was nothing he could do to prevent it.

"Look at 'em." Jensen was pointing again.

The fighters came zooming past the jumbo jet, turning sharply, then sliding away to the left. They looked playful, in a lethal sort of way: mechanical babies cavorting around the lumbering giant. They came again, one after the other, close enough so that the oil stains and scars were visible on their metal bodies.

"Keep your goddam distance!" Jensen barked, as the 747 rocked in a jet's wake.

One thing about the later-model B-17: the gunners could warn you if fighters were coming up from the rear. In a 747 you had no advance warning. You just had to sit there and take it.

"A large city ahead," said Nowakoski.

Mallory wet his lips. A minute or two's grace. They'd be unlikely to shoot him down over a densely populated area.

"You must change course to three-three-zero degrees." said the East German controller.

"Negative. I can't turn . . . and you damned well know why."

"Flight nine-zero-one, you are ordered to turn to three-three-zero degrees. . . "

"Negative, negative, negative! . . . we are unable to comply!"

"Very well, Trans American Flight nine-zero-one. You have precisely one minute. If you have not altered course at the end of sixty seconds, your aircraft will destroyed."

Destroyed?!

He had seen film clips of old bombers hit by such missiles. In a split second they became a bewildering collection of metal fragments fluttering forlornly through the air.

The fighters had disappeared again.

"Our aircraft are taking up firing positions behind you, Flight nine-zero-one."

"I can't obey your orders. If I could, I would. But there's a gun at my head! Do you understand that?"

"Forty seconds."

Mallory twisted in his seat. Fadia was standing behind him, her pistol raised.

"For God's sake . . ."

"Don't change course, Captain. You have your orders."

"But you heard the man. . . ."

"Stay on this course. The slightest turn and somebody dies."

"Thirty seconds."

Nowakoski started to get up from his seat; she flicked the gun barrel in his direction. "Stay in your seats, all of you. We will maintain this course."

"But the goddam controller. . ."

"Fifteen seconds."

Evasive action . . . The idea ran through Mallory's mind. Ridiculous. Evade air-to-air missiles in this sluggish thing? Impossible.

There was nothing to do but sit and wait and hope.

And think of the poor sons of bitches of passengers who didn't know what the hell was going on.

On second thought, they were the lucky ones.

"Five seconds, Captain. Four. Three. Two. One. Zero."

"Jesus . . . . "

Silence.

Mallory squirmed, anticipating the awful shattering explosion that would tear the great jet to bits, the rockets bursting through her fragile skin, a fireball searing through row after row of passengers, the torn bodies spinning through the air. . . .

Jensen's fingers were digging deep into his legs, the skin on his knuckles taut and white.

Then the East German controller called again. Excitement and relief bubbled in his voice.

"Trans Am Flight nine-zero-one, you have permission to overfly East Germany. Maintain present heading. Good luck."

Mallory breathed again . . . a reprieve.

"Thanks," he told the East German. "Give my regards to the military commandant."

The MIGs flew alongside. The lead pilot raised a gloved hand and saluted. Then they peeled off and were gone.

Mallory turned to Fadia.

"We damn nearly got ourselves blown to hell."

She seemed unconcerned. "We didn't, though, did we?"

Jesus, they didn't make them any cooler than this one. He said, "How could you be so sure those guys wouldn't open fire?"

She shrugged. "Do you really think there was any chance they would shoot at *this* aircraft? No, I don't think so."

"You're cool," Mallory admitted. "I've got to hand it to you: you're cool."

But he wished she had gone into some other line of work.

* * *

The East German general reported immediately.

"Our aircraft inspected the Boeing at close quarters. It carried no unusual camera ports or detection antennae and appeared to be a standard, passenger-carrying 747SP of Trans American Airlines. The captain refused to deviate from course in the face of imminent destruction by our interceptors. We are confident, therefore, that he was indeed flying at the point of a hijacker's gun. His only chance for survival was that we would let him through at the last moment, which we did. I am certain that the aircraft was not on a spy mission. I would stake my military reputation on that."

As he hung up the telephone, he silently congratulated himself for his expert handling of a delicate situation loaded with political dynamite. Nevertheless, he paused for an uncertain moment before walking outside.

chapter 14

Old man Nowakoski had fallen asleep. Sprawled in his chair, mouth open, head resting on one shoulder, he looked like a corpse. He made no sound. Concerned, Jane had gone to him and had listened to satisfy herself that he was still breathing. Poor old guy. What was he dreaming about? What did old men dream about? All the things they did when they were young? Or all the things they didn't do?

There was no sound from Telly or the others; nevertheless, Jane and Virginia Jensen kept talking about houses and food prices, operations and lingerie—anything but the subject that was uppermost in their minds.

How long would it take to get help? More than three hours had elapsed since Craig had escaped. If indeed he had escaped. There was no evidence to confirm it. The truth was, he might have suffocated in the chimney; his body might be stuck up there....

She hoped the thought hadn't occurred to Virginia Jensen.

A plane flew over. It sounded low. The two women exchanged glances. For a moment they conjured up images of helicopters full of assault troops, speeding to their rescue. But the plane kept going, its sound diminishing until it became a rumble; then it merged with the wind's murmurings.

A step outside. A key turned.

The women sat upright; Mr. Nowakoski stirred.

Scarface came in.

"What do you want?" Jane demanded.

He looked at her, then at the others.

"Anyone still hungry?"

"No. We don't want any more of your lousy sandwiches."

149

He shrugged. "As you wish. Does anyone want to go to the bathroom? The baby? The boy, perhaps?"

Fear darted through Jane's body. "He's asleep."

Virginia Jensen muttered something about his always sleeping a great deal.

"Like the old man, huh?"

Virginia nodded. Too enthusiastically. A poor actress, crummy liar.

Jane said, "How long are you going to keep us here?"

"Not long, I told you."

"How many hours?"

He shook his head, irritated. "You know I won't tell you. Why do you keep asking?"

"Because you might slip up."

He regarded her with a steady gaze. "No, I won't slip up. So it is a waste of your time to keep trying. You're certainly a talkative female; foul, too."

Jane said, "I suppose you all think you're heroes."

"Heroes?" He seemed to flush a little in spite of his shrug. "No, we are not heroes. We don't pretend to be heroes. We are just soldiers."

"Soldiers don't kidnap women and children and old men."

"Sometimes such things are necessary. Isn't it true that after the attack on Pearl Harbor, the American authorities kidnapped all citizens of Japanese ancestry?"

"That was wartime," said Jane, wishing she had a more cogent response.

"We are at war," he said. "We have been fighting it for thirty years."

"You haven't made much progress, have you?"

"Perhaps you won't say that after tomorrow."

"What's going to happen then?"

"You'll find out."

"Will my husband be all right?" Virginia Jensen's voice had a pleading tone.

"Yes, everyone will be fine. This operation has been brilliantly planned. Everything is going smoothly."

He sat down and leaned the chair back against the wall. He

crossed his legs; his left shoe slipped at the heel, revealing a large hole in his sock.

"You'll get a blister there," said Jane.

"A what?"

"A blister . . . where your sock has a hole."

"Ah . . . I didn't notice."

"War is hell," she said.

He did not smile. "Of course it is," he said, clearly thinking the remark superfluous. Then he studied the room, a corner at a time, as if looking for some evidence of escape attempts.

Old man Nowakoski woke up. He was startled to see Scarface.

"What has happened?"

"Nothing," Scarface told him. "You can go back to sleep."

"Why are you here?"

"I came to discuss politics with Mrs. Sutton."

"You had a good sleep," Jane remarked to Mr. Nowakoski. And instantly regretted it.

Scarface had turned toward the blanket.

"The boy is sleeping very soundly."

"He often does," said Virginia, her cheeks brightening.

"Is he sick?"

"No, he's fine. I . . . checked just before you came in."

Scarface gazed at the still form. Then he uncrossed his legs and stood up. The chair clattered as it found equilibrium on the bare floor.

Jane trembled. In a moment he would go over and look closer. An instant later he would discover that there was no boy there. Then what? Immediate retaliation? Panic twisted and turned her insides. She tried not to catch Virginia Jensen's eye. Nowakoski seemed to have forgotten about the boy; he was busy loading his pipe.

Scarface moved in the loose, lazy way of someone who sees little urgency in his mission but who performs it because it is his duty.

He walked between Jane and Virginia Jensen, looking at neither.

Now he was only six feet from the blanket and the two

cushions beneath it.

Stop him! For Christ's sake, do something! Anything!

Jane blurted, "I thought you wanted to get laid." Her voice cracked; she coughed the tickle away.

He stopped, stared. "What? . . . What did you say?"

Her try at nonchalance wasn't totally convincing, but he didn't appear to notice. "You seemed pretty interested in my body a little while ago."

His mouth dropped half-open. He was momentarily speechless.

Nice, she told herself. Keep going; it's working.

"There's no time like the present," she suggested.

"Now?"

"Sure. Why not?"

He frowned at her as if not believing what he was hearing. "What are you saying?"

"To be blunt, I'd like to get laid." Wordly-wise shrug of the shoulders. She felt the others' eyes on her. "It's boring as hell sitting around here. It'd help pass the time."

Old man Nowakoski sputtered, then wheezily sucked in air.

Scarface gaped. "You want to pass the time?"

Jane nodded. "And you might turn out to be a good lay. It could be enjoyable. In that case it will be more than just a way to pass the time. But at this point I don't know what you're like, so I can't say."

"And . . . you *want* to find out?"

He tried to sound flip, but he didn't quite succeed. The excitement showed.

"If you like," she said.

Scarface seemed to be fighting a battle within himself. Duty versus lust? For some reason, Jane wondered if he thought in Arabic.

His tongue moved along his lower lip. He half nodded.

"Come with me," he said.

His big hand closed on her shoulder. She got to her feet. He led her to the door. She turned to the others.

"See you later."

"Sure, sure," the old man muttered, bewildered, his world awry.

Virginia Jensen looked at her, shaking her head gently as if to convey the fact that she didn't know what to say.

Telly was sitting in the hall, reading a newspaper. He and Scarface exchanged a few words. Telly looked angry. More words. Now Scarface looked angry. He said something. Telly looked away in disgust.

"I take it he doesn't approve," said Jane.

"I'm not concerned about him. He is a difficult person."

"Are you?" she asked.

"I don't think so," he said seriously. Then he looked at her. "Was that a joke? I am never sure when you are joking."

"I wasn't joking," she assured him. God, God, God, what the hell had she gotten herself into?

He led her out through the ramshackle kitchen that still held hints of countless meals made God knows how long ago. A faded 1965 calendar was still pinned to a wall. Outside, the air was warm and dry. It was delicious, after the chill dampness of the house. She felt the warmth enveloping her. She breathed deeply. Above, the stars were a billion tiny pinpricks of light. She wondered if her father was looking at the same stars and wondering about her. Just as well he didn't know what was happening. What would he say? "Well done"? "Three cheers for our side"?

Her heartbeat was beginning to settle down again. More or less normal. Okay, she was committed. She had seen what had to be done, and she had done it. Maybe it was too compulsive, too self-sacrificing; but at least some time had been bought. But was it worth the price? A good deal? Seller and purchaser both pleased? Time, she supposed, would tell. The sordid fact was that she should do her womanly best to keep the guy out here as long as possible. Which, she admitted candidly, might not be such an ordeal. He was far from repulsive.

"Are you afraid?"

She shook her head. Resolutely. "Afraid? No, why should I be afraid?"

"I thought you might be."

"How about you?" she asked.

"Me?" He laughed. "What do I have to be afraid of?"

"Perhaps you won't be able to get it up. It happens sometimes, particularly with a new partner."

He gazed at her. "You are an extraordinary woman. Never have I encountered anyone like you. You say whatever is on your mind."

"There's nothing wrong with the truth."

He nodded. "Then I will tell you something that is true."

"Go ahead."

"You excite me greatly. You are beautiful."

"Thank you."

He held her waist and drew her to him.

"See," he said, "I do not have the problem you mentioned."

"So I notice. But let's get away from the house. . . . We don't want your friends disturbing us."

He nodded in an oddly formal way and, hand in hand, they walked a hundred yards to the edge of a clearing.

His hands roamed her breasts. Powerful yet gentle hands. Soon he had unbuttoned her blouse and unfastened her bra. She tugged his shirt free of his pants. In a moment they were both struggling out of the rest of their clothes.

He looked her up and down, his eyes gentle with wonder.

She felt herself responding, softening, awakening.

Together they tumbled onto the soft grass, their limbs entwining, their hands urgently exploring. He was strong and firmly muscled; she reveled in his maleness, and the devotion of his hands and body.

"There's no hurry," she tried to tell him. "Baby, we've got time."

But his thrust was immediate. Big, insistent. A delicious intrusion that seemed about to pierce her entire body.

Then it happened . . . explosively. In the midst of the physical act, an uncontrollable metamorphosis overcame her. It was no longer sexual self-sacrifice. It was no reluctant parting of the legs. It was a willful and total partnership. With every thrust she responded vigorously with one of her own and the increasing intensity drove her thoughts beyond her wildest fantasies. This was the ultimate freedom, the culmination of all the passion and desire she had stored for a lifetime.

Emotions quelled and stifled by parents and peers, by teachers and churches were now screaming their release and the pleasure of it all was overwhelming. Her legs were wrapped around her liberator, not her captor.

With each savage thrust, she felt a rebirth of her deep-seated rebellion against society, against the system. He became the personification of her hatred for Viet Nam, Watergate, the establishment and all the values she was forced to accept but had grown to despise.

This was new freedom, an escape from conformity . . . and she loved it. Fucking Scarface was the fascinating embodiment of fucking the system. This was her own private revolution and she became the consummate revolutionary.

There was no holding back now. There was only the relentless rhythm of desire. Like a tribal dance, its tempo intensified. There were rolling tides and hot, powerful winds; deep blues and rolling crimsons; warmth that exploded and disintegrated and formed intricate patterns that danced along every nerve and fiber.

Then peace.

He was breathing hard; his cheek lay on one breast; his tight, curly hair tickled her chin.

She rubbed his lightly sweating back. He snuggled closer to her, like a child to its mother.

"You are a very beautiful woman," he said.

"Thank you. You are very beautiful yourself."

"No. Men are not beautiful."

"They are to women." She touched his chin lightly. "That's a beautiful scar. How did you get it?"

"An Israeli bullet," he said shortly. "It only grazed me . . . but it killed my mother."

"I'm sorry."

"It was many years ago." He was silent for a moment. "I would prefer not to talk more about it."

"I understand."

He smiled.

"That was good for you, huh?"

"Very. You've had practice."

"Some," he admitted.

"Here in America?"

"Sure. A few times."

"Do you live here?"

"Yes."

"Where?"

"In a university dormitory."

"You live where? . . . *What*?"

"A dorm. What's so strange about that?"

She sat up. "You mean, you're a student in an American university? Which one?"

"I'd rather not say. I was sent here by UNESCO. They pay the bills."

"I wondered what they did with all that dough from the Christmas cards."

"What?"

"Never mind. So you took time out for . . . this?"

"Of course."

"What's your major . . . assassination?"

"What are you talking about? I study political science." He frowned. "It seems to annoy you, the idea of me going to one of your universities."

"I'm not sure whether it annoys me or not," said Jane. "It just seems so . . . *bizarre*."

"Bizarre? Isn't that a place to buy things?"

"No. That's a *bazaar*. Never mind. I guess I shouldn't find it hard to think of a guy who goes to a university doing things like this. They all do, it seems. Why don't you get out of it?"

"Get out?"

"Sure. You're a bright guy. You have your whole life ahead of you. Why risk it all for . . . politics. It's not worth risking your life."

He shook his head like a teacher disappointed with a student. "You don't understand, do you? It's worth a million lives like mine. Ten million. Didn't your soldiers feel that way during World War Two?"

"That was different. That was *real* war."

"*This* is real war."

She sighed. "But you're involving innocent women and children. . . ."

"Didn't your bombers involve innocent women and children?"

She thought of her father. Of Dresden, of Hamburg. Of Hiroshima. Of Nagasaki.

"What's your name?"

"I will tell you only the name by which my comrades know me. It is Abou Gabal. My real name is unimportant."

"It belongs to your other life?"

"Yes, you might say that." He fondled one of her nipples, examining it with interest as it became rigid, then flaccid, then rigid again. "Your name is Jane. Jane Sutton. You are twenty-four years old, and you are divorced from your husband."

"Very good."

"Why are you divorced?"

"We got bored with each other."

"You are, I think, a little ashamed of that fact. You try to sound very bold and brazen about it. But it troubles you."

"Maybe. It makes me wonder if I will always be like that. Perhaps I'm just not able to care for someone for a lifetime. Maybe some people can, but I'm not so sure about me. Sure, it troubles me at times."

She was uncomfortable with this analysis and changed the subject. "You're quite a versatile guy. University student, psychiatrist . . . and terrorist."

"American women are strange."

"Strange?"

"On the one hand, very materialistic—greedy in some ways for the products of their husbands' labors. On the other hand, very honest, realistic, I suppose."

"Aren't Palestinian women like that?"

"Some. The younger ones are learning Western ways. But the majority still think like their mothers. They are content to be shadows of their husbands. In some ways, I suppose, it is pleasant; in others, annoying. My mother was a woman of keen intelligence. But she never had the opportunity to use that intelligence. A pity, I think, a terrible waste."

"Is your father alive?"

"Yes. He married again and lives in Beirut. I see him sometimes, but not often. We argue. He has become comfortable and settled with his new wife. He sends the PLO as little as he can get away with—a token, you would call it. He has lost heart for the fight."

"Maybe he's the sensible one."

"No. The fight for Palestine must be intensified. It is *our* land, you must understand that."

"I do. At least, I guess I do. But I know a lot of Jewish people, and I like them."

"I have nothing personal against the Jews."

"Then how can you think of killing them?"

"I won't—the moment they leave our land. I promise."

"Land isn't worth dying for."

"On the contrary, it it the only thing worth dying for—that, and a beautiful woman."

"You're a smooth-talking bastard."

He grinned.

They began to caress one another, fingers and lips traveling boldly.

"I do believe he's beginning to show signs of life again."

He groaned with the pleasure of it. "Hardly surprising."

"He's a tasty morsel."

Abou Gabal laughed. He had a pleasant, open laugh, like that of a boy without a care in the world.

* * *

The helicopter's rotors were still turning as Mr. Beale jumped down to the grass and ran to the boy who was waiting with a group of highway patrolmen.

"You're Craig Jensen?"

"Yes, sir."

"Good boy. My name's Beale. I'm with the FBI." His black-gray hair became a tangle in the wind. He looked like a teacher at Craig's school, from the tweedy sport jacket to the metal-rimmed glasses. "You did a great job, Craig. Your father will be very proud of you." He spoke the words quickly, automatically, as if they were something that had to be said before the real business at hand could begin. "Now, we're going to get your mother and the others out of that house, but we need some more of your help. Okay?"

"Yes, sir."

"Can you take us to the house?"

"I think so."

One of the patrolmen said, "From what he said, it sounds like it's on the fifth side road. Maybe five miles. There's only one house. Used to be a farm. Family moved. No one's wanted to buy it."

"What's the best way to approach it?"

"Not sure. It's right smack in the middle of ten acres."

"There are trees on one side," said Craig. "That's where I ran to. The other sides are just low hedges."

"Thank God it's dark now," murmured Beale. "That's a blessing."

They pored over a sketch that a patrolman had prepared with Craig's aid. It depicted the layout of the ground floor, or as much of it as Craig had seen and could remember.

"This room where your mother and the others are kept—is there only one door?"

"Yes, sir."

"How many windows?"

Craig tried to remember. "They were covered with boards. . . . Two or three, I think."

"And you're not sure which side the room is on?"

"No. They brought us in the side door, there, and then straight through the hall into the room."

"Okay," said Beale, "we'll just have to make some assumptions." He turned to Craig. "I want you to come with us; you can be very helpful. We're going to get your mother out of there. Will you come along?"

Craig felt his stomach flutter, and he knew he was frightened. But he had to do it. He felt like the marshal in a Western: the moment of truth. He nodded.

"Good boy," said Beale approvingly. "Let's go."

chapter 15

Mallory nodded to Jensen.

"Let's have an update on the weather, Cliff."

"Okay." He reached for the high-frequency transceiver, tuned in the appropriate frequency and requested the information.

Terse. Very uptight was Mr. Jensen. Of course the poor bastard could hardly be blamed; he had problems; but so did everyone else; they all had families to worry about. And the fact remained that no one could do anything to help any of them except get his airplane down at El Maghreb in one piece.

Mallory watched as Jensen absorbed the incoming data.

"Not good," was the report.

The *simoom* was still blasting its scorching, suffocating way through the Middle East. Weather stations closest to El Maghreb were reporting occasional visibility as low as a sixteenth of a mile—far less than the minimum necessary to safely land a 747.

Mallory rubbed his eyes. He turned to Fadia. She regarded him with a level gaze. The gun rested in her lap.

"I'll tell you the truth, lady, we've got to start thinking about an alternate airport."

She shook her head. "There will be no alternate."

"There's going to *have* to be if we can't land at El Maghreb."

"No."

Stubbornness always irritated Mallory. "Christ Almighty, do I have to draw pictures for you? Conditions are bad. Really bad. It may be impossible for us to land at El Maghreb and if we can't land there, we're going to have to land someplace else. And to do that, we're going to have to start making plans. So for God's sake, tell me where you want us to go if we can't land at El Maghreb."

Again she shook her head. She refused to even consider the thought of going elsewhere. "We will land at El Maghreb. Nowhere else. Is that clear?"

"It's clear," said Mallory. "It's also ridiculous to try to land on a runway that you can't find."

"Those are my instructions," she snapped. "You will obey them."

Jensen turned on her. "You don't give a damn if you kill everyone on this airplane. All you care about is following your stupid orders!"

"The orders may seem stupid to you," she smiled triumphantly, "but they will result in Israel's total surrender of the West Bank."

"*What*?"

"Immediate and complete withdrawal from the West Bank," she said, "is the price demanded for the Pope's life."

Mallory's spine seemed to turn momentarily to ice.

"You're a mental case," Jensen told her. "All you goddam revolutionaries are mental. You can't see straight. You can't think straight. You belong in psycho wards, all of you!"

"Be quiet. You are becoming tedious, Mr. Jensen."

Her calm, almost bored tone seemed to exacerbate Jensen's anger."

"You lousy bitch!"

"I warn you!"

"Fuck your warning!" Before Mallory could move to stop him, Jensen had flung his safety belts aside and was scrambling out of his seat. But there is little room for rapid movement in the confining quarters of a 747 flight deck. Getting up took time. Before he could take a step back toward the jump seat, Fadia had, with astonishing speed, darted forward and hit him a cracking blow across the forehead with the butt of her pistol. Even as Jensen collapsed back into his seat, she withdrew to the rear of the flight deck. There she stood, semicrouched, holding the pistol with both hands, fanning it from side to side.

She shouted, "Next time I shoot. I promise. Do you understand? Do you?"

Mallory leaned across to Jensen. "Are you all right?"

Jensen was dazed and rubbery. The flesh on his forehead had split; blood streamed down his face, spattering his white shirt.

"I'm okay . . . sorry. . . ."

"Give him a hand," Mallory told Nowakoski.

"Next time I shoot," Fadia repeated.

Mallory told her to shut up. He picked up the interphone.

"What are you doing?"

He ignored her and summoned Dee to the cockpit. The senior stewardess had done some nursing before joining Trans Am.

Nowakoski was fumbling with the first aid kit.

"You'll be okay," he kept telling Jensen. Mallory wondered how he knew.

Jensen apologized. "Sorry. . . . I shouldn't have done that."

"Forget it," Mallory told him.

"It was goddam stupid. . . . Lost control of myself."

When Dee comes in, Mallory thought, will Fadia look behind her? And will that give someone time to rush her and snatch the pistol out of her hand? Then what? Go to the door, throw it open and blaze away at the two Arabs guarding Cousins and his men? Speedy execution. Aerial St. Valentine's Day massacre? Problem solved? Situation saved? And who, he wondered, would be the heroic volunteer? A glorious opportunity to die for your company. No doubt the president of Trans Am himself would be present at your funeral. Big deal. And anyway, it was hopeless; it wouldn't eliminate the dilemma. There was at least one more hijacker somewhere in the passenger cabin. And no doubt that hijacker had a *plastique* gridle just like Fadia's. Any trouble, and the plane might be blown to bits.

He sighed wearily as Dee was admitted by a guard. Fadia still stood at the rear of the cockpit, the gun still in her capable hands.

"Jesus Christ," Dee exclaimed when she saw Jensen. "What the hell happened?"

"He decided to play games," said Fadia. "I warned him, but

he didn't listen."

In other words, she seemed to say, he's only got himself to blame.

Dee took the first aid kit and ministered to Jensen's head.

"It doesn't look *too* bad," she said when she had finished. "We'd better get it checked when we land, but I think you'll live."

Jensen smiled thinly. "Thanks."

"Don't mention it. I'll send my bill."

Fadia resumed her station on the jump seat.

"You can go now," she told Dee.

The senior stew asked Mallory if there was anything else she could do.

Mallory shook his head. "See you later. And thanks."

"You know," Nowakoski told Fadia, "one of the things that really pisses me off about you is your goddam accent."

"I've been to some of the finest European schools," she said.

"You sound like one of the broads from *Upstairs, Downstairs.*"

"Really," said Fadia in her level way. "You, Mr. Nowakoski, remind me of a character in *All in the Family.*"

* * *

Beale studied the place through his binoculars. It looked dark and empty. Not a sign of life.

"That's the house all right," said the Jensen boy. "They've got the windows all boarded up. That's why you can't see any lights."

"Okay," said Beale. A good kid, lots of guts. "I understand."

The SWAT team was moving swiftly and silently, close to the trees.

"You came down off the roof?"

"Yes. There. On that side. There's a pipe."

"Then which way did you run?"

The boy pointed. "That way. See the fence?"

Beale nodded.

"I followed that for a while but it brought me right back here again. So then I went that way." He pointed in a different direction.

"All right," said Beale. "Now, we're going to move up closer. I want you to come with me. Okay?"

"Yes, sir."

"We're going to do this just right so that your mom and the others don't get hurt." He turned his back to the house and examined the floor plan that had been drawn at Craig's directions. He had a flashlight that threw a pencil-thin beam of light. "That's the room where they're all being kept. Is that right?"

"Yes, sir."

"And that room is on *this* side of the house, the one nearest to us now?"

The boy stared intently at the drawing, then at the house. He nodded.

Beale felt the sweat collecting around his collar. It was a hell of an assignment, no matter how you looked at it. Somehow those hostages *had* to be rescued. But the dismal reality of the situation was, the chances of getting them all out in one piece were slim. There were too many unknowns, too many unpredictables. The only certainty was that the matter couldn't be discussed with the gunmen inside. Firepower was the only argument those sons of bitches understood.

He pointed out the shed beside the house.

"Is that where they put the Sears truck?"

"Yes, sir, I'm sure of it."

"It's not attached to the house, is it? Do you know if we can get in that way?"

"I can't remember. . . . Sorry."

"Did they bring you out of the shed and then into the front door of the house?"

"No. We went in the side door." His small finger pointed it out on the floor plan. "It's right beside the shed."

"And that leads right into this little hallway beside the kitchen?"

"I think so."

"You're not sure?"

"No . . . not really. I only saw it once."

Beale massaged his nose. The kid was doing his best. "But we've got to be as sure as we can about where your mother and the others are. You say they're across the hall on the other side of the house."

"Yes. There."

"And the kitchen is at that point."

"Yes." The boy was nodding. "I saw the kitchen when they brought us in."

"There's a door there?"

"I think so. Or maybe it was just an opening, you know. I remember I looked right into the kitchen."

"Very well." Beale turned to the tall, helmeted figure beside him and indicated the side door on the sketch. "There. That's the point. Start it near there. It's about as far from the hostages as we can get."

"Yes, sir."

Crisp nods; quick, nervous breathing.

"Remember," said Beale, "there are four terrorists that we know about for sure. There could be others." He nodded to a man on his left. "Reager, I want you to position yourself outside this room here." He pointed out the spot on the floor plan. "When the noise starts, remove a plank from the window as quickly as you can and make damn sure the hostages know enough to lie down on the floor. You cover them. If any of those terrorists try to get into that room, kill them. Good luck."

"You too, Mr. Beale."

* * *

Telly went into the kitchen to pour himself another cup of coffee. He was angry with Abou Gabal for going outside with that American bitch. He was also angry with himself for not having prevented it. A blatant breach of discipline; that was the only way it could be described. Shameful behavior, a gross capitulation to the baser instincts. Abou Gabal would pay for it, that was certain. But the fact remained, it should have been prevented. A word from the leader should have been sufficient.

But the leader's words had been ignored. The thought rankled. It became a knot that worked its way around his guts. How could a man call himself a leader if he was incapable of preventing such a petty incident? Damn! Perhaps he belonged in the ranks, after all; perhaps his fondest, most private hopes were in vain; perhaps he would never rise in the organization, never possess real power. . . .

He turned on the radio.

Abou Khelil emerged from the toilet. He stood for a moment outside the hostages' door.

"Everything still quiet?"

Abou Khelil nodded. "The little girl and the mother are talking. The old man says nothing."

Telly nodded. He sipped the coffee. Feeble American stuff, not to be compared with the Turkish coffee of his homeland.

Abou Khelil sat down at the kitchen table. He listened to the radio, cocking his head at an odd angle. There was a bulletin about the hijacking, but it contained no real news.

"All they talk about is 'unconfirmed reports,'" Abou Khelil complained.

"I know," said Telly. "But they won't be unconfirmed much longer. We will know the outcome soon enough."

"Do you really think the Israelis will give in?"

Telly sighed. Foolish, pointless question. Time alone would provide the answer. In the meantime, conjecture achieved nothing but a breaking of the silence. . .

He frowned. A thought occurred to him. "You say the little girl is awake."

"Yes."

"Talking to the mother?"

"Yes."

"But not the boy?"

"No. He has been sleeping."

Telly felt an uneasy stirring deep within him. How long had the boy been sleeping? Had he slept right through that sickening conversation between Abou Gabal and the American woman—a conversation that had been so clearly audible from the hallway?

Something wasn't right.

He remembered the form lying under the blanket, so still. But was the form a boy?

"Come with me."

He took two paces. They carried him out into the hall. His footsteps were like drumbeats on the bare floor.

Abou Khelil's voice stopped him.

"Smoke! I'm sure I smell smoke!"

"What?"

The young man was standing in the center of the kitchen, turning slowly, warily, his arms half extended. "Something's on fire! Jesus, the house is burning!"

Abou Bakr and his fucking cigarettes! The damned idiot! So stupidly careless! He was always tossing cigarettes around, forgetting them. . . .

"Perhaps it's in the garbage."

Abou Khelil was frantically searching the kitchen cupboards.

Telly rushed to the back door.

"No, I think it's outside."

God, imagine the consequences of a fire! If it wasn't contained at once, the fire department—and possibly the police—would be on the scene in no time at all. Where was Abou Bakr?

He appeared. Smoking, of course.

"What's wrong?"

"Look! A fire! That's what's wrong! Get some water!"

They hurried outside. The smoke was coming from behind the old wooden basement siding, the skirting that was rotten and falling to bits. A pile of oily rags was burning. . . .

Telly paused. If the boy *had* escaped, perhaps he was responsible.

"You take care of the fire," he ordered the others.

"Where are you going?" Stupid, aggrieved tone.

"To see about the boy. You concern yourselves with the fire. It's not that big. Put it out."

He hurried back through the smoke-filled kitchen, into the hall.

The smoke had drifted in there, too; it was visible, suspended like a wispy cloud.

He grabbed the doorknob and turned the key with his other hand.

And at that moment, the front door burst open.

The man wore a soft-peaked cap and a flak jacket. He carried an automatic rifle.

"Freeze!" he commanded.

He barked the words. A shortish man with broad shoulders and a thick neck.

"Get away from that door or I'll shoot your ass full of holes."

Even as he made his move, Telly knew it was hopeless. He didn't have a chance. He was throwing away his life, tossing it like some defiant gauntlet in the face of the enemy. And there were so many of them, so many dark figures crowding by the front door, rifle barrels jutting out like eager limbs. Suddenly, horribly, they infested the place; they had materialized, appeared out of the night. . . .

He felt the first bullets as they sped by a few inches from his head. He heard the cracks as air rushed to fill the vacuums created by the hurtling projectiles. As he hit the floor he dragged at his pistol. At that instant, a bullet hit him; it sliced neatly through his calf, in one side and out the other. He hardly felt it. He pulled his gun free and fired. A man in the doorway went down without a word. Telly scrambled. His feet skidded on the bare floor. Frantically he rolled, twisting his body to one side. A hail of lead cut through the woodwork above him. Hardly able to believe that he was still alive, he managed to wriggle to temporary safety beneath the staircase. He gasped in air. The floor shivered under the weight of heavy boots. Men shouted in hoarse, clipped voices.

Telly hurled himself across the passageway into the kitchen. In time to see Abou Khelil die.

He was slumped against the table, streaming blood from God knows how many wounds. He seemed to gaze at his pursuers without seeing them. He tried to fire but his gun was empty. He folded as bullets thudded into him, his legs twisting as if trying to change direction. His weight tipped the table over; the coffee pot's contents splashed over his wide-eyed face.

Instinctively, Telly scrambled backwards, away from the intruders. Jamming another clip into his Colt.

It was a nightmare, a cataclysm of shots, of bullets striking flesh and thudding into walls, of boots and figures abruptly materializing, of struggling to move faster, of cries and exhortations, of the shattering of hope. . . .

He grabbed a rifle that he had left propped against the wall.

Swine, Abou Gabal! He should have been here with his comrades, instead of consorting with that cunt! There was no way out. He flung himself at the stairs. Bullets snapped through the bannisters, but he moved too rapidly for the marksman. In an instant he was on the first landing, his feet skidding on the old, rotten carpeting. Half a dozen more steps.

He fired at a man slithering across the hallway below. He saw the man's mouth drop open; he looked indignant; then he slumped clumsily to the floor, his rifle clattering loosely as if the fall had broken it.

Telly heard the men on the stairs, following him.

Bastards!

He pressed himself against the wall, withdrawing slowly toward the room he had been using as a bedroom and temporary office. Now he had a good view of the top of the stairs, and he was protected by two walls. It was like the wedge-shaped windows they used to cut into castle walls to help the marksmen, giving them a good field of fire but at the same time providing cover.

Here he would make his stand. He would kill them all if he had to, one at a time. He had plenty of ammunition. It would be a magnificent stand, one to go down in the annals of military history. . . .

He wondered why his vision was becoming blurry.

He blinked furiously.

It was then that he noticed his shirt. It was soaked in blood. The stuff was streaming down onto his pants, half congealing in ugly, sticky streaks. Desperately he tried to find the source of the blood, to stem it. God, why didn't he feel any pain? Why hadn't he been aware of the hit?

He was still asking these questions when he slumped to the floor.

He had a faint pulse when they found him but he was dead before they got him downstairs.

* * *

The shots sounded like someone beating on a galvanized roof with a stick. Sharp, staccato. One, two, a fusillade. A man screamed something, then seemed to choke.

Jane gasped. She covered her mouth with her hand, as if afraid that it would cry out. Something flickered. The glow came from the direction of the house. God, it had really happened! Craig had made it!

Abou Gabal sat up. Eyes wide. He muttered a curse and fumbled in his clothes for his gun. Finding it, he sprang to his feet and began to run toward the house.

"Don't go. Stop," she shouted.

He did . . . and turned toward her. He was stark naked and appeared to Jane like the statue of a Greek runner she had once seen.

More shots. And shouting.

Frightened, Jane scrambled for her clothes in the semidarkness. She wondered why she had called out to Abou Gabal? Why was she trying to protect him?

Thoughts continued to race through her mind. Would the police come searching for them? Would they blaze away at anything that moved? And would Abou Gabal turn on her, suspecting that she might be responsible for all this? Should she try to hide from him, somewhere back there, among the trees?

A bullet hit something at an angle and buzzed away into the night like some angry insect.

"Bastards!" He stood there, his slim body touched by a dusting of moonlight.

"What . . ."

"They must have set fire to the house. The place is swarming with cops. God knows what is happening to my comrades."

He winced at every shot, imagining.

He scrambled into his pants and threw on his shirt. He held the pistol high as if poised to bring it down on the head of an attacker.

She thought he might still go to the aid of his friends. But he hesitated. He looked back at her. She realized that she felt sorry for him at this moment. Poor son of a bitch, he had all the law enforcement agencies in America stacked up against him. She ran to him.

"Don't go. They'll kill you. . . ."

He smeared a hand across his face. The truth of the statement was all too obvious. He looked at her, biting at his lower lip as if wanting to punish himself, inflict pain, make himself bleed like his comrades.

Abruptly he whirled around. He began to run directly away from the house, away from the fire and the shooting and the killing. But he stopped. Again he turned. Now he looked at her as if having just remembered her existence. A few steps brought him back to her side. He took her arm—firmly but not tightly.

"Come."

She didn't resist; it didn't occur to her to do so; her mind seemed incapable of independent decision. She simply nodded, agreeing.

"This way."

She felt herself rushing through the trees. Branches snatched at her, leaves slapped at her face like soft, dead hands. Her thought process was almost leisurely. *Get away from him.* That's what you've got to do. Just pull your arm away from him. *Do it!* He isn't holding you tightly, for God's sake. She knew she could do it. But she kept running, following. It was as if his strength of purpose, his desperate striving for survival, had taken command of her being as well as his.

The trees gave way to scrubby bushes.

Abou Gabal stopped. He seemed to shrink back as if afraid to leave the protection of the trees. His breathing was loud; he clenched his teeth as he stared ahead. A bird squawked. Jane shivered.

There was no shooting now. The night was tranquil. A night for moonlight dances and concerts in the park.

When he spoke, his voice startled her; she felt her heart pound, almost painfully.

"How the hell did they know where we were?"

She said, "I don't know." Lies, lies—and surely he must know it.

"Bastards!" He muttered something in Arabic as he examined the pistol, doing something with the butt. He let go of her arm. But she didn't run.

He snapped the clip out and back in again, checking it; then he beckoned to her.

She followed him. Only a step or two.

They stopped. The lights of a car sliced the darkness, splashing through the bushes. A car swept by, with a glimpse of the driver, apparently holding the roof on with his left hand.

"There's a road there!" Abou Gabal declared. "I didn't know that."

"Nor I," said Jane. "I had no idea, no idea at all." Stupid, pointless words, but they kept bubbling out as if they had a will of their own.

Cautiously, he moved forward. He took her arm again. A few steps down an incline brought them to the road. Narrow and rough, it certainly wasn't a major highway.

"We'll stop a car and get a ride," Abou Gabal announced as if it were the simplest thing in the world.

"Sure . . . good idea."

But, she wondered, would a police car come racing down the road? And would they riddle them both with bullets, Bonnie-and-Clyde style? Or would they only kill him? And would she laugh . . . or cry? Or fight back with his gun? She didn't know; she damn well didn't know anything anymore. The very foundation of rational behavior had been removed. In some physical way she was no longer connected with the world she had known.

"Car coming!"

His grip became viselike. He turned her so that she looked directly at him. His fingers seemed to inject urgency into her arm.

"You will try to stop the car . . . will you?"

An odd order-plea. She nodded. He released her arm just as the twin lights swung into view around a curve. They swept the road ahead.

A police car! It could be police! It most likely *was,* for God's sake. . . !

The brakes squealed.

She still stood there, arm extended.

It wasn't a police car. It was an old Plymouth—'58 or '59. A rattletrap.

The window creaked as the driver lowered it. He was a nondescript individual of about fifty. And slightly drunk. He beamed foolishly.

"Wanna ride, honey?"

"Yes, please."

"Hop in . . . my pleasure . . . delighted as hell, lemme tell you. . . ."

The pathetic attempt at gallantry became a splutter of fright as Abou Gabal suddenly emerged from the shadows.

He held the pistol on the man with one hand as he opened the car door with the other.

"Drive!"

chapter 16

Beale was immediately connected with the Emergency Command Center.

"Well?" The Director was a man of few words.

"It's done, sir. But one terrorist got away—with one of the hostages."

"Jesus. Which one?"

"Captain Mallory's daughter, sir: Mrs. Sutton. The two of them were. . . . " Beale shook his head; he still refused to believe what the Jensen woman had told him. It was jealousy or something like that. It had to be. "For some reason, they were outside the house, sir, when we attacked. We surrounded the place, but they must have been some distance away."

"Jesus," muttered the Director again. "And the others?"

"The hostages are okay, sir; shaken but okay. The three other terrorists are dead."

"It would've been interesting to talk to one of them. You see my point, don't you?"

"Yes, sir." Beale nodded into the police radio mike; you always saw the Director's point. "But they refused to surrender. Those Black September people aren't the surrendering type. They're like the Japs at Tarawa."

"What about this bastard who got away? Any leads?"

"Not yet," Beale replied with uneasiness. That son of a bitch of an Arab had vanished. No one had the slightest idea where he was or where he'd taken Mrs. Sutton—or even whether she was still alive. There was no telling what the guy might do to her. "We think he'll most likely contact someone before long. We're placing all known PLO sympathizers in the area under surveillance and

175

setting up several key roadblocks. . . ."

"Of course."

But, thought Beale, what about the PLO sympathizers who were *un*known? How many were there? Where did they live? The truth of the matter was, the terrorist could disappear forever. He might never be found. In fact, it was probable that he wouldn't be found. The hostages' description wasn't going to be much help—about twenty-five, powerful build, average height, dark, curly hair, regular features. About half a million young men in California alone fitted such a description.

The Director paused. Beale could hear him breathing, cogitating. He was tapping the mouthpiece of the telephone in little bursts of rhythmic patterns.

At last he spoke. "So where do we go from here, Mr. Beale?"

Weary, Beale said, "There are several courses of action, sir, but I'm not sure at this stage just. . . ."

"I am," said the Director.

"Sir?"

"I'm going to urge that some way be found to tell the flight crew that their families have been rescued."

"But they haven't been, sir, at least not all of them. . . ."

"I'm aware of that. No need to remind me about Captain Mallory's daughter, Mr. Beale, no need at all. But at times we have to circumvent the truth to resolve a crisis. It's sure as hell justified in this case. Everything possible must be done to relieve the minds of those men. If they *believe* their families are safe, they may be able to do something. God knows what. But the thing is, right now those poor bastards are helpless. They're afraid of what might happen to their families if they make a move. See what I mean? That burden must be lifted in some way."

"But Captain Mallory . . ."

"It's essential."

"Sir, telling a man that his daughter is safe and sound when she isn't. . . . Jesus, sir, it's immoral and improper."

"So is hijacking an airplane full of innocent people."

Beale shook his head. "Captain Mallory's daughter isn't safe and it's . . . *wrong*"—the word sounded so damnably weak—"to tell him she is."

The Director sighed. "I know, I know. But it's essential to ease Captain Mallory's mind, if you see what I mean."

"Perhaps."

"But you disapprove."

"Yes, sir."

"I appreciate your candor. Nevertheless, Mr. Beale, it's something to be discussed with the President. So if you'll excuse me . . . ."

* * *

Mallory kept remembering the slim, slightly stooped figure, the pale face, the eyes so alert, so absorbed in what they were perceiving. He had asked intelligent questions as he had examined the flight deck. What was the power of the jet engines? Why were the wings swept back? What advantages did the swept-back shape provide? How could the pilot check on his position at any given moment during the flight? How high could the 747SP fly? How fast? How far? The old man had enjoyed himself; he had reveled in the technicalities, the systems, the gauges, the forests of levers.

I *like* him, Mallory thought.

Somehow liking him seemed vaguely sacrilegious. People— ordinary mortals—don't usually get involved with popes.

Nevertheless, Mallory had liked him . . . and now the Pope might be killed.

Mallory knew the Israelis well. He had flown the world's air routes for years and had become a serious student of international affairs. He knew damned well that the Israeli government would never accede to this demand no matter whose life hung in the balance. The realization of the dilemma was chilling. By flying this aircraft to Jordan, he was personally handing the Pope a sentence of death, one that could easily include the passengers and crew.

That was the ugly truth of the matter. Black September had miscalculated. The Israelis don't submit to blackmail. Mallory knew that this policy was as important to them as the Ten Commandments.

And so the gentle old man would die.
Damn the world and its scheming, clawing, grabbing. . . .

* * *

The gun lay in his lap, his fingers resting loosely on the butt
and the trigger guard. Jane didn't look at the weapon, but she was
all too conscious of its presence. She wondered if the shaking of
the old Plymouth might cause the thing to be fired accidentally.
She hated guns—and suddenly her world seemed full of them:
ugly, dark, merciless metal. . . .

"I told you, man, you can *have* the goddam car. . . . Just
lemme go, huh?"

It was the third time the man had uttered the words.

"Be quiet," Abou Gabal told him for the third time.

"I got four bucks on me, thassall—shit, I'm not worth
robbing, man, and you can have the goddam money. . . . Here, I'll
get it outta my pocket for you. . . ."

Fear made the man's lips tremble; his teeth chattered when
they touched.

Abou Gabal told him to keep his money.

They were speeding along a quiet country road. They had
seen only one other vehicle, a Cougar convertible full of windswept kids. At every corner, Jane had expected to see the flashing
red lights of a roadblock, but none had materialized.

Abou Gabal spoke to her in a low voice. "Do you know this
area?"

She shook her head. "I don't recognize anything." She
shrugged. "Where do you want to go?"

"Near San Francisco—Oakland. Do you know it?"

She nodded. "Is there someone you want to see there?"

"Possibly," he replied with care. "I see you're still asking
questions."

"When I'm running away from the police," she told him, "I
like to know where the hell I'm going."

He accorded her a brief smile. "I told you before—you have
a strange sense of humor."

Then he leaned across her. "Stop the car," he told the driver.

The man's mouth dropped open; his eyes were damp with
terror. "What. . . . Whatcha gonna do. . . ?"

"Nothing. Just stop the car."

The man looked about him. "Jesus, mister, this is the middle
of nowhere. . . . "

"Stop the car, I said!"

Shocked by Abou Gabal's tone, the man hit the brakes too
hard. The car swerved, bounced against the grass shoulder and
skidded to a halt.

"Sorry . . . shit, sorry. . . ." The man kept mumbling
apologies. He switched off the ignition. It was dark and perfectly
still.

Abou Gabal motioned with the pistol.

"Get out of the car and stand beside the door. Understand?
Don't try to run or I'll shoot you."

"Sure, sure. . . ."

For a brief moment both men were out of the car—the driver
on one side, Abou Gabal on the other. The thought raced through
her mind: start the engine, slam the shift into drive and go! But it
was impossible; there simply wasn't enough time.

"You get out too, please," Abou Gabal told Jane, "and get
the keys. Then open the trunk."

"Aw, Christ, *no*. . . !" The man twisted awkwardly against
the side of the car; his mouth had dropped open; he kept staring
at the gun. "No, don't do it, mister, *please;* I got a *family* . . ."

Abou Gabal shook his head impatiently. "I'm not going to
shoot you."

". . . and two kids," the man babbled on. "One's gone now . . .
livin' in L.A. or someplace, I think, but the other one's still at
home . . . a boy, seventeen, see, and the old lady. . . ."

"I'm *not* going to shoot you," Abou Gabal said again.

"Huh?"

"Just get into the trunk."

"Huh?"

"You heard me. In the trunk!"

"In *there?*"

Half a dozen prods with the pistol barrel overcame the man's
reluctance. He scrambled into the trunk, pushing aside a

collection of tools and metal boxes to make room for himself. He curled up against the spare tire.

Abou Gabal slammed the lid down.

Jane looked at the trunk; the closing of the lid had seemed so final.

"Is he going to be all right in there?"

"Yes, yes. Don't worry. Now drive, please."

The Plymouth had seen heavy duty. It creaked and sagged as it picked up speed. The steering wheel felt disconcertingly wobbly in Jane's hands.

"I think we got a lemon."

"A lemon?"

"A lemon is a crummy car."

"Never mind. It runs."

"How long do you plan to keep that man in the trunk?"

"Not long." He shrugged as if he were powerless to alter circumstances. "We don't want him telling the police about this car and giving them the license number. He'll be all right."

She stared ahead. "Do you want to keep going this way?"

"Are we heading toward San Francisco?"

"I saw a sign to San Jose. We can pick up the freeway to San Francisco there."

"Good. Let's do it."

She glanced at him. He sounded depressed. The tension of escape had evaporated, leaving only the knowledge of failure.

They drove in silence for several minutes. Then Jane asked, "What will happen to my father?"

"Nothing, I assure you."

"Why did you kidnap us?"

"It was as we told you."

"But what do you want with the Pope?"

"I do not wish to discuss it."

"Not even *now?*"

He shook his head. "You must understand that this changes nothing. You see, your usefulness ended the moment your father found out you were in our hands and agreed to do as we instructed. It is unfortunate that three brave comrades have died, but it changes nothing as far as the main plan is concerned." He sighed, ruing the incalculabilities of this life. "We anticipated problems, of course. But we expected them early on, when we had to take people from their homes and cars. So many things could have gone wrong then, yet it was accomplished without any difficulty at all." He punched the palm of his hand. "How did the bastards know we were there?"

"I don't know," Jane replied carefully.

"Those deaths were so *needless.* God, we would have released you in a few hours."

"I wonder. I think that bald man would have killed us."

"Never."

"He'd have killed us because we knew you all by sight."

"No. I would not have permitted it." He pointed at her. "You are like the rest of the Western world. You think of us as ruthless killers, without any regard for life. And yet it is because we care about our people that we do what we do. . . ."

"And lots of innocent bystanders seem to be getting killed in the process."

"But not without purpose."

"What the hell does that mean?"

He shook his head. "Your minds are closed. You see and understand only what you want to see and understand. When you Americans fight and kill to achieve your goals, that's all right. But when *we* fight and kill to achieve ours, you call it murder."

"It *is* murder when you kill innocent men, women and children."

"What do you call it when you Americans massacred thousands of men, women and children who were here long before your people ever came?"

"What are you talking about?"

"The White Man butchered the Indian people and drove them out of their lands. You were conquering territories to which you had no right. We were driven out of our land, too, but now we're fighting to get it back."

Jane turned to say something, but Abou Gabal raised his voice and declared with finality, "The only thing that matters is the cause, the goal."

"Your life is more important than any cause."

"Nonsense. You do not understand."

Anger tightened her fingers on the wheel. "Damn it, you're just throwing your life away for a stupid cause that no one will even remember in ten years."

"What do you mean? We've been fighting for our land for centuries and what happens today will be remembered forever. What we are doing is eminently worthwhile; in fact, there is nothing more worthwhile; we are fighting to restore what is rightfully ours."

"What do you mean?"

"I can't tell you any more. You will find out soon enough."

"That's not fair."

He smiled. "As you yourself said, war is hell."

"What difference will it make if you tell me now?"

"Perhaps none; but I prefer not to."

"Because I might think less of you?"

He gazed at her for what seemed minutes. "You really turn me on. It is unfortunate that we have met under such circumstances."

"I guess it's unlikely we would have met under any other circumstances."

"Then perhaps we should simply be thankful. Damn!"

Her heart leapt. Ahead, a flashing light punctuated the darkness.

"Roadblock," she said.

"Yes . . . I think so."

"Do you want me to turn around?"

"No, no. Not yet. Keep going. Let's get closer."

She nodded, vaguely aware of the excitement inside, the sense of being more keenly alive than ever before. Jesus Christ . . . the realization grew that she was almost enjoying this. Defying law and order—with the perfect excuse if she got caught. I had to do it, she could say, because there was a man at my side with a gun ordering me to do it.

It wasn't a roadblock. It was nothing more frightening than a tow truck pulling a car out of a ditch.

Abou Gabal whistled his relief.

"The red light . . . just like a police light!"

She wanted to laugh because the roadblock had turned out to be a tow truck.

They drove on. Soon the road joined a highway. Heavy traffic; scores of cars rushed by, innocent, ordinary. No police cars. No armored vehicles. It was as if they had found sanctuary in the middle of a war zone.

Abou Gabal said, "You could have run away."

He made the statement quietly, unemotionally, as if it were a matter of no great importance.

"I know."

"Why didn't you?"

"Just lazy, I guess."

"Not very convincing."

"Okay, I figured you'd never be able to find your way to Oakland on your own. By the way, why do you have to go there?"

"There's a man there. I must see him."

"Why?"

"Never mind." He grinned. "You still ask far too many questions."

"I like to know things. For my diary."

He laughed. His not-a-care-in-the-world laugh.

I'm not exactly protecting him, she thought. I just don't want to help them catch him.

What the hell are you saying? This is a terrorist, for God's sake, someone who kidnapped you, who killed your dog, who helped cause the shooting, the dying. . . .

She stated the facts to herself, but they seemed to have no significance. It was a scene on television, a picture in the newspaper, a frightening event and a shocking commentary on the world in general, but something with which she had no personal connection. . . .

Personal connection? It couldn't be a more personal connection. The sex had been great; she still glowed from it; she had reveled in it and responded joyously in the oldest of rituals, but there had been more to it than a *lay,* for God's sake.

She kept remembering how, as a child, she had been haunted by the thought that circumstances might make her something called a wanton. She wasn't exactly positive how it happened, but as far as she could tell, it was a condition that would overtake you if you weren't extremely careful about something or other. But then she had wondered why there seemed to be no such thing as a wanton boy. As time rolled on, she unearthed the truth that the world regarded the male equivalent of a wanton as a hell of a guy. Unfair. Just another on the seemingly endless list of injustices. Unjust that her mother had died at age fifty-four. Unjust that life with Frank had turned out to be much less than what society's myths had led her to believe it would be. Unjust that she was kidnapped by Arab terrorists. . . .

She sighed. Too much had happened. She was no longer capable of appraising anything. Life had turned itself upside down. And in a curious, perverse way, she was glad it had happened. Everything had taken on a new significance; things would never be quite the same again.

If she hadn't been outside with him, he would have been slaughtered with the others. A barrage of bullets perforating him, slicing through his firm, beautiful body, smashing his face. Every one of those cops would have fired into the body, if only to be able to talk about it later. Carcass of despicable Arab terrorist, to be carted off, the trophy, symbol of Right triumphant over Wrong.

"By the way," he said, "I must apologize."

"Apologize?"

"I behaved crudely when you were first brought to the house."

"You seemed very horny."

"I was . . . and you looked delicious. Too delicious. And you were in my power. . . ." He shook his head as if still not quite believing what had happened. "I'm sorry."

"I'm not," she said.

*   *   *

"There should be a law against it," the drunk declared.

"I really think there is such a law," Vernon Squires told him.

"Goddam hijackers shouldn't be allowed on airplanes in the first place. That'd keep the sons of bitches out of mischief."

Mr. Squires sighed. The only saving grace in the whole

unhappy business was the publicity it would generate. For a few days, he would be the best-known actor in the world. All of a sudden no one would confuse him with E. G. Marshall. Everyone would want him on talk shows. And every producer would have parts for him. For a time. It wouldn't last. That, Vernon Squires knew, was certain. A couple of months perhaps. Then it would be forgotten, filed away among the innumerable sensations that had preceded it.

Mrs. Lefler was talking. . . . He hadn't been conscious of it. He had tuned her out. Now, as if the antenna had turned in her direction, her voice, her insistent, machinelike voice, became audible again.

It transpired that the whole thing was her husband Manville's fault.

"Of course," said Mr. Squires.

"He's to blame."

"Naturally."

"I wanted to come back via London," she declared.

"Understandable."

"I mean, a couple more days: could it make all that difference? I just thought: Wouldn't it be nice to do a little shopping along Bond Street, it wasn't too much to ask, just two more lousy days, after all, it's on the way, I told him, but he doesn't listen; that's always been his trouble. Right now he's waiting in San Francisco, and I'm going the other goddam way!"

"Poor fellow."

"Now he's going to regret it. Now he'll wish he'd listened. Oh God, he'll wish he'd listened. He'll be beside himself at this moment. . . sick with worry. . . . God, of all the things that ever happened, I never thought I'd ever be hijacked . . . never, not once. . . . I mean, you think of traffic accidents and earthquakes and fires and burglaries, but who ever thinks about getting hijacked. . . .with the Pope, no less? God, it's got to be the most terrifying thing I've ever experienced."

"Do you have a weak heart?" inquired Mr. Squires.

"No, thank God for small favors."

"Amen," said Mr. Squires.

"But what good does a strong heart do if you're murdered by

goddam terrorists? They don't give a damn. They'll slaughter us all without thinking twice about it. You, you and you ... they'll just pick some of us at random, and it'll be curtains ... and Manville will never be able to live with himself again."

"Poor Manville," said Mr. Squires, who thought it likely that Manville was almost certainly humming a cheerful tune as he wrote out a handsome check in favor of Black September.

"If he hadn't been so goddam persistent ... I could have taken a plane to London, spent a couple days there, shopping, seeing Buckingham Palace and the Queen and everything, and then I could have caught TWA or British Airways or something and gotten back to California from there, right?"

"Certainly."

"And now, God only knows when we'll get back."

"And He isn't saying."

"Huh?"

chapter 17

0601 GREENWICH MEAN TIME
ABEAM TIMISOARA, ROMANIA
45°39' NORTH LATITUDE, 20°49' EAST LONGITUDE

Joe Nowakoski entered the latest fuel-consumption figures on his log sheet. Now that the engines had been throttled to economy cruise, kerosene was being consumed at the relatively modest rate of seventeen thousand pounds per hour. There was sufficient fuel remaining for about five more hours of flight—which meant a maximum of about four hours, for no pilot would dare cut things any finer in a 747. About three hours to El Maghreb. Then what? Would the Pope be whisked away? Would the crew and passengers be left to look at one another?

Once again, he cross-checked the complicated matrix of gauges that revealed the heartbeat, pulse and respiration of each engine and each system. He was the technical watchdog.

What was happening to his father? Poor old guy, he didn't deserve this kind of crap; he'd had a hard life; now he just wanted to rest, to be left alone, for God's sake. . . . Was he dead? No, definitely no. Nowakoski told himself that he would have known—somehow—if his father had died. A pain, a chill: *something.* The sort of link that exists between father and son can't be broken without any reaction; he was sure of it. And yet visions of his father's face still haunted him: the familiar features white and still in death, eyes only half closed.

No, hell, he wouldn't permit such invading thoughts. But they kept slipping through his mental guard.

Behind him, the girl Fadia sat motionless in the jump seat. Usually the seat was occupied by FAA inspectors, company check pilots or other Trans Am pilots deadheading somewhere. She hadn't said anything for a long time. He glanced at her, but she regarded him without interest. Cold, calculating bitch.

She seemed to know how to handle that gun of hers. Had she killed with it? At one point he had come close to asking, but at the last moment decided not to. A little cowardly, he supposed. But maybe it was just as well, better not to know the answer. There was something intensely frightening about a good-looking broad with a gun. In a way, it would be easier if she was ugly or the lesbian type. The disquieting thing was, she was just the sort of chick you might try to hustle in an airport bar. Hell, she could be a stew; she was the type. Capable looking. Too goddam capable.

The flight was oddly peaceful now. No one said anything. The East German fighters were long gone. Over Hungary, a pair of jet escorts had appeared and flown a parallel course for ten minutes, then they had abruptly turned west and disappeared. At the moment there seemed to be nothing in the sky but the 747. Since they had been flying all night, the sun was especially harsh and glaring; below, the clouds had begun to dissipate.

Nice day shaping up for Eastern Europe.

Nowakoski supposed that the entire world was at this very moment watching the progress of this airplane. The hot lines were probably busy in every capital, the politicians knocking themselves out trying to figure out the right things to say and not to say. In Nowakoski's book, politicians didn't rate much respect; they were salesmen, always handing out endless gobs of bullshit— all sounding as sincere as hell—for the sole purpose of gaining your support. Everywhere, politicians would be calculating how this particular development shifted the balance of things in the world and how they could come out of it ahead of the game and looking as if their actions throughout had been motivated by nothing but concern for mankind and courage and generosity and all the other qualities that none of them possessed.

He was only half-conscious of the high-frequency static, the air traffic control chatter, the background stream of Morse code. He paid little attention; the noise was a constant companion that had to be tolerated on every flight and was of no direct interest to the flight engineer.

Then, idly at first, he began to listen to the Morse signals. There was an unusual pattern, a rhythm that seemed to flow from the speakers in repetitive waves. To the casual observer it was just the usual scramble of dots and dashes, but Nowakoski had spent thousands of hours listening to similar transmissions on international flights; these signals sounded oddly different. He picked up a pencil and nonchalantly began to copy down the letters.

. . .AFEYOURFAMILIESARESAFEYOURFAMIL. . .

His mouth dropped open as if the jaw muscle had suddenly snapped.

My God! He realized what was being transmitted. A few strokes to separate the words made all the difference. A marvelous, fabulous difference!

. . . AFE— *YOUR — FAMILIES — ARE — SAFE — YOUR* . . .

Somehow, they'd done it! They'd freed them! Fantastic!

He covered the grin with a cupped hand and moved his shoulders so that he was turned directly toward his panel and away from the girl. He prayed there was nothing unusual in his posture. It felt as if his entire body was aglow. Cool! Be cool! As casually as possible he moved to turn down the volume of the high-frequency receiver. Now that he knew what was being transmitted, it seemed as obtrusive as hell, a raucous bleat simply begging to be heard.

The problem was to convey the information to Mallory and Jensen. Useless just passing a note; she'd be on it in a flash.

So distract her.

"I could sure use some coffee," he said. He turned to Fadia. "Okay?"

A curt nod.

Okay. So push the stewardess call button. Then fold the paper. Neatly. Take deep breaths while waiting. And pray.

He heard the flight deck door handle turn.

He glanced back. So did Fadia. Just long enough to nod assent to the guard.

Jensen looked puzzled as the folded piece of paper was suddenly tossed into his lap. But he had the sense not to look down or to comment.

"Yes, sir?"

Dee was looking inquiringly around the flight deck.

"Could you spare a cup of coffee?"

"Sure thing. Anyone else?"

The others shook their heads.

"No," Fadia snapped. "Get out and close the door."

"Sure thing, honey," said Dee, "since you ask so nicely."

* * *

Relief swept over Mallory. He had to restrain himself; he wanted to cheer and clap Jensen and Nowakoski on their backs; he longed to discuss this new development openly. It changed everything. Now the battle was to be fought on one front only, so to speak. Thank God Jane was okay—and a million thanks to whoever they were who got her out. Lovely words: YOUR FAMILIES ARE SAFE. Jensen had cupped the piece of paper in his right hand; the message had been easy to read from the next seat, yet Jensen's body had concealed the note from Fadia. Mallory saw the dots and dashes above the individual letters and knew instantly how the message had been smuggled aboard the aircraft.

Now, at least, whatever action they chose to take, it wouldn't jeopardize the safety of anyone at home.

Great. But what action could be taken?

Think, goddam it, think!

His euphoria began to dissolve. What could possibly be done that wouldn't endanger the lives of his passengers or the aircraft? His orders were straightforward: fly directly to El Maghreb.

The topographical chart provided with the hijack note showed the location of the airport, just inside the Jordanian border, in an area that for years had been known as PLO territory. The approach to the field would involve a flight directly across southern Israel, from northwest to southeast. Most of the approach and descent would, in fact, take place over Israeli territory. So what? Did that help in any way? If so, he failed to see how.

"Anything new on the weather?"

"Still bad," Jensen reported.

There was only one runway at El Maghreb: numbered "22"

on the chart because it was aligned in a magnetic direction of 220 degrees. The runway was nine thousand two hundred feet long; long enough for a 747—a further indication that whoever had planned this abduction had more than a casual knowledge of matters aeronautical. Two questions remained to be answered: would he be able to find the strip in the sandstorm, and would the runway be in good enough condition for a safe landing in such a heavy aircraft?

He asked Fadia if she knew anything about the runway surface.

She shrugged. "It is adequate. That is all I know."

"It was once a military field, right?"

"I believe so. I understand the British built it."

"Now it's abandoned?"

"Partially," she said. "It is sometimes used."

By Boeing 747s? Mallory wondered. He doubted it. God knows, the runway might crack and collapse at the instant of touchdown. Which would unquestionably be messy. He sighed. There was nothing to do but rely on the perspicacity of the Black September planners. Hopefully, they realized that a good, strong runway was necessary to successfully land a 747.

The *simoom*. The biggest worry of all. Sandstorms are erratic, vicious things. Local winds could change direction and speed in an instant, creating nightmarish conditions for a pilot on final approach. But, he thought, if the storm is making things tough for us, presumably it's also creating problems for the people on the ground. Because of the limited visibility, it might even be possible for an aircraft to approach and land without even being seen by anyone on the ground. He considered the fact. Was it of value? Could it be put to use? In other words, could the storm serve him in any way? He racked his brain, trying to figure how. He considered Fadia. What would she be able to see of El Maghreb when they landed? No more than the pilots—practically nothing. A few yards of runway, not much more. In fact, he thought, momentarily stirred by the germ of a notion, since she doesn't seem to know much about the specifics of the airport, she's probably never even been there. And in a sandstorm like this, she probably wouldn't even know the difference if I landed in Katmandu.

But it wouldn't take her and her buddies long to determine the truth. Then what? It was a discouraging thought. But he kept remembering the world leader whose life was in the balance. Damn it, something had to be done!

The Israelis had to be contacted prior to penetrating their airspace; that was for sure. Perhaps they even had an idea that could be conveyed to the aircraft as surreptitiously and successfully as the message about Jane and the others.

He turned to Fadia.

"I'm going to contact Israeli Air Traffic Control."

She was instantly alert. "Why? We aren't over Israel yet."

"I know. But the Jews are goddam trigger-happy. You must know that."

She nodded.

"We'll be making most of our approach over Israeli territory," Mallory continued. "I want to be damn sure that we're expected and they know just where we're going to be at all times. You remember that Libyan Airlines' Boeing 727? Flight 114 from Tripoli to Cairo back in 1973?"

"Yes."

"Poor bastards were forced to detour because of severe thunderstorms and inadvertently flew over some secret Israeli military installation in the Sinai Desert."

"Bir Gafgafa," murmured Fadia.

"That's it. Israeli Phantoms shot 'em down. I don't want to happen to us, so I want to make sure our overflight is okay with the Israelis. See what I mean?"

She nodded, apparently satisfied.

Mallory sighed silently. So far, so good. It had been a good move, dredging up the Libyan 727 story. He reflected on how the Israeli Phantoms had used international flight signals to instruct the 727 to land; how, when they were ignored, the Phantoms had fired warning bursts across the airliner's nose. Still no reaction. The 727 had been heading flat out toward Cairo. Convinced by now that the airliner was in fact a spy plane, the Phantoms fired at a wing tip. The idea was to inflict minor damage, forcing the 727 down. But the shots crippled the airliner and it crashed twelve miles east of the Suez Canal, killing most of those aboard.

He told Jensen to contact Israel Control on the HF transceiver.

"No tricks," said Fadia.

"Tricks?" Mallory shrugged. "I wish I had some," he said truthfully.

The Israeli controller sounded as if he had been expecting to hear from Flight 901. "We are aware of your situation," he said formally.

Mallory told him, "We have been ordered to land at El Maghreb. I am concerned about the condition of the airport and whether a landing is feasible there in this storm."

"Roger, Trans Am. We have no current information on the single runway at El Maghreb. All we can tell you is, the field used to be a military base, but it's been rarely used for several years. We don't know of any large traffic ever using it. We can assure you, however, that the weather in that area is very poor at the moment. There's quite a sandstorm down here. It's severe; one of the worst we've seen in recent years. Winds are up to fifty knots. The only good news we can pass on is that the storm is expected to abate later on in the afternoon. For your information, Ben Gurion International Airport near Tel Aviv has been closed to all aircraft for the last seven hours because of blowing sand. We suggest you proceed to an alternate airport or delay your approach until the storm eases."

"Thank you," Mallory acknowledged. "Unfortunately we don't have enough fuel to wait out the storm. And our hijacker here in the cockpit isn't keen on the idea of an alternate."

"No!" Fadia was suddenly at Mallory's shoulder. She grabbed the mike from his hand. "No alternates! We will land at El Maghreb. Do you hear that, Jew?" She spat out the words.

"I hear it," retorted the Israeli controller. "But you're not making much sense. The weather here is bad, really bad."

"They've closed Tel Aviv Airport," Mallory added. "So how the hell do you think we can land at a crappy little strip in the desert without any of the sophisticated approach aids they've got at Tel Aviv?"

"You will do it," Fadia snapped.

"But . . ."

"Don't argue!"

Mallory thumbed the transmit button again. "Negative, Israel. We've been ordered to land at El Maghreb, so we'll have to try it, I guess."

"I understand, Trans Am."

"We'll be heading direct from over Gaza to the Beersheba VORTAC and then direct to the radiobeacon at El Maghreb."

"We understand, Trans Am. Stand by for your clearance."

Mallory studied the chart, wondering about the abandoned field with its single runway. Glumly, he decided there were so many variables that the only sensible course was to try to find the place first and worry about setting down later. At that moment an idea occurred to him. An incredible idea. He dismissed it. But. . . . He thought about it again. Another look at the chart.

No. Not with the *Pope* on board . . . and yet, hell, it was to *protect* the Pope . . . or at least to attempt to protect him. . .

He glanced at Jensen. The first officer was gazing ahead, gloomily contemplating the immediate future and a landing that could well be his last.

Was it worth a try?

Yes. No . . . yes. Yes!

He pressed the transmit button.

"It's a hell of a wind, but thank God it seems to be blowing straight down runway thirteen. I know it's only seven thousand fifty feet long, but with that headwind blowing straight down the runway, it should be long enough. Over."

He kept his finger glued to the transmit button on his microphone.

And prayed. It was a hell of a gamble.

* * *

At Tel Aviv, Chief Air Traffic Controller Chaim Hirsch was puzzled. What was the guy talking about? Runway 13? There wasn't a runway 13 at El Maghreb. He examined the chart once more to confirm the fact. Yes; check. One runway only: 22.

He turned to the other controllers grouped around him, all

eager for information about the world's most famous airliner.

"What the hell is he talking about?"

"Maybe he's confused."

"Who wouldn't be?"

"Better get him to repeat. . . ."

"Can't, at least not now. We're getting a carrier wave from the aircraft which means that his microphone button must be stuck down. This prevents him from receiving any of our transmissions. . . ."

Transmitter held open, but nothing being sent from the big jet with the big problems. Why? A crew error? Or could it be intentional?

"That runway direction and length is wrong," someone said, "but it sounds familiar."

"Familiar?"

"Who's got the airport directory?"

Chaim Hirsch had a growing conviction that the transmit button on the Trans Am plane was being held down on purpose, for one reason and one reason only: to prevent the reception of a correcting message from the ground stating that El Maghreb doesn't have a runway 13. What was the American pilot trying to tell him?

"I've got the directory."

"Let's have it."

"Is there a field in the area with a runway thirteen, seven thousand fifty feet long?"

Someone said he was looking; there was a flurry of pages.

At last Trans Am's transmitter snapped off.

Silence. Hirsch scratched his chin. What now? He swallowed. He would go along with the game for a while and see where it led.

He said, "I agree with your appraisal, Trans Am. Latest weather information from a station not far from El Maghreb reports the wind out of the southeast at thirty-seven knots with gusts to forty-eight knots. So your landing on runway thirteen at El Maghreb will be into the wind."

"Roger, Tel Aviv. Thanks."

The pilot sounded relieved. Something was definitely

cooking. But what? Chaim nodded to himself, as if approving his own action.

Someone touched his shoulder.

"I got it! Runway thirteen—seven thousand fifty feet long!"

Fingers stabbed at the spot on the chart.

"Ramat Shamon."

It was in the Negev only a mile or so from the Jordanian border, halfway between the southern tip of the Dead Sea and the northern tip of the Gulf of Elat. Once it had been a bustling Israeli Air Force base. Now it was deserted, a few acres of sand with a concrete runway and some empty, echoing hangars.

"Almost on the Jordanian border."

"That's why they closed it. And that must be why the Trans Am captain chose it."

"He's going to try and land *there?*"

"I guess so."

"He's nuts. The place is derelict."

"Maybe he thinks no one will notice it's the wrong field."

"He could be right," mused Chaim Hirsch. "Look at the weather. You can't see more than a few meters."

"Maybe he's just got the wrong chart."

"Wrong chart?"

"It's possible. The pilot hadn't intended to come to this part of the world when he took off. He could have some out-of-date charts on board."

Chaim nodded. It was possible. But the transmit button hadn't been pressed accidentally.

"No," he said, half to himself. "He's trying to tell us that he's going to have a crack at deceiving the hijackers. He intends to land in Israel, and he's hoping we'll be able to do something to help him."

"What can we do?"

"God only knows."

"He's nuts," said someone, "but you've got to admit, he's got *chutzpah.*"

Chiam picked up the telephone. "Get me the Prime Minister's office," he said as matter-of-factly as he could. "It's top priority."

chapter 18

The Intelligence Chief grinned; ingenuity and innovation always delighted him. "We assume, Mr. Prime Minister, that what Captain Mallory is telling us is that he is going to land at one of our abandoned air force bases. It's close to the Jordanian border, only a few kilometers from the place he has been ordered to land by the hijackers. You see, it's the only airport in the area with a runway thirteen that's seven thousand fifty feet long."

The Prime Minister nodded. His head ached; he had been talking on the telephone for more than an hour discussing various alternatives with the President of the United States. One option was tempting: accede to the demands, withdraw from the West Bank. The United States could be the peacekeepers; they, and possibly other Western powers, would guarantee the security of everyone concerned. Weariness had come close to prodding him into acceptance. But in the end he had declined; the Americans were too vulnerable to blackmail by petroleum; what might seem to be a solution to a dilemma today might well become the genesis of an even more hideous problem a month, or a year, or ten years later.

"You've got to hand it to Mallory, thinking up that way of deceiving the hijackers."

A political advisor snorted. "He's playing games with the Pope's life!"

"So are the hijackers."

"Can the jet land at Ramat Shamon?" the Prime Minister asked.

The air force general nodded. "Yes, sir, as long as the runway is in reasonable condition—and that's a big question mark in my mind at the moment."

"The biggest risk," said the army general, "is after they land. How long can they hope to convince the hijackers that they've landed in Jordan? Hell, they're liable to blow up the airplane and everyone in it."

The Prime Minister considered this. "Your point is well taken, General. What do you suggest?"

"I wish I knew, Mr. Prime Minister."

The Intelligence Chief said, "Look, the pilot of that airliner saw an opportunity. And he's taking it. He doesn't have time to wonder about it or consider every eventuality. Now he's thrown the problem in our laps. It's up to us to do with it what we can."

"In my opinion," said an army general, "we can't do a damn thing about it."

"Let's not forget the weather," said Intelligence. "There's a vicious sandstorm blowing out there. From the air the whole surface of the earth is invisible. Just a swirling mass of sand. My guess is that Captain Mallory is considering that storm as a sort of ally. If it makes it tough for him to find the field and land, then it will also make it tough for the hijackers to be able to sort out precisely where they are."

"True," said the Prime Minister. "But surely there must come a moment when the pretense must come to an end. When the aircraft has landed, it must eventually taxi to a terminal of some sort. . . ."

"No, sir, actually there is no longer a terminal at El Maghreb," the air force general replied. "In all probability he will simply park at the end of the runway. . . ."

Intelligence peered intensely at the Prime Minister and concluded methodically, "We must attempt to determine the logic in the captain's plan. Undoubtedly, he believes he has a better chance of survival by landing on our side of the border. And— considering the mentality of those who have seized his plane—he is undoubtedly correct. We are, I think, suddenly part of a very difficult combined operation. That pilot is going to do everything he can to land that jetliner at Ramat Shamon."

He paused momentarily, deep in thought. "Yet clearly, the captain must delude the gunmen on board into believing they are in Jordan. The *simoom* may help, but only if the aircraft can be landed in the first place. But what then?"

Intelligence studied those about him as he prepared to answer his own question. "Gentlemen," he pronounced, "that is precisely where the captain hands the problem to us. Once that plane comes to a stop, it will be up to us to neutralize the terrorists with a minimal loss of lives to ourselves and the innocent people on board the aircraft. It will not be easy. . . . We don't even know how many fanatics we have to deal with. But one thing seems clear . . . we must have one small advantage if we are to succeed. We must have the initiative at the outset . . . or we can do nothing. Consequently, Mr. Prime Minister, we are compelled to help that unfortunate crew to complete the deception."

"But what can we do with so little time left?" asked the Prime Minister.

"The first thing we must do, sir, is to make Ramat Shamon look like El Maghreb."

"And how do we do that?"

"Put up Jordanian flags, sir, and have vehicles and commandos dressed as Arabs all over the place. Hell, we've got plenty of captured uniforms and equipment. Let's give them an airing!"

"Impossible. . . ."

"Why?"

"There isn't time. That aircraft will be landing in less than three hours."

"We've got to do it."

The men looked at each other.

"Maybe . . ."

"We have a military base in the Negev south of Dimona. . . ."

The Prime Minister's finger jabbed the air, as if pushing a button. "Yes. We'll do it! I want it arranged immediately. Get a Jordanian flag, the biggest one you can find . . . and trucks and armored vehicles—anything that will support the illusion. A company of commandos—send them on their way at once. They can be briefed en route. Get the necessary garments there by the time they arrive. I don't care how. Just do it! We've got to convince the hijackers that they're on Jordanian soil. Once they're off the aircraft we can dispose of them; we'll worry about that part of it later. . . !"

* * *

There was no time for briefings.

"Get your men into the vehicles, fully armed. Do it in five minutes. Or less. Then proceed immediately to Ramat Shamon. It's an abandoned airfield near the Jordanian border, in sector K14H. You will receive further orders there."

Rumors materialized—verbal spontaneous combustion. It was another war. It was an invasion. By us. By them. By the Russians. No; on second thought it had something to do with the hijacking of the Pope's plane. . . .

Some men were still gulping down midmorning snacks as they threw their Uzi submachine guns over their shoulders and followed their comrades outside. There, they recoiled as the sand whipped around them, stinging, biting. This was madness. How could they get out to Ramat Shamon in these conditions? How would they find it? What would they do even if they did find it? What lunatic issued these orders?

* * *

The Pope looked at each of them in turn. He spoke quietly, as if the subject was of only academic interest.

"I have been informed that when we land in Jordan I shall be taken from the aircraft. The rest of you and the other passengers will remain."

"That is outrageous. . . !"

"Please. Let us not waste time and breath condemning the culprits. We can do nothing to prevent their actions; we can only put our faith in God. The Black September organization is responsible for our plight. Now, it is my belief that I shall be held as hostage in an attempt to force Israel into some action, but I do not know what. It is, however, a simple matter to think of the possibilities." He frowned slightly, but his voice was soft. "I insist," he declared, "that none of you make any attempt to protect me."

"But these people are murderers. . . ."

"Yes. And they are heavily armed. They will not hesitate to shoot. You are no match for them. If you take any aggressive action, you will be killed. And your deaths will have been for no purpose. I therefore order you to obey their instructions. I shall have enough to occupy my mind in the next few hours without having to mourn any of you." The tiniest hint of a smile touched his lips. "You are all my good and trusted companions and colleagues. I think I understand how you must feel. It is natural and admirable to want to defend those who are dear to you. But you will be doing a great disservice to the Church if you throw away your lives in vain attempts to fight with armed terrorists. I categorically forbid any such action. Is that clearly understood?" Again he looked at each face. Abruptly, he smiled, an irrepressible smile. "Besides, you are all much too old and plump even to consider such antics."

There were reluctant nods. A cardinal, a man of seventy with gray curly hair, said, "It is one thing to accede to your wishes at this moment, Father; I'm afraid it might be quite another matter when the moment comes for them to take you away. You ask us to stand by and do nothing. . . ."

"On the contrary," said the Pope. "I order; I do not ask."

More nods. They would obey.

"Now," he said, "I would like to say a few words to the passengers. I feel that my presence has resulted in much jeopardy and anguish for them. Perhaps you would be kind enough to find out whether it is permitted and if it is felt that such a message would be appreciated, under the circumstances. . . ."

*   *   *

Mallory ignored her. To hell with her hand that gripped the back of his seat; to hell with her gun; to hell with her suspicious gaze that kept roaming the instrument panel. Maybe she thought there might be concealed weapons up front. Maybe she just wanted to remind everyone that she was in charge. A show of strength.

God only knows how long ago, teachers in classrooms had breathed over his shoulder in the same way, peering, prying.

The muscles in his neck and back were tied in knots and needed exercise. But he refused to reveal his tension. No; never let the opposition know they bother you.

At last she returned to the jump seat, apparently satisfied that all was normal. Mallory glanced across the cockpit. Jensen sat quietly, still groggy from Fadia's pistol-whipping and the strain of it all. The poor bastard was out of it. But the fact remained that he was still alert enough to possibly recognize that Mallory would not be approaching El Maghreb. Christ! One wrong word from Jensen could blow the whole plan. So how could he get the message to his first officer? But . . . maybe he wouldn't have to.

"Say, Cliff, you're in no shape to be of much help to me during the approach to El Maghreb. So don't take it personally, but I'll handle it all the way down. All I want you to do is monitor the radio altimeter and call out altitudes during the descent. I'll keep the chart on my side of the cockpit, and you keep your eyes glued on the altimeter. Let's avoid the sand dunes and the camels. Okay?"

Jensen seemed relieved and nodded without speaking.

Mallory winked. A hang-in-there wink. It would have been good to talk over the situation with him. But, as captain, Mallory had to make the decisions. No democracy, an airliner; no forum, the flight deck. Herr Dictator Mallory. Again he studied the chart of the region. It showed navigational aids and the locations of major cities. But it was sadly inadequate for an instrument approach in such conditions and in such an aircraft. He caressed his chin as he tried to picture the situation he would soon face. The only navigational aid was a radiobeacon just northwest of Ramat Shamon. Because the beacon offered little in the way of precision navigation, it would be imperative not to descend below 500 feet until the runway was actually in sight—if it ever was. He mentally sketched the approach; a straight shot in from the Mediterranean, intercepting the Israeli coast at Gaza, then a line southeast across the country, almost to the Jordanian border while homing in on the beacon—if the Gods who look after foolhardy aviators were willing. At the beacon, a sharp left turn, heading three-one-zero degrees, an outbound leg of precisely ten miles, then a standard procedure turn to bring the 747 back to an inbound track of one-three-zero degrees to line up with the runway. Q.E.D. He hoped. He imagined the ADF needle trying to point to the beacon, swinging, quivering; it would be a matter of trying to interpret the thing, judging just where it would be pointing if the nose of the airplane weren't being buffeted by the storm. The depressing truth was, he might easily fly a few hundred yards on either side of the field and never see it.

Then what? It was a phrase he seemed to be employing a lot in recent hours.

He might have to abandon the attempt to land. If conditions were just too bad, he'd have no choice. Sorry, lady, I hereby refuse to endanger my aircraft and my passengers by attempting to land under these horrendous conditions. . . . Let's be reasonable. I can't land on a runway I can't find, can I?

Great. Firm and decisive. A credit to the profession.

Then what? Would Fadia put a bullet in his brain? Possibly. But maybe she would decide to kill Joe Nowakoski instead: a little subtle demonstration to discourage further argument from any other members of the flight crew. . . .

He glanced at her. Her earlier calm had given way to uneasiness. Who could blame her? Her big assignment was approaching its climax. So far, everything had worked perfectly—except for the *simoom*. The sandstorm, the cursed unpredictable storm, was jeopardizing all the meticulous plans. And no doubt she was reasoning that he, Mallory, would make the most of it as an excuse for aborting the approach. She had to be firm. She had no choice. It was all or nothing now. Shooting one crew member was probably standard operating procedure for hijackers and terrorists in her league. . . .

The unpleasant fact was that a great many people might die because of what he was about to do. Already he had committed people's lives—without consulting them. Some nerve. He was gambling everything on the Israelis' coming up with some bright idea. And yet he had no way of knowing if the Israelis could or would do anything. God-awful odds, when you thought about it.

Already he seemed to hear the righteous tones of the investigators. . . .

Q: Wouldn't you say, Captain Mallory, that you were taking one hell of a chance with your passengers' lives?

A. I was trying to protect them.

Q: How did you determine that you were protecting them?

A: Because I thought that a landing in Jordan was like handing down a death sentence to all on board, and anything was better than that.

Q: How did you arrive at such a conclusion, Captain?

A: You don't have to be a genius to know that Israel never deals with terrorists. In the short time since these fanatics took over my aircraft I could tell they wouldn't stop anything to achieve their goals. Murder was merely an expeditious tool of their trade. Better to have *some* chance by landing in Israel, than *no* chance by landing in Jordan!

Q: And did you suppose for one moment that the hijackers would permit you to do that without reacting?

A: I . . . I hoped that because of the extremely poor visibility, they might not realize that they were down on the wrong airfield . . . until it was too late.

Q: Too late? What, precisely, do you mean by "too late," Captain?

A: You see, I hoped that the Israelis might understand what I was attempting . . . and that they would be ready at Ramat Shamon when we landed.

Q: Ready Captain?

A: Yes, I hoped that they would have an assault team in readiness . . . to swarm aboard the aircraft . . . and disarm the hijackers . . . or something.

Q: And did you have any assurance that this was, in fact, the case?

A: No . . . I didn't.

Q: Nevertheless you proceeded to land at Ramat Shamon?

A: Yes.

Q: And is it a fact that when the hijackers realized where they were, they slaughtered the Pope, the passengers and the crew . . . except *you?*

He shuddered.

Land at El Maghreb and let events take care of themselves? Or land at Ramat Shamon and risk everyone's life for some dumb, tiny particle of a hope of fooling the hijackers and saving the day? Who the hell do you think you are? James Bond? God, he could hear those investigators again. How would the passengers vote if anyone chose to give them the opportunity? What about the Pope? Chances are, he would order the plane to El Maghreb, to minimize the danger to the other passengers. But would it? They only had the hijackers' word that the passengers would be released. Undoubtedly they too would become hostages. A little extra leverage.

You've got a lot of crust, Mallory, making up everyone's mind.

True. Undeniable. Yet every fiber of his being rebelled at the thought of meekly flying to Jordan and surrendering, giving the sons of bitches what they demanded.

And he kept seeing that old man's face; the inevitable execution . . . . And would the passengers and crew be freed? . . . Or would there be mass murder?

Damn it, Ramat Shamon it would be!

* * *

Dee Pennetti tried to wear a confident smile as she strode along the aisle. Rows of faces turned toward her, like spectators at a tennis match. But surprisingly few of them spoke to her. Every passenger seemed to be wrapped in his or her own thoughts. Dee kept thinking of rows of French aristocrats going to their executions in tumbrils. They probably didn't talk much, either, poor guys. This was sure a strange hijacking. Here in the cabin it was hard to believe it was really happening. Not having armed hijackers running around made all the difference; somehow it seemed to imply that the coach passengers were not personally involved in what was happening up front. It was somebody else's problem. Reality was kept at bay a little longer.

Vernon Squires beckoned to her.

"Stewardess, would you be kind enough to get a message to

NBC via the aircraft radio?"

Dee stared. "NBC? Are you kidding, sir?"

"Certainly not," said Mr. Squires. "I want to get in touch with them because I was supposed to be on the Johnny Carson show this evening. *The Tonight Show.* You've undoubtedly seen it."

"Yes, but . . ."

"Clearly I shall be unable to honor the engagement. I'd like to tell NBC that I shall do my very best to get there tomorrow."

Dee shook her head. This guy was too much. "I'm sorry, sir, there's no way we can use the radio for that purpose."

"Why not?"

"Sir, there's an armed hijacker in the cockpit who isn't about to let anyone transmit personal messages. It could be code or something."

"But it isn't," declared Mr. Squires, annoyed. "It's a perfectly straightforward message."

"I know that and you know that—but that hijacker doesn't."

Mr. Squires wondered aloud what the world was coming to.

"Is there anything else I can do for you?" Dee asked.

"I'd appreciate a Scotch and water," he said.

"I'll get it for you right away."

Mrs. Lefler said, "Have you actually *met* Johnny Carson?"

"Several times."

"Tell me, what's he really like? I mean, *really.* You know what I mean."

"Perhaps," Mr. Squires told Dee, "you'd better make that a double."

* * *

The *simoom* enveloped the convoy, lashing it with stinging, burning sand and dust as fine as talcum powder. It was a billion minuscule bullets that seared their way into flesh, poured into every buttonhole, behind goggles, up sleeves. Industriously, the sand etched the paint on every vehicle. It caked on lips; it crept into throats and noses. It plugged up ears and matted hair. Eyes burned and skin itched. The world became a mass of swirling, blinding yellow.

Sensible men sought shelter from the *simoom* and bathed their faces and eyes in diluted vinegar, waiting for the storm to abate. No one in his right mind attempted to defy it.

But still the Israeli commandos plowed on. Twice they lost their way, confusing landmarks.

The thirty-one-year-old colonel who led the convoy was of the opinion that the whole world had gone completely mad. How could anyone land an airplane in this? How could the pilot even find the field? And even if the aircraft landed successfully, was there really much chance of fooling the Black September maniacs into believing that they were in Jordan? He had been told that a separate convoy would meet him at Ramat Shamon; it would be carrying suitable apparel for the troops, plus captured Arab trucks and equipment.

"Your biggest advantage will be surprise," they had told him.

And my biggest disadvantage will be total confusion, he had thought. But he hadn't said it. He had promised that he would do his best. They had assured him that they expected nothing more. But it wasn't true. They expected success. The pride, the morale of the Jewish state, rested on his shoulders. Failure was unthinkable. But more than a little likely, in his unhappy opinion.

chapter 19

0815 GREENWICH MEAN TIME
OVER THE EASTERN MEDITERRANEAN SEA
32°18' NORTH LATITUDE, 34°03' EAST LONGITUDE

The Israeli coast was barely visible ahead, shrouded by the hazy edges of the storm. Beyond, a film of beige stained the land from Haifa to Port Said. From forty-five thousand feet it looked innocent enough, but Mallory had no illusions. He had experience with sandstorms, and they scared the hell out of him. The only sensible thing was to avoid them like the plague.

"Shitty," Jensen grunted as he looked forward.

Mallory didn't reply; the copilot had said it all. He glanced at the DME as it ticked off the distance to the Beersheba VORTAC, an en route navigational aid situated in the heart of the Israeli desert. Thirty-five minutes to the beacon at Ramat Shamon. Soon it would be time to start the descent, the first step in the involved business of getting the great 747 down to earth. He considered the matter of destination again. Yes. Ramat Shamon, for sure—unless the storm took it into its head to abate at the last moment. Then he might *have* to divert to El Maghreb.

Okay. Course of action definitely decided.

The storm looked solidly entrenched.

He wondered when the Israelis would communicate with him. Inevitably they would. But when? He would have to be as alert as that Tel Aviv controller. If they could do nothing, they might tell him to abandon Ramat Shamon by saying that runway 13 was unusable. But if no such message was transmitted, could he assume that they were prepared for him to land at Ramat Shamon?

It could be crucial for him to know, one way or the other.

Anyway, thank God Jane was safe. Jane, the problem child who had finally begun to grow up.

* * *

They chose a dark, deserted street. A sinister place of old warehouses and hopeless businesses. When they opened the trunk lid, the man gazed, pop-eyed with terror, convinced that the moment had come for his execution.

Jane told him to relax. "It's okay. We won't harm you."

"Honest?" The man's voice was a squeak.

"Honest."

They helped him out of the car.

"Where the hell are we?" His mouth fell open as he gawked about him.

"San Francisco," Jane told him.

"You're kiddin'."

Jane assured him she would never kid him about a thing like that.

He turned watery eyes on her. "So what . . . what you goin' to do with me, huh?"

"We're going to take you to the movies."

He stared. "Movies?"

He sat in the back of the Plymouth with Abou Gabal. But the man said nothing. He just kept opening and closing his mouth and swallowing as if he was having trouble disposing of a particularly large chunk of food.

A dozen blocks further on, Jane found an all-night theater. It played X-rated movies; *Nooky and Cranny* and *Weekend Hookers* were the current attractions. Inside, the place was almost empty, but it reeked of the drunks and deviates who habitually slept there.

"We want you to sit down in this row," Jane told the man. "Then we're going to sit behind you, in the back row."

"Wha' for?"

"It's a new kick. A blast."

"What d'you do?"

"Can't tell you. It wouldn't be fun if I did."

"What do I have to do?"

"Not a thing. That's what's so great for you. All you do is sit and watch the movie and stay there until we tell you to get up. But you mustn't move . . . or we'll have to hurt you."

The man kept nodding, agreeing, pathetically anxious to please. They slumped him down in the seat so that he was only partially visible to the other patrons of the place. He seemed comfortable enough, and he had a good view of the screen.

Abou Gabal whispered to him, "Don't make any attempt to get up. Understand?"

More nods. He understood.

They watched the show for a few minutes, grinning at the gasps and groans and simulated passion of the performers; then they slipped out of the place and went back to the car. The man was safe there for a while; he was too scared to move. Jane suggested stopping at an all-night restaurant for cheeseburgers and coffee before setting off again, but Abou Gabal was in too much of a hurry.

The radio newscaster was agog with the latest on the papal hijacking.

"At last report," he declared, "the Trans American 747 jumbo jet was heading for an undisclosed destination in the Middle East after having been hijacked during a flight from Rome to San Francisco, where the Pope was to attend the World Conference on Population. It is believed that a radical Palestinian terrorist group is responsible for the hijacking, but this has not yet been confirmed. Still to be learned is the reason for the hijacking. Official sources have not yet indicated what demands have been made by the Palestinians. Leaders around the world have expressed the most profound shock. The President has called upon Arab leaders to exert their influence to effect the immediate release of the aircraft and all passengers; refusal will, he declared, result in the abhorrence of decent people all over the world."

"Decent people all over the world felt the same abhorrence about Viet Nam," said Abou Gabal, "but did it make any difference?"

"Maybe," said Jane.

The city was quiet at this hour. The buildings looked tranquil and snug, resting comfortably in spite of the Pope and his problems.

"I must find North Allwyn Street in Oakland," said Abou Gabal. "See if there is a map in the glove compartment."

She found a road map under an empty flask; it was dog-eared and disintegrating but fortunately it provided the information they needed. The street was in Oakland, a half hour's drive away. Parked under a streetlight, they planned the route.

As she studied the map, she wondered why she was being so damned helpful. What was she aiming at? Why didn't she run like hell? Well, she told herself, that would be unwise because he might shoot as I ran. But at once she had to admit it was a phony reason; she didn't believe he would shoot; no, he *cared.* Didn't he? She didn't know. Things didn't make any sense. The world simply wasn't the same place it had been twenty-four hours earlier. Too much had happened. All balance and logic had vanished. A strange excitement simmered within her. Sexual? Plain old terror? She wasn't sure. She wasn't sure of anything anymore.

She asked him what was going to happen to him.

"I'm not sure. The man I am going to see will advise me."

"Where will you stay?"

"I don't know. It will of course be necessary to remain in hiding for a long time. The authorities will be looking for me. And for you," he added.

"Maybe I can help you escape."

"You?"

"Sure. If I go home I could cook up a story . . . about how I escaped from you. I'll throw them off the track, say you headed for Canada or someplace."

"Yes, I suppose you could say that."

She glanced at him. "But you don't think I would."

"Why should you? I am your abductor."

"I know. . . . Don't ask me to explain it."

"You are really strange."

"You're not exactly typical yourself."

He smiled.

She asked him, "Will you return to the Middle East?"

He nodded. "No doubt I shall be told to go, when it is safe."

"Do you want to go back?"

"I'm not sure," he said, not looking at her.

"So stay."

He smiled, a thin, sad smile. "You make it sound very easy."

"Maybe it's easier than you realize."

"No, I think I shall be told to lie low for several weeks until the 'heat,' as you call it, is off. Then I shall head for Mexico, and from there I will return to Beirut."

"Why must you see this man tonight?"

"Because it is my duty."

"Haven't you done enough?"

"What do you mean?"

"You've already risked your life . . . so quit now."

He grinned; the idea was amusing. "One does not quit Black September, I can assure you."

"Maybe they'll think you were killed back at the house with the others. They'll forget about you. Jesus Christ, man, this is an *opportunity* for you to get *out*. . . !"

He turned to her. "You sound angry. Why?"

She breathed deeply; it calmed her. "I guess it's because we're talking about waste. Waste of you. Waste of life. Waste always makes me angry. If you go back, you'll eventually get killed. You'll end up just like your buddies at the house. I don't like that thought . . . because in a peculiar sort of way—and I do mean peculiar—I don't want you to get killed. Besides, it's foolish to keep fighting about Israel and Palestine and everything. Why, they're talking about it right now, negotiating; any day they'll settle the whole dumb business once and for all, and then all those people who have died fighting will have died for nothing. . . ."

His mouth hardened. "You do not understand. They will never reach a lasting peace with the Palestinians because Israel will never agree to *disappear.*"

"Disappear? You mean, you want Israel wiped off the map?"

"Precisely."

"Why, for God's sake? There are lots of nice, innocent people living in Israel. Why do you keep killing and maiming. . . ?"

"Those people have no right to be there. That is Arab land. It is the land in which my father was born. It is our land. You talk about us committing atrocities. What about Deir Yasin?"

"What the hell is that?"

"It was a Palestinian village west of Jerusalem. About four hundred people lived there. In April of 1948, the Irgun—the Jewish underground—massacred two hundred and fifty of them. Men, women and children. Menachem Begin, who was then the Irgun leader, justified the incident and said there would never have been a State of Israel without the 'victory' at Deir Yasin. What do you think of that?"

"I don't know," said Jane helplessly. "I don't understand any of it."

*   *   *

Dee Pennetti's voice came over the interphone.

"Captain, the Pope wants to say a few words to the passengers. It'd be nice, I think; they'd appreciate it. Is it okay?"

Mallory glanced at Fadia. "Well?"

She shook her head. "He cannot come here to the cockpit."

"It isn't necessary," Mallory told her. "He can use a hand mike in the first-class cabin to talk over the public address system. I think it'd be a good thing; it might help keep the passengers calm."

She considered the question, then shrugged. "I have no objection."

"It's okay," Mallory told Dee.

"Thanks, Captain. It'll help."

"You might say he's got a captive audience," Fadia added, with a smile.

No one laughed.

The Pontiff spoke for a few minutes, first in English, then in Italian, his thin voice intoning ancient words of prayer. There was utter silence in the passenger cabin, broken only by the faint hum of the jet engines. His Holiness told the passengers how grieved he was that his presence on the airplane had created this situation. He asked for their understanding and for them to grant forgiveness to those of God's children who have gone astray. "I have been promised that when we land, you will not be harmed; in due course you will be permitted to go on your way. I will be detained, for how long I do not know. My faith is in the Lord, however, and I am not afraid." He blessed the passengers and wished them well. The PA system went dead.

"That's all," came Dee's voice. "He's gone back to his compartment."

Mallory thanked her. Then he picked up the PA handset in the cockpit. He fingered it as he contemplated the things he had to say.

"Ladies and gentlemen, this is your captain speaking. In a few minutes we will be starting our descent. We will be landing approximately half an hour later." *If* we land, he thought. "I can't overemphasize the importance of everyone remaining in his or her seat until instructed otherwise by a member of the crew." Or some son of a bitch with a gun, he wanted to add. "There's no reason to be scared. It's not a pleasant experience to have your flight turned around and find yourself flying to the Middle East. But these things have happened quite a few times in this crazy world of ours. And just about everybody has survived. Remember that. We are going to cooperate, and we're going to come through this just fine. But I must tell you that we're going to run into some turbulence on the way down. It could be a rough descent, so be sure your seat belt is firmly fastened. Thank you. We'll see you on the ground."

He clicked off and sighed.

"Great," Jensen murmured. "Just right."

"Thanks."

"You should have been a politician," said Fadia.

"And you should have been a hangman."

"A what?"

"Never mind."

Israel Control interjected.

"Trans Am, descend to and maintain flight level two-four-zero."

"Descending to two-four-zero. Request the best altimeter setting you can provide for our destination."

"Roger," said Israel Control. "We'll try."

"Okay, here we go," Mallory murmured as he eased the thrust levers back to idle and lowered the nose gently.

Fadia came forward again; she stood almost between the two

pilots and gazed ahead into the murky distance as if hoping to see her comrades waiting. Mallory glanced sideways at the pistol in her hand resting easily on the back of Jensen's seat. Could he reach out and grab it fast enough? He would have to be incredibly fast—and accurate. If she had time to react, it might mean a chestful of bullets for his trouble. And even if he did manage to grab the thing, she would probably manage to let off a few rounds. God knows where they would go. Jensen, Nowakoski: either or both of them might get themselves shot without having done anything to provoke it.

She moved back to the jump seat. Thank God.

No guts, he told himself. He thought about it. True. He couldn't steel himself to tussle with an armed terrorist, male or female. Sweat had broken out on his forehead. He wiped it away with the back of his hand.

Gently the altimeter needle continued to unwind as the 747 lost altitude.

Nowakoski was busy adjusting the cabin pressurization system.

Ahead and below, the mist was now the color of sulfur. A dirty, dangerous color. A hellish color. God knows what the visibility would be close to the field. Zero, possibly. In which case there wouldn't be any hope of landing the airplane safely.... Very sorry to disappoint you, lady, but, after all, you can visit El Maghreb some other time. . . .

If she came for him, maybe he could slam the controls forward, send the plane into a dive and throw her off balance. But she wasn't alone, damn it. There was nothing to be gained by that train of thought . . . for sure. Worry about getting the airplane on the ground, if it's possible; then you can start figuring what to do next.

He nodded to himself. Logical instructions.

Every moment brought the 747 closer to the storm—the savage, merciless *simoom*. Mallory had heard of men losing their sanity after being caught in the desert by such storms. Their minds couldn't cope; it was too awesome, too all-enveloping. No horizon, no sun, no sound but the ceaseless thunder of the wind. A world of whirling, lashing sand, numbing mind and body, sucking energy and hope, leaving nothing but mere shells. . . .

Jesus.

He turned to Fadia. "Look, you come from this part of the world. You know how bad these storms can be. . . ."

"You will land!" she snapped, her eyes bright. She looked almost feverish.

"For God's sake, understand," he replied. "If the visibility is much below a half mile, I can't do it. There's simply no way. I'll have to go someplace else. If I can't see the goddam runway, I can't land on it!"

"I will not discuss it," she said, the color rising in her cheeks. "It is imperative that you land at El Maghreb."

"But . . ."

"We have talked too much about it already." She emphasized the words with little, abrupt movements of the pistol. "You *will* land there . . . or die trying."

"We'll see," he muttered, turning forward again.

Mallory pressed the transmit button. "Trans Am nine-zero-one, leveling at two-four-zero."

"Roger, nine-zero-one," came the voice from Israel Control. "Continue descent to flight level one-six-zero. Contact Tel Aviv South Sector, one-two-five point zero-five."

"Roger. Down to one-six-zero. Contacting Tel Aviv on one-two-five point zero-five." He adjusted the frequency on the VHF transceiver to the new wavelength. "Tel Aviv South Sector, this is Trans American nine-zero-one for one-six-zero."

A fresh voice came over the radio. Correct but full of concern. For some reason, Mallory pictured a bearded man with cavernous cheeks and the darkest of eyes. A Biblical individual. "Roger, Trans American nine-zero-one. The calculated altimeter setting is two-niner-six-niner. Report leaving flight lever two-zero-zero." Somehow the technical phrases became a message of sympathy and encouragement.

"Roger, Tel Aviv. Altimeter two-niner-six-niner. Will check out of flight level two-zero-zero."

Mallory turned on the Seat Belt sign and asked Nowakoski for a landing weight. It was time to ignore Fadia and her colleagues. The 747 had to be brought back to earth; all attention and skill had to be devoted to this task.

Nowakoski consulted his data. "Looks like we'll weigh three hundred ninety-five thousand pounds, Captain."

Mallory nodded and checked the placard on the panel before him. Rows of computer-born figures informed him at what speed he should land, depending on the aircraft's weight.

"One hundred twenty-nine knots on the bug."

Mallory made a mental note to make the final approach at 15 knots above the recommended speed, to compensate for the airspeed-robbing gusts and probable wind-shear conditions.

"Let's have the preliminary checklist, Joe."

"Okay, Skipper. Pressurization is set and checked. Landing data?"

The two pilots confirmed that their speed bugs were set.

"The fuel panel is set for landing. Annunciator lights are checked. Altimeters?"

"Set and cross-checked. Two-niner-six-niner."

"Inboard landing lights?"

"They're on."

"Radio and navigation instruments?"

"Set and cross-checked."

"Radio altimeters?"

"They're set to five hundred feet."

"Preliminary checklist complete, Skipper."

"Thanks."

Jensen nodded ahead. "There's the coast. Gaza."

It was almost invisible beneath the ugly yellow stain. Already the *simoom* was visible as a swirling mass, the highest peaks almost translucent, the merest wisps of dancing dust. But lower down the stuff looked solid. Solid and evil. To be avoided by all those in their right minds. . . .

The 747 was descending at twenty-five hundred feet per minute. Its path was smooth; the broad swept-back wings hardly rocked. But in a few moments, Mallory knew, the air would be buffeting the big airplane, slapping it with vicious updrafts, elbowing it, doing its utmost to tear the whole structure apart. It was not structural failure that Mallory feared, however; the 747 was incredibly strong, more than capable of absorbing any punishment the *simoom* might care to hand out; the next few minutes might be decidedly uncomfortable but not dangerous. It was the landing. The goddam, unpredictable landing. There was just no way of knowing what lay in store.

The Tel Aviv controller came on the air.

"Trans Am nine-zero-one, you are cleared present position direct to the beacon. Maintain six thousand; contact Amman Control on one-two-zero point one for approach clearance."

"Roger, Tel Aviv," Mallory responded.

"A. C. Ross says good luck. And may God be with you."

"Er . . . thanks, Tel Aviv. Understand cleared direct."

Oh, shit! Mallory shook his head, cursing himself. He hadn't considered this complication—having to talk to a Jordanian air traffic controller in Amman.

But there was nothing he could do about it without raising Fadia's suspicion.

"Amman Control, this is Trans Am nine-zero-one descending to six thousand, over."

"Good day, nine-zero-one, this is Amman. Understand you are descending to six thousand. We are unable to provide radar assistance in your area because of intervening high terrain. You are cleared for an approach to El Maghreb. Can we be of further assistance?"

Relieved, Mallory responded. "Negative, Amman. But thanks anyway."

He returned the microphone to its hook. A break: without radar coverage of the area, the Jordanian controller would be unable to track the path of Flight 901 to Ramat Shamon in Israel and announce that fact for Fadia to hear.

So far, so good. Mallory worked his shoulder muscles. Fatigue was beginning to take its toll.

Suddenly Mallory realized that he would no longer be communicating with an Israeli controller. And there was nothing he could find in the last transmission from Tel Aviv to bolster his determination about landing at Ramat Shamon.

Jesus, he thought, I've been handed over to a Jordanian controller. Is this Israel's way of telling me that I can't or shouldn't land at Ramat Shamon? Maybe they don't want me to land there for some reason or other. Maybe the runway there is totally unsafe.

Beads of perspiration were in full production now. Captain Steven Mallory felt a kind of controlled panic.

"And," he wondered, "what the hell was the Tel Aviv controller talking about? A. C. Ross? Who the hell is he?"

* * *

The gusts kept sweeping through the open hangar doors, sending the heaps of clothing rolling and contorting like bodies in agony. It made them dirtier than they already were, which was a feat in itself. The commandos' faces twisted in disgust as they examined the garments.

"This jacket *stinks!* A donkey must have worn it!"

"This one is worse, I swear."

"I'm going to puke."

"Go ahead. It'll smell better after you do."

"We'll have to be disinfected after wearing this garbage."

"God knows what diseases these sons of bitches had."

The sergeants exhorted the men to hurry.

"Move! Put something on. *Anything!* It doesn't have to *fit!* This isn't a fucking fashion show! Move your asses! Hurry! Hurry!"

"This thing hasn't got any buttons."

"So find another one. Move, move! There's plenty to choose from! In two minutes I want all of you to be looking like Arafat's heroes!"

Struggling, cursing, bumping into one another, the commandos sorted the items of clothing and pulled them on. The stuff was old; it had been captured during terrorist raids and previous wars. For reasons no one could recall, it had never been destroyed; it lay in storage for years. And had become progressively riper.

Half a dozen trucks captured during the Yom Kippur War had set out on the journey to the airport. Only three made it; the others fell victim to various mechanical failures along the way.

A man tried to climb up the flag pole beside the hangar; he carried a Jordanian flag, carefully folded. But when he was halfway up, the old, brittle pole snapped; he fell; he was lucky to escape without injury. They stuck the remains of the pole on one of the trucks. When they released the flag, the wind tore it away; half a dozen men went scrambling into the storm to retrieve it. Two of them collided in the maddening sandstorm; one was knocked cold by the impact. He was carried into the hangar.

Casualty number one. Already the damned operation was like a Three Stooges film. Cursing his luck at landing this lunatic assignment, the colonel ordered the truck drivers to keep their engines running. "Don't switch the bastards off or you'll never get them started again!"

He kicked a couple of empty ammunition boxes together to form a rough stage; he nodded at a sergeant to collect the men. It was time to brief them.

They gathered around him, still fumbling with the fittings of their unfamiliar garb, examining the Soviet and Czech arms they had been given, grinning in disbelief at the sight of their comrades impersonating the enemy. The ramshackle hangar clattered and creaked, battered by the storm.

The colonel had the highest regard for his men. Resourceful, intelligent, they were probably the best soldiers in the world. There were no troops he would rather have had for this job. But no matter what the caliber of the troops, Lady Luck was going to play one hell of a big role in these proceedings.

"Every moment counts," he announced, "so I'm not going to waste any time. You've all heard about the hijacking of the airliner carrying the Pope to America." The men exchanged I-told-you-so nods. "At this moment that airliner is approaching this area. Now, here's the plan. The hijackers think they're coming in to land at a place called El Maghreb, not far from here, just across the Jordanian border. But the fact is, they're coming here!"

The gasp was audible. Already the troops were grappling with the ramifications of the statements. "The storm is helping us, of course. Without it, the captain couldn't hope to deceive the hijackers into believing they were landing in Jordan when they were really landing in Israel. But the storm is also creating a very difficult situation for the pilot. I'm told that he could very likely crash trying to land that big jet during these conditions. It's not even certain that the runway can take the weight of the airplane. So the whole thing is a big gamble. But let's suppose they *can* get the airplane down in one piece. The visibility is terrible. So there's a good chance the hijackers won't suspect that they aren't at El Maghreb . . . until it's too late."

Nods, sober and thoughtful. An Everest of uncertainties was forming in every man's mind. "Black September is behind this. And it's been well-planned. The hijackers even went to the trouble of kidnapping the families of the flight crew. We've had word, however, that they've been rescued. Good news, but it doesn't help us. Now, Black September's demands are outrageous. They want nothing less than our complete and unconditional withdrawal from the West Bank in return for the Pope's safe release. If the withdrawal doesn't take place within twenty-four hours, the Pope will be executed. That's the deal. We have no way of knowing whether it is possible to negotiate a way out of this. That isn't our concern. All we have to think about is convincing the hijackers that they're at the right airfield . . . just long enough to give us time to eliminate them before they can harm the Pope or anyone else on on the airplane. As soon as the jet comes to a halt, I want the trucks with the Arabic markings to park near the nose of the aircraft. The tall truck will back up to the front passenger door. I am told that this will appear to be a normal procedure because, without conventional ramps, it's about the only practical way to get in or out of a 747. We'll enter the airplane from the roof of the truck. It's just about the right height. Shouldn't be any problem. The whole object of the operation will be to get inside that airplane and disarm the hijackers as rapidly as possible."

"Forcibly, sir?" A nineteen-year-old commando asked the question in a casual tone, as if inquiring about the time lunch was to be served. "Do we go in shooting?"

The colonel shook his head. "Not unless it's the only way. Presumably, we will disarm them *psychologically.* Let me explain. Now, think about the hijackers for a moment. They're tired and tense as hell. And probably feeling sick from the turbulent approach. What's more, they may not know what to expect. They've done their job; now all they want to do is unload their responsibilities onto someone else. Our hope is that they'll see all you scoundrels swarming around the plane. As far as they're concerned, you are all Palestinians. You look like Palestinians. And," he added with a grin, "you sure as hell smell like Palestinians. And remember, only those who speak Arabic will board the airplane. So we think they will almost certainly believe they are where they're *supposed* to be, namely, El Maghreb. If this thing is going to succeed, it must be in the first few moments. We must go into that airplane without hesitation; we're acting on direct orders from Allah himself. We go in. We take the Pope away; then we help the hijackers out of the plane, congratulate them on a fantastic job and get them into the trucks. The plan is, I will escort the Pope out of the airplane and into the lead truck. We will drive back here into this hangar. The other two trucks are for the hijackers. They will also be brought here. We'll have a reception committee waiting for them. A squad will remain on the airplane with the passengers. When we get the Pope and the hijackers off the airplane—and *only* then—the passengers can be told the truth. All right, so much for the basic plan. Questions?"

The faces before him wore expressions ranging from mildly incredulous to downright pessimistic.

"Colonel, do you *really* think the hijackers are going to believe they're at El Maghreb?"
place intimately. He might realize it isn't El Maghreb the moment the plane touches down. It's possible. But the odds are, none of them has ever been there before. And think what a job we had just finding this place. In such a storm it is almost impossible to distinguish one abandoned airfield in the desert from another."

"Sir, isn't it possible that the hijackers will be expecting a certain individual to meet them? I mean, the whole enterprise seems to have been so well planned and executed, wouldn't they also have organized the reception at the airport?"

"Could be. We have no way of knowing. But remember the storm. The blessed storm. It's the one factor that makes almost anything possible. If necessary, we say that the original reception committee got lost. I can't overemphasize the absolute necessity of every man looking as if he *belongs* on that airplane. Any hesitation, any uncertainty, will instantly create suspicion. God only knows what might happen then."

"It's possible, sir, that they may blast us out of our socks the moment we go near the plane."

"Correct. Expect the unexpected."

"Sir, is our first duty to protect the Pope or the passengers?"

"My guess is, if we can get the Pope out of the airplane, we will have solved the main problem. The danger is, there could be a hijacker or two aboard the airplane who will realize what has happened after we get the Pope out. I could see such an individual holding the rest of the passengers hostage, threatening to blow up the airplane or something of the sort. So it's vital that we neutralize all of them. Quickly. What complicates this is that we don't know where in the airplane they are located. However, we can do some educated guesswork. There has to be at least one on the flight deck, to keep an eye on the pilots. We have also been informed by the Americans that five Secret Service agents are aboard the aircraft. We have to assume that all or some of them are under guard. That accounts for at least one more hijacker. Now, it's conceivable that one or more Secret Service agents might still be under cover, pretending to be passengers. They could offer some help, but I wouldn't count on it. Black September has done a first-class, thoroughly professional job— and I am certain the planners wouldn't have forgotten about the Secret Service agents who always travel on flights like this. There may be a hijacker or two in the passenger compartment keeping an eye on the passengers. God knows. The idea is for us to create the proper atmosphere so that the hijackers are able to relax. They believe their job is done. They'll be elated with victory and probably will come forward, revealing themselves voluntarily . . . I hope. We simply collect the assholes and take them for a short ride. *Élan* is what will carry the day. You go in; you take over; they relax and go out to the truck."

"Colonel, isn't there a danger that we'll hold our fire too long?"

"Of course. But I can't give you a timetable. Each individual may have to decide when to start shooting, if at all. I'm relying on every one of you. Remember, once any shooting begins, the game is up. I pray we can carry this thing off without firing a shot. But we've got to be realistic. It could be a bloodbath."

"Let's make sure it's the blood of Black September," said one commando with a wry grin.

Another man raised his hand. "Sir, where will the airplane park?"

The colonel pointed out toward the sand-gripped field. "The plane will land in that direction—northwest to southeast. We'll have a truck waiting at the end of the runway. Sergeant Herzog has volunteered to assist us. He's air force, but okay." He indicated a burly man in one corner of the hangar. "He is a signalman; he carries baton lights so he can signal to the pilot of the plane and show him the way to taxi. We'll take the plane straight over to the far side of the field and park it facing the fence. Direct route. Nothing to be gained by letting the hijackers see any more than they have to.

"The instant the aircraft comes to a halt, we move in. Just remember, the plane is full of innocent, frightened people. We're going to tell them to stay seated, but God only knows whether they'll obey. Some may panic and try to get the hell off that airplane, and I can't honestly say I can blame them. So I'm going to be asking a lot of all of you. Everyone has been on the plane for more than twelve hours. They're all nervous and edgy. The hijackers *and* the hostages. God knows, some of the women may be hysterical by now. Maybe the men too, for all we know. You'll have to be alert." He smiled apologetically. "And that's putting it mildly."

"Sir," a commando indicated the weather, "how the hell is that airplane going to land in this stinking weather?"

"That," said the colonel, "is the pilot's problem."

chapter 20

At first the turbulence was insignificant. A nudge, a gentle dip. But as the 747 sank deeper into the swirling storm, the air became angrier. The sun shriveled to a yellow glow. The aircraft wobbled uneasily. Then the blows came in rapid succession. Rocking, skidding, the 747 was like a truck traveling at top speed along a bumpy, potholed road. The structure groaned, absorbing sudden, vicious stresses, directing them from component to component, apportioning them, dividing them, subdividing them until they were tamed. Through the streaming sand and dust, the passengers could only stare in fascinated horror as the giant wings flexed, their four turbines shuddering beneath them, the slender pylons trembling. They just weren't strong enough; it was obvious to anyone with eyes. There was no way they could endure that kind of torture and still stay whole; in a moment the entire airplane was going to break up into tiny, futile fragments.

For the flight crew it was like hurtling straight at a wall—a magic wall that kept opening at the last possible scintilla of an instant. The wall became a door of dancing sand and dust . . . and beyond them, more doors, more walls. No horizon; no up, no down; just sand. On the instrument panel, silent, responsive gauges were the only way to know anything of the aircraft's altitude, position and speed.

"Out of eleven thousand," Jensen announced.

Mallory nodded. Gradually the airspeed was reduced.

A. C. Ross? Who was he? What was the Israeli controller talking about?

Two hundred and fifty knots indicated.

"Out of ten thousand."

For an instant the storm abated. They flew into an aerial oasis of calm air. A glimmer of sun thrust its way through the sand to perch on the 747's nose. A glimpse of dry, dusty ground below. Then it was gone. The sand enwrapped them again. The sun vanished. A steel fist seemed to smash into the right wing. The 747 lurched, righted itself, staggered again as it thrust its way through the turbulence.

He wanted to look back, to see what Fadia was doing. But, no. Ignore her. Do nothing to tell her she matters. Chances were good that she wasn't enjoying the ride any more than any of the other passengers. He had to act normally, go through every motion as if totally disinterested in her presence.

But did she know the frequency of the El Maghreb radiobeacon?

There seemed to be only one way to find out, short of asking her.

He tuned in Ramat Shamon. And waited to see if she knew that he had tuned in the wrong frequency.

No reaction.

So far so good. But what would he do if she noticed? What could he do? Was there anything he could say? He tried to think. No good. To hell with it. He would hope for the best, hope she didn't notice.

Speed down to two hundred forty knots indicated.

A. C. Ross. The name seemed familiar but he couldn't place it.

Ross, Ross, Ross. His memory worked at the puzzle, sifting through uncounted fragments from the years. Then it occurred to him. It wasn't A. C. Ross at all. It was A/C Ross. A/C—Aircraftsman. Aircraftsman Ross. The name T. E. Lawrence had used when he had joined the Royal Air Force after World War One. And the name he had used as author of *The Mint*—a book Mallory and Henderson had argued about at a cocktail party a year or two ago. A long, heated argument. Nan had been mad as hell. Henderson *must* have remembered the incident and *must* have suggested it to Tel Aviv. T. E. Lawrence. Lawrence of Arabia!—the man who disguised himself as an Arab! That was it! That had to be it! The Israelis were disguising themselves as

Arabs and would be waiting for the plane at Ramat Shamon! And, come to think of it, that Jordanian controller must have been an Israeli communicating on one of their own frequencies. Of course!

He grinned to himself. Too bad he couldn't pass on the good news to Jensen and Nowakoski. Shame. But too risky.

The sand seemed to be denser, more solid. But Mallory reasoned that it was simply that it was darker down here, closer to the earth, deeper in the ocean of sand, farther from the sun—wherever the hell it was.

Smart guy, Henderson. Goddam brilliant when you thought about it.

"Flaps one," he commanded.

Jensen shifted the flap handle to the first notch.

On the leading edges of the broad, swept-back wings, flat surfaces moved out into the slipstream, subtly affecting the shape of the wing and improving its ability to perform at slow airspeeds by helping to accelerate the vital, lift-giving flow of air over its expanse.

The Morse code identification of the radiobeacon had a plaintive bleat. Mallory turned the volume down. No point in helping Fadia to realize that the aircraft was homing in on the wrong beacon. He glanced at the needle of the ADF, the automatic direction-finder used to home in on radiobeacons. The 747's receiver was picking up the signal from Ramat Shamon well enough, but the violent turbulence was making it next to impossible to steer an accurate course. As the 747 was buffeted by the storm, so the homing needle tried frantically to compensate. But by the time it had corrected, another lurch had shifted the aircraft's nose once again. More confusion. And even when the air was momentarily still, the needle seemed to shiver in anticipation of the next lurch. In normal visibility the turbulence wouldn't create such a problem because the field would eventually come into sight. In the *simoom*, however, the 747 could easily miss the field by a mile or more on either side. It was part skill, part guesswork, wearying guesswork, trying endlessly to interpret the right direction from the waverings of the needle.

He allowed the speed to slip to two hundred twenty knots.

"Flaps five."

Jensen shifted the lever to the second notch. On the panel, a green light winked, indicating that all the leading-edge flaps had extended fully.

"Two hundred knots."

"Flaps ten."

Mallory could feel the aircraft shifting its posture in the air as the massive trailing-edge flaps moved aft and down, altering the lift and drag characteristics of the airplane. He eased the thrust levers forward to maintain altitude.

A generous scotch on the rocks would have been welcome.

The topographical chart showed only the principal features of the terrain. God knows what obstacles might lie on the approach path. After all, the field was abandoned; no one had to worry about airplanes on final approach. . . . He mentally confirmed his earlier decision to go no lower than five hundred feet until the runway was in sight.

If it ever came in sight.

His eyes ached with the strain of staring at the damned, shivering ADF needle. Beside him, Jensen gazed out at the storm; how long before the poor bastard became hypnotized by it?

The big airplane suddenly dropped, hit by a ferocious downdraft. An instant later it soared, boosted upward by an equally lusty upcurrent. The metal airframe squealed, complaining. The gauges on the panel vibrated; for a moment they were unreadable. He breathed a sigh. No doubt a few meals came up in coach.

Five miles to the beacon . . . more or less.

He turned on the No Smoking sign.

No sound from Fadia. What if she got sick? Would there be an opportunity to disarm. . . ? No. Forget it. Worry about landing the airplane.

He loosened his collar and ran a hand around his neck. It was soaking. Maybe he *was* getting too old for this racket. But at what point did the accumulated treasure of experience and skill become overtaken by faster reactions and better eyesight? The airlines should construct their pilots, he thought: six-million-dollar airmen: ninety-year-old brains with twenty-year-old limbs.

Jesus, he told himself, *concentrate!*

The only thing to be said in favor of this stinking storm was that the hijackers couldn't see any more than he could. El Maghreb? Ramat Shamon? It could be Kennedy or Heathrow. . . .

Was the Pope praying at this moment? He hoped so. Any assistance gratefully accepted. . . .

"Should be there by now," Jensen observed flatly.

The ADF needle fluttered.

Abruptly it flipped one hundred eighty degrees. They were over the beacon. More or less.

Mallory turned the big craft to a heading of three-one-zero degrees.

"Flaps twenty."

The speed dropped to one hundred eighty knots as the trailing-edge flaps edged to twenty degrees, creating a huge barrier to the rushing air. Still there was nothing to see but wall after wall of dancing, swirling sand. And nothing to feel but bumps and jolts.

Three thousand feet. Level off.

Heading still 310 degrees.

Was there still a world beyond the goddam sand? No wonder men lost their minds in sandstorms. It was bad enough in the air-conditioned, pressurized comfort of a 747's flight deck; God knows what it must be like in the choking, blinding roar outside.

Mallory flew ten miles on the clock from the turning point. Then he swung to the right, to three-five-five degrees.

Straighten out. One minute at three-five-five.

Down to 2,200 feet.

Next, reverse course to the left.

Straighten out again on one-seven-five degrees.

Then the last turn, on to final approach, heading one-three-zero degrees to the airport.

"Gear down and flaps thirty, Cliff."

Jensen acknowledged as he activated the systems. "Landing gear coming down, Captain . . . flaps thirty degrees . . . green light. . . ." Formal, was Mr. Jensen.

"Final checklist, Joe."

"Okay, Skipper," came Nowakoski's voice.

Auto brakes, ignition, cabin signs, speed brakes, landing gear, flaps, hydraulics . . .

The familiar interchange of technicalities was curiously reassuring.

"Final checklist is complete, Skipper."

"Thanks." Mallory eased off more power; the 747 sank lower into the yellowness. To his right, Jensen was leaning forward, peering ahead, trying to see something, anything, of the ground.

He settled the speed at one hundred forty-five knots and began to descend. According to his calculations, the runway was dead ahead, less than ten miles away.

"Keep your eyes open," he told Jensen unnecessarily.

"Okay."

Hands slick and slippery on the controls. Lips dry. Mouth sour-tasting. Armpit itching. For God's sake, why would an armpit choose such a moment to itch?

Descent rate: eight hundred feet per minute.

Every nerve tense.

"Cliff, for Christ's sake, watch that radio altimeter. I don't want to go below five hundred feet unless the field's actually in sight."

"One thousand feet to go, Captain."

Still nothing but sand: an endless parade of billions of grains of the goddam stuff. A silly thought occurred to him: the Maintenance guys would be happy with him after this trip; the turbine blades would be bright and shiny; the sand would have given them a thorough cleaning.

But after this trip the airplane might be completely beyond help from Maintenance.

Three minutes to go.

Nuts.

The whole goddam thing was nuts. Groping around in the dark in a two-hundred-ton airplane. . . . The eyes kept playing tricks. The swirling, whirling sand became a huge tower, a church spire, the Tower of London, Hugh Hefner's mansion, another airplane heading in exactly the opposite direction, having just taken off from the runway in question. . . .

He should have told that Arab bitch to go to hell and abandoned the whole thing; he had no business endangering the lives of the Pope and his passengers trying to put this thing down in such conditions.

Two minutes to go.

God, by now the ground should be in sight.

Where the hell was it? Please . . .

"I can't see shit," muttered Jensen, hands clutching the panel before him as if bracing himself against the inevitable impact.

"You're not the only one," said Mallory. His voice sounded odd. Tinny.

"Five hundred feet."

"Yeah."

Five hundred feet. The magic altitude. No lower! Add power to maintain altitude.

Now that the aircraft was close to the ground, the turbulence was murderous. Mallory felt his head bouncing forward and back as the flight deck trembled. Every metallic muscle of the 747 was straining. And complaining. And aching. Could a 747 really take this kind of punishment and stay in one piece? How could all the systems keep operating? There had to be limits, for Christ's sake; there came a point where things had to start giving way. . . .

The Stearman used to make noises like this. . . .

Suddenly Jensen pointed.

"There! I got it! One-thirty—but you're too high!"

Mallory caught barely a glimpse of the concrete strip. Off to the right, less than half a mile away. A glimpse of concrete runway, the suggestion of a building or two. Hopeless to attempt to turn in. . . . Too high. . . . Too close for such a turn. . . .

"No way!"

He advanced the thrust levers.

"Flaps twenty!"

"Roger."

After an agonizing pause, the great engines delivered their full surge of power. Mallory rotated the 747's nose up to fifteen degrees.

"Gear up!"

"Gear coming up."

"It's there . . . at least the goddam place is there."

Jensen was grinning as if all their troubles were over. In a way, Mallory thought, it would have been safer if the airfield hadn't appeared. Then there would have been no question about turning for another field. Now the whole agonizing business had to be repeated. To make matters worse, he hadn't seen a sign of life on the field. There was a gnawing possibility that even if he got the 747 down, he'd find himself on an abandoned airfield—in Israel. Jesus, A. C. Ross might be the Trans Am station manager at Tel Aviv and he might have met him five years ago and it might be nothing more than a good-luck message and. . . .

Don't think about it! That's an order!

"Radiobeacons are useless in this crappy weather."

Jensen was nodding now. Agreeing. Grin gone. Still groggy.

"Not enough precision."

"Right."

Mallory engaged the autopilot and entered a holding pattern north of the beacon at five thousand feet. That ought to be safe enough, he thought.

Mallory sat back. He sighed. His eyes felt tired and prickly. There had to be another way of tackling the problem of the approach.

He asked Nowakoski for a fuel check.

The news wasn't good. Nowakoski sounded apologetic, as if it was his fault that the fuel was running dangerously low.

"Looks like we've got enough juice for one more try, Skipper. But if we don't get down real soon we'll be sucking fumes."

And pushing up daisies, Mallory thought bleakly.

*   *   *

The noise of the jet was deafening—but still the damned airplane couldn't be seen. It was as if the noise itself was flying about. The din seemed to spring from every direction simultaneously. Was a squadron of jets converging on the field?

A soldier pointed.

"There! There it is!"

The colonel caught a glimpse of the airliner. Wings rocking, it materialized like some prop in a magic show; then it was gone again, swallowed by the storm.

"He was nowhere near the runway!"

"I'm sure he'll try again."

The colonel recoiled in pain as dust stung his eye. Cursing, he went back into the hangar. "He didn't make it," observed Sergeant Herzog, the signalman.

"Let's hope he does next time."

Sergeant Herzog nodded. He had a sad face; he should have been a junior clerk in some accounting office, not an airport technician.

"I guess the fire trucks and ambulances got lost, huh?"

"They'll be here," said the colonel.

"I wouldn't count on it," said Sergeant Herzog mournfully.

The wind was blowing the sand into weird, whirlwind patterns around the hangar doors. The swirls found their way inside, wriggling, snaking until, robbed of the wind, they were still. Then they lay dormant on the floor, to be crunched beneath the commandos' boots.

The colonel had sent one of the trucks to the northwest end of the runway, with orders to park to one side, headlights on. It was probably pointless, he knew, but the lights might constitute a modicum of assistance to the pilot during the final moments of his approach. Unlikely, but possible. Therefore worth the effort.

He sent the second truck to the southeast end, with Sergeant Herzog aboard. When—if—the Boeing landed, it would travel along the runway that could just be seen from the hangar through curtains of sand and dust. When it became visible it would be time to dispatch the last truck. The stinking sand seemed to rattle the brain. The colonel found himself yawning. He covered the yawn with his hand, hoping no one had seen it. Thank God the army photographers hadn't arrived yet. Those sons of bitches would have been sure to immortalize the yawn on film. A man could spend the rest of his life trying to explain away such a thing....

He took a deep breath to wake himself up. He grimaced. It tasted of dust.

The radio team stood in a corner of the hangar. Their

equipment lay on the floor. The colonel had ordered them to leave it untouched. He wouldn't even permit them to switch it on for test purposes. No, absolutely no. Interception of any sort of signal from a place that is supposed to be abandoned could blow the whole operation even before it began. No communications with the outside world until after . . .

He wondered if there would be an after for him.

It wasn't the first time he contemplated the distinct possibility of his imminent death. It didn't trouble him. He accepted the risks of his profession; some soldiers were luckier than others; it was that simple.

What were the Black September people doing at this moment? Standing on their airfield at El Maghreb, waiting, just as he was? There was a disturbing possibility that they might be in communication with the airplane. Perhaps they were already asking why they couldn't hear the plane if it was so close to the field. . . . Perhaps the thought of being over the wrong airport was even now causing angry questions and guns being pointed at the flight crew.... He shrugged. It didn't help to conjecture along such lines.

The men waited, watched, nursing their weapons in the natural, instinctive way that soldiers have with guns and mothers have with babies. The colonel was of the opinion that if any soldiers on earth could pull this stunt off, it was these men. He felt great affection for them.

He again considered the technicalities.

Assuming he managed to wrest the Pope away from the terrorists, how should he handle him? After all, the Pontiff was an elderly man. He had to be gentle, yet he had to be firm if the terrorists weren't to become instantly suspicious. A moment of some delicacy.

He sighed. He would do what seemed right at the time.

Was there anything else he should have told the men? He couldn't think of anything. They had absorbed the message, the facts, the risks. They were thinking about them, each reassuring himself, organizing his actions before they were needed.

Sergeant Herzog stood by the hangar doors, peering outside as if expecting a hail of bullets. He had asked the colonel if there would be any further need for his services once the 747 had parked. The colonel had told him no. Sergeant Herzog seemed relieved. Hard to blame him. All he had for weapons were two batons with which to guide the jet to a parking place.

A jeep squealed to a halt outside the hangar. The photo unit had arrived. Their presence irritated the colonel. How could the goddam photographers manage to find the place if the crash vehicles and ambulances couldn't?

"If you show your faces too soon, I'll personally blow them off! Is that understood?"

Yes, it was understood.

* * *

"What are you doing, flying in circles?"

Breathing hard, her forehead pasty and sweaty, Fadia clutched the back of Mallory's seat to steady her as the flight deck bounced and pitched.

"You'd better sit down," Mallory told her.

The remark angered her. She thrust the pistol in his face.

"Land the airplane! Now! Don't play games!"

"I'm going to land," Mallory snapped. "In fact we've damn well *got* to get down the next time. We used up one hell of a lot of fuel during that missed approach. We can't afford another go-around. Do you understand that?"

"Of course I understand it!"

"Well, then, I'm trying to figure a better way of doing it. And all you're doing, sister, is wasting my time and our fuel. So sit down and shut up!"

"You—" For an instant she seemed about to retort angrily. Then she thought better of it and returned to the jump seat.

"You'll be safer there," said Nowakoski in his friendly way.

"Shut your mouth!"

"Okay, okay." He shrugged, hurt.

The INS, the inertial navigation system, Mallory thought. Was it a possibility? He wondered. The airborne navigational computer system was designed to guide airliners around the world, not to provide pinpoint guidance to a runway in such horrendous weather. But it might be utilized. . . . There were no electronic approach aids at Ramat Shamon, and the radio beacon was almost useless, so something *had* to be done. . . .

The aircraft carried three inertial navigation systems. One of them was located in front and slightly to the right of him—and therefore largely concealed from Fadia's gaze by his back. He consulted the chart and used his plotter to determine the precise longitude and latitude of the radiobeacon. He punched this information into the INS keyboard. He assumed that since she didn't know the runway number of El Maghreb or the frequency of the radiobeacon there, she sure as hell wouldn't understand the complexity of inertial navigation procedures. Thankfully, Fadia didn't react. She didn't consider his action suspicious. She didn't notice that Mallory had programmed the INS computer with an Israeli destination.

Mallory disengaged the autopilot and turned once again toward the radiobeacon.

Plowing determinedly through the storm at 5,000 feet, the big machine angled its wings and turned to the new heading.

Mallory caressed his chin.

It *had* to work. He had told Fadia the truth: there wouldn't be sufficient fuel for a third landing attempt. So if they failed this time, the last gallons of kerosene would be sucked away during the climbcut, when a 747 consumes fuel at several times the normal cruise rate.

An unpleasant thought. No one had ever made a dead-stick landing in a 747. He shook his head as if dismissing the notion.

The ADF needle began its snake dance again. It was hard on the eyes, watching it. But necessary. Ah . . . it snapped one hundred eighty degrees. Simultaneously, Mallory pushed the Insert button on the INS keyboard. Thus he informed the electronic brain of the precise location of the aircraft so that the errors that inevitably crept in during a long flight would be erased and the computer could start its work anew. Next, he inserted the longitude and latitude of the airport, selecting a final approach course of 130 degrees, the direction of Ramat Shamon's runway thirteen. In theory, the INS would lead the 747 through the murk to a rendezvous with the concrete strip. With the added precision,

Mallory elected to descend to a lower altitude when on final approach, two hundred feet . . . until the runway was in sight.

Mallory closed his eyes for a long moment, resting them for the task ahead. The INS would keep telling him his precise distance from the airport, in tenths of a mile. In theory, then, he could gauge his descent with accuracy. The big questions were: Would he be able to see the runway in time? How violent would the storm be at the time of touchdown? And would he be able to get the airplane down on the first part of the runway so that there would be enough room to stop the hurtling mass before it ran out of concrete?

And would the runway take the 747's weight?

And . . .

God, no; no more unanswerable questions.

Ten miles from the beacon. Mallory turned to a heading of three-five-five degrees.

Flaps, gear, speed brakes, cabin signs, hydraulics . . .

Now the 747 was turning to the left, sweeping through 180 degrees to head back toward the final approach course to the runway.

* * *

Mr. Squires pulled his seat belt extra tight and gazed up at the ceiling, trying to persuade himself that he was enjoying a ride on an elephant in India, perched up high in the *howdah,* a regal personage, object of envy and awe, nodding charitably to the mere peasants on the roadside. It began to work quite well. The motions of the 747 were not dissimilar to those of the elephant. He could almost smell the peculiar mixture of incense and elephant dung; a dusky Indian princess was suddenly beside him in the *howdah,* eyes moist with admiration. . . .

But Mrs. Lefler chose that precise moment to announce that she wasn't feeling well.

Mr. Squires said he was sure she would be all right.

"I don't think so," she said. She had turned a yellowish gray. She turned to Mr. Squires and started to say something else.

But she didn't have time. In one ghastly convulsion, she

demonstrated just how unwell she felt.

For once Mr. Squires was speechless.

Recovering with remarkable rapidity, Mrs. Lefler spluttered an apology and started dabbing at Mr. Squires' suit with a Kleenex.

"It'll dab off," she assured him.

"Dab?" he said. *"That?"*

"I should think so," she replied, unabashed.

He felt his hands assuming the approximate circumference of Mrs. Lefler's neck. Never before had the desire to kill surged so potently through his nervous system.

"Excuse me," he snapped and unfastened his seat belt.

He got to his feet and started for the nearest lavatory.

He got about six feet.

Then the aircraft lurched. His legs buckled beneath him. In an instant he was flat on the floor, rolling against a fat man's legs.

Now a stewardess was shrieking at him from a seat.

"You mustn't get out of your seat, sir!"

"What?" He was dazed.

"Regulations, sir! You could get killed walking around in this turbulence!"

"But my suit!"

Again the plane staggered in the sky. Mr Squires felt himself flung off the floor like the female partner in an Apache dance. Frantically, he grabbed at the nearest handhold. It was the stewardess' skirt. It ripped, but it stopped him from being dashed against the ceiling. Mr. Squires found himself draped over a seat, his head in someone's lap.

Hands grasped him and thrust him back into his seat. The seat belt was fastened about his middle.

"Thank you . . . thank you," he gasped, breathless. God, a fellow could be killed in this crazy contraption! He shut his eyes. Tightly. His sanity was in imminent danger of snapping, like a rubber band stretched too far. Was it possible that the whole thing was an incredibly bad dream? The product of some visceral upheaval? He opened his eyes. No, unhappily, the swaying, yawing tube was still there, still crammed with people, still stinking of their vomit. The flying torture chamber. And Mrs.

Lefler was still there too, still babbling, now saying she felt a little better and that there was no question that the mess would dab off in no time flat, absolutely.

The drunk from across the aisle proffered his bottle.

"Nothing to drink, thank you," replied Mr. Squires.

"Steadies the old stomach. Listen, have you ever been in Buffalo, New York?"

"Not for many years, I'm delighted to say."

"Great town."

"Really?"

"You bet!" The man frowned. "You know you dropped something on your suit?"

* * *

"Well you might say that first pass was a reconnaissance, ladies and gentlemen. We wanted to look over the field and make sure that everything would be okay for our landing. This time we'll be landing for sure. It's going to be bumpy again, all the way down, so keep your seat belts as tight as you can pull them. We will be landing in just a few minutes now. Don't be alarmed if we touch down a little harder than usual. In these conditions it's important to put the airplane firmly on the ground so the gusts don't get an opportunity to blow us around. And I must remind you, ladies and gentlemen, to remain in your seats after landing. It's vital for the safety of everyone aboard. Okay, just hang on for a few more minutes and we'll be on good old solid Mother Earth again. See you later."

Jensen shifted uncomfortably in his seat; as he did so, he glanced at his watch.

"Behind schedule?"

Jensen smiled crookedly. "I was just wondering what time it is at home. Silly, I guess."

No, Mallory thought, not silly.

"Five miles on the nose."

Mallory nodded, his eyes darting from dial to dial, checking airspeed, rate of descent, altitude and attitude. The 747 was nicely set up for the descent, or as nicely as she could be, slogging her gallant way down through this maelstrom. She would, with luck, meet the runway in just two minutes.

Two vital minutes. It had to be right this time. Another attempt was out of the question.

Please, INS.

But even if the INS did its stuff, he still might not be able to see the goddam runway when he reached it.

Then what?

And suppose all this thumping and banging had affected the operation of the INS? It was part machine, for God's sake; those delicately balanced gyroscopes and accelerometers could only take so much. . . .

Correct, it was indeed possible that things were no longer working properly. Probable, even. But it wasn't worth thinking about because it would almost certainly mean that the landing would have to be aborted and that would almost certainly mean that the airplane would run out of fuel while it was bumbling about in the goddam, stinking storm and that would almost certainly mean that it would hit the desert with an almighty bang which would almost certainly mean that no one on the airplane would ever be faced with another problem ever again in all the eons of eternity. . . .

No doubt it would all be blamed on pilot error. A foolhardy attempt by the captain. Ill-judged in the extreme. Unwise. Poor judgment. The investigating committees had their own jargon for the verbal crucifixion of those who erred.

"Four miles."

"Nice day to go flying, huh?"

"Wouldn't have missed it."

"I figured."

The same swirling, dancing sand; still doing its evil best to hypnotize him.

Now the turbulence was even more violent, as if the storm knew it might have only a moment or two left in which to tear the persistent airplane apart.

Below him, the floor seemed to crack. The flight deck shuddered.

This airplane, he thought, is going to need a complete overhaul after this. And so am I.

"Three miles to go," said Jensen. Still the INS dutifully ticked off the digits, representing the shrinking distance to Ramat Shamon.

Any time now the field could come into view. He peered until his eyes stung. Could you injure your eyes by staring too hard? It would, he thought, be a hell of a time to go blind.

Sand. Wall after wall of it. Looming, hurling, parting. The lousy stuff was thicker, wilder than before. Christ, the goddam visibility was nil!

"Jeez, I don't know, Skipper. . . ."

A let's-abandon-the-whole-thing voice from Mr. Jensen.

Maybe he was right.

"Your speed's slipping down to one-two-five. . . "

"Yeah." More power.

"That's better. One-forty. Two miles."

Jensen leaned forward, biting his lower lip, contorting it.

Mallory found himself remembering his first solo landing. The same soul-chilling tension. But, for God's sake, he could at least see what the hell he was going to land on. . . .

The INS could have been banged out of alignment. It could be taking them straight into a hill, for Christ's sake! This was suicidal!

"It's got to be wrong. . . ." Now Mr. Jensen was thinking the same way. Mutual panic.

One mile. Altitude, three hundred feet.

God, please let's see something through this mess; if we don't...

"There! Yeah!"

Dead ahead. Bless the INS's little metal heart!

And there were lights—pale, watery things—on one side of the runway. A blurring instant later, Mallory saw the truck behind them. A man was leaning out of the cab, waving.

"Jesus—on the nose!" Jensen pointed, grinning, fully awake now.

Weirdly, the scene seemed to halt for a fraction of a moment, an infinitesimal fragment of time. There was no color; the layers of sand and dust had excised it. The truck, the man waving, the concrete strip: gray and lifeless, a still from an old black-and-white movie.

"Hang on!"

Why the hell did he say that? What choice did they have, for Christ's sake?

No flaring out just above the runway, no gentle kissing of the concrete with the tires. Forget smoothness, forget finesse. The object of the exercise was simply to reconnect the airplane with solid ground as rapidly and as firmly as humanly possible. . . .

The concrete ribbon sped beneath him. Dirty, smeared by rivulets of curving, twisting sand. The number "13" almost illegible, the paint dulled and chipped. Potholes, chunks missing from the runway's surface. Too late to worry about them.

Now!

The truck vanished behind.

Power off. Down!

The aircraft's sixteen-wheel main gear took the impact. And shuddered. The structure howled, agonized. Wings flexed as if the plane was readying itself to take to the air again. The nose dipped, the front landing gear bottoming noisily. For a frightening instant it sounded as if the nosewheel had failed.

More than one passenger thought the airplane had crashed. Surely such a bang, such a crunch couldn't be intentional. Then relief replaced alarm. The airplane was unquestionably traveling along a runway. On earth. On fantastically, beautifully, absolutely solid earth! They were down!

Now the engines roared into reverse, dragging at the speeding monster, fighting its colossal momentum. The din was frightful: sand and dust exploded around the screaming turbines. Then, unbelievably, it seemed to be over; it was just a normal landing now.

Someone cheered. Someone else started to applaud.

Then everyone was clapping and cheering. God, it was marvelous to feel the solidity of terra firma. No more bouncing. How delicious breathing was!

On the flight deck, Mallory worked the brakes without mercy. No doubt they were glowing down there, smoldering, voicing their complaints about such abuse. But he had no choice. He just didn't know how much runway remained. He couldn't see the end of it; it kept unwinding, a gray, scarred ribbon that disappeared somewhere in the uncomfortably near distance.

But at last the aircraft's momentum was tamed. She became docile, trundling along like a huge baby carriage. The end of the runway came in view.

Time to relax. For the moment.

"Nice work, Steve," said Nowakoski with fervor. "Goddam nice work."

"Amen to that," breathed Jensen.

Fadia came forward. "You did well. I knew you could manage it." She gestured with the pistol. "Everyone remains in his seat."

Nowakoski assured her he wasn't planning on going anywhere.

Jensen pointed. A truck.

A signalman stood beside it, beckoning with his batons: the 747 was to turn off to the right.

"Your friends are waiting for you," said Mallory.

"Of course they are," she said. She sounded brighter. You could feel the relief in her every movement. Soon the last, big responsibility would be lifted from her shoulders.

"This is the terminal?" Jensen wondered aloud.

Fadia told him not to question the signalman; he was to be obeyed.

Mallory frowned, biting his lip. As the 747 came to a halt, armed men swarmed forward—and, God, they looked uncomfortably like Palestinian guerillas, each man with an *okal* on his head and a Soviet AKM 7.62-mm assault rifle in hand. Uncertainty gnawed at him. Where had he landed? Could the INS have led him miles off course? Anything was possible under these crazy conditions. Even the ultimate irony was possible: the INS might have taken them straight to El Maghreb.

He couldn't bear to think about it.

He told Jensen to shut down the airplane.

Then he picked up the public address handset. "This is the captain, ladies and gentlemen. I apologize for the horrible landing but there wasn't much we could do about it. We've arrived in Jordan." He took a deep breath. "At a place called El Maghreb. In a few moments Arab troops or PLO people—I really don't know who—will be coming aboard the airplane. Remain in your seats, please. I believe the Pope will be taken off the plane very shortly. Please don't make any attempt to interfere. You won't help things. We're going to witness a despicable act, but there's nothing we can do about it. I want to emphasize that fact, ladies and gentlemen. You can't fight heavily armed men with bare fists and purses. We've obeyed their demands because we had no choice. Now, I don't believe that the hijackers have any further interest in us. But we'll determine this just as quickly as we can. I want to apologize for this happening on our flight. I thank you for your courage and forbearance. I know these last few hours haven't been easy for any of you. You're a great group. Now I want one more thing from you: I want you to remain in your seats until we tell you otherwise. Thanks. We'll be talking to you again very soon."

Jensen and Nowakoski were intoning the technicalities of the shutdown checklist as if this had been a normal landing at a normal airport.

"Speed brakes?"

"Down."

"Flaps?"

"Up."

"Radar?"

"Standby."

"Ignition?"

"Off."

Fadia's finger jabbed Mallory's shoulder. She demanded that he instruct the cabin crew to be ready to open the forward door when she so ordered.

He nodded, preferring not to look directly at her. He passed the instruction to Dee Pennetti via the interphone.

Now Fadia was rapping out orders to the men in the lounge area.

One man entered the flight deck, machine pistol raised.

Jensen and Nowakoski continued:

"Start levers?"

"Cutoff."

"Window heat?"

"Off."

"Probe heat?"

"Off."

"Oxygen regulators?"

"Off."

Another truck moved in on the 747. More armed men. Palestinians?

They sure as hell looked the part. Maybe Mallory didn't fool anyone. Maybe they knew what he was doing all along—and sent an invasion force to occupy Ramat Shamon just long enough. . . .

Nowakoski said, "Secure Cockpit Checklist complete."

At last the long flight from Rome was over.

chapter 21

She slept fitfully while he drove. Strange, disjointed bits of dreams floated through her mind. Swimming against impossible currents; parking her car and not being able to remember where; dancing with a man who had four feet; trying to fire a revolver with a broken trigger. . . .

It was a relief to wake up. She blinked the sleepiness out of her eyes.

"You dozed."

"Sorry," she said.

"It's all right."

"Are we nearly there?"

"I think so. We've just come off the Bay Bridge."

"I guess our friend is still watching the movie."

He smiled.

It was nearly two o'clock. In a few hours, the first glimmerings of dawn would be visible over the coastal mountains. Another day. Second in the new series. She switched on the radio. There was still no additional news of substance concerning the kidnapping of the Pope. The hijacked airliner was said to be heading for an undisclosed destination. According to the newscaster, Black September had claimed responsibility for the hijacking, but the terrorists' demands had not yet been made public. Another station mentioned an unconfirmed report of a shoot-out at a farmhouse near Salinas. Further details would be forthcoming.

He said, "They should have landed by now."

"Where?"

"In Jordan."

246

"Will they take the Pope somewhere?"

"Yes."

"And will they let the others go?"

"Yes."

The lights of an airplane slid through the night above them, heading east.

She thought of her father. God, if only he knew what she was doing: riding along with a Black September terrorist. And *liking* it, in spite of everything. Mentally she shook herself. She was absolutely nuts; the man was armed and dangerous as hell. No one in his right mind . . . then perhaps her mind was no longer right. . . .

He touched her hand, squeezing it gently.

"It is all very confusing," he said.

"Confusing?"

"I do not know precisely what is so different about you, yet you are the one woman who has made me wonder."

"Wonder about what?"

"About . . . my purpose in life. I vowed that I would never let any woman interfere with that."

"Have I interfered?"

"You have. You have made me think seriously of abandoning my duty and my comrades and running off somewhere with you."

On second thought, maybe it wasn't so crazy to be here with him; in fact, the more you thought about it, the more exciting it became. . . .

"So let's do it," she said.

"It would be very pleasant."

Would be? She waited for the inevitable "but."

"But," he said, "I must tell you that I don't think it is possible."

"Why?"

"Because I am what I am and you are what you are."

"Why go back?" She caught his arm and ran her fingers along it. "You've done enough. Hell, if you go back, you'll get yourself killed. I couldn't bear it."

"How would you know if I were killed?"

"I don't know, but I think I would. Somehow. For God's sake, think about living your own life for a change. Let's go away together."

"Where would we go?"

"I've been thinking. We could head up into the Sierras. Rent a cabin for a while. No one would know we were there."

"How long would we stay?"

"I don't know. A week. A month. We could decide later."

"I think people would get suspicious if we stayed long."

"So we'll go somewhere else."

"Where?"

"This is a big country. There are a million places to hide."

"And would we settle down in one of these million places and live happily ever after?"

The odd thing was, his voice didn't mock. It was as if he genuinely wanted to know.

"It's possible," she said.

"But the police and the FBI and God only knows who else will be looking for me, and I don't think they will be satisfied until they find me."

"Maybe they'll never find you. Lots of people have never been found."

He had slowed the car. Now he rolled it on to a shoulder and stopped.

"It's a delicious dream," he said, cupping her face in his hands and kissing her.

"We can make it happen."

He sighed, leaning back until he was staring at the roof of the car.

"It's extraordinary," he said slowly, softly. "Never in my wildest dreams did I ever imagine this dilemma. I was far too strong ever to be diverted by a woman. Women were to be petted and bedded, then forgotten. And an *American* woman at that!"

"Three cheers for the red, white and blue!"

He grinned in his boyish way, then kissed her again. "I don't think there can be another woman in the world quite like you."

"Thank you."

He gazed at her. "I'm not at all sure it is a compliment. You are a temptress. You are leading me astray."

"You led me astray."

"So I did."

"I'd like to go astray again. Now."

"Now? Here?"

"Why not?"

"I can think of a number of reasons."

"Name some."

"This is a main highway and the cops will undoubtedly catch us in the act, so to speak."

"If they do catch us," she said, wagging a triumphant finger, "they'll never think for a moment that you're on the run."

He shook his head in admiration. "There's a kind of lunatic logic in what you say!"

They kissed again, fiercely this time. His hand grabbed her breast, his fingers caressing the nipple through the thin material of her shirt. Suddenly he pulled away.

"God, I am definitely going crazy!" He laughed, a booming, wholehearted laugh. "It is, however, a most pleasant form of lunacy. Come on; let's get out of here. We're driving a stolen car. I think it would be sensible if we remembered that. You drive for a while. Okay?"

"Sure you wouldn't rather stay here and get laid?"

"Of course I would prefer it. But I think you'd better be patient. I have to see the man at North Allwyn."

"Is this guy so important?"

At once she regretted asking the question. It sounded too much like interrogation, prying for information, compiling dossiers and reports. . . .

"He's important to me; I must see him. He will help. He'll give me money and another car. We'll need those things if we are to get away from here . . . together."

Her heart bounded. "You mean it?"

"Perhaps; I don't know. I must hide somewhere. Why not in the mountains with you?"

"But . . . this man you're going to see—will he go along with the idea?"

"He is not my commander. He is a sympathizer. I am going

to see him only because he can tell my superiors that I am alive. They, I hope, will convey the news to my father."

"And as soon as you're through with him, can we leave?"

"Yes, of course." He smiled. He was happy, she could tell.

"We'll find a place to go." She gripped the wheel hard, as if clutching reality. The headlights gobbled up the white line, faster and faster as she accelerated. God knows what tomorrow would bring. To hell with it. She would worry about tomorrow tomorrow.

* * *

It was a quiet street: typically middle-class homes with neat, well-trimmed lawns and late-model automobiles in orderly driveways.

Nothing distinguished 1347 from the others. It might have been the residence of a store manager or an accountant. Perhaps it was, Jane thought as the car slowed. An ordinary businessman by day, terrorist by night. . .

They stopped, but the engine still ran.

He looked the house over. It was in darkness. Jane looked at the windows. She thought she saw the stirring of a drape.

He pulled out his shirt and slipped the gun inside, under his belt.

"Shall I stay here?" she asked.

He looked at her a moment, thoughtfully. Then he shook his head.

"No, you come too."

He reached over and switched off the ignition. There was a weary clattering as the engine died; it sounded as if parts were loose and ready to fall off. Perhaps they were. But Jane felt an odd affection for the old Plymouth. It had served them well.

"Let's go."

She got out of the car. The air was sweet and cool. She thought she heard voices, but then she realized it was the breeze feeling its gentle way through the trees above her.

Abou Gabal took her arm. Tenderness? Security? She wondered whether to ask him but decided not to.

"Everyone asleep?" she whispered.

"I doubt it."

The crunching of the gravel beneath their feet reminded her of stepping in frozen snow.

"Don't be afraid," he told her. His face was marblelike in the soft moonlight. It was beautiful enough to be sculptured: a perfect balance of convexities and concavities, the shadows creating a delicate pattern around his eyes and mouth.

She told him she wasn't the least bit afraid; he nodded approvingly and pressed the doorbell.

The door opened at once. A short, middle-aged man stood there. His hair was gray, but he had a thick black mustache. He wore a purple robe and bedroom slippers.

The two men exchanged a few words in Arabic. They spoke in low, cautious tones, with glances toward the street. Then the man beckoned.

Again Abou Gabal took her arm as he guided her inside.

The man regarded her with ill-concealed suspicion. He closed the door.

Abou Gabal said something to the man, something about her, mentioning her name. The man shrugged but didn't look at her.

They were shown into a small room that seemed to be an office. A desk stood against one wall, but there were no papers on it, just a telephone, a radio and a leather notepad. Jane looked around, vaguely expecting pictures of Yasser Arafat and posters condemning Israel. But the only wall decoration was a set of old English hunting prints, handsomely framed. Although the room was furnished, it had an oddly sterile look, like something out of a home show.

"Can I get you something?" asked the man, in near perfect English.

Abou Gabal shook his head. "You?" he asked Jane.

"No thanks, nothing." The only thing she wanted was to get the hell out of this damned house as rapidly as possible.

The man was shaking his head. "It is a bad business," he said in English to Abou Gabal.

"You know what happened?"

The man nodded. "A late-breaking newscast just gave some details of the raid. You were indeed fortunate to escape with your life."

"I suppose so."

"You are sure you were not followed?"

"Of course." Abou Gabal sounded irritated that the question had to be asked.

"Where do you propose to go?"

"To the mountains, I think."

"With her?"

A nod.

"I am not sure that is wise."

"She can be trusted, I am sure."

The man examined his fingernails. He was silent for some moments. When he began to talk again he spoke in Arabic. His tone was soft, but there was heavy emphasis on certain words. As he spoke, Abou Gabal listened intently, frowning, evidently pained by what the man said. Now the tone became even quieter. Abou Gabal, still frowning, kept glancing at Jane.

Fear jabbed her like a battery of needles.

He turned to her. He said nothing. He just looked.

"What is it?"

Still he said nothing. His breathing was harsh and loud; his face reddened.

Now the middle-aged man sat down at his desk and folded his arms. Outside, a car passed by.

Somewhere in the house a clock chimed.

Abou Gabal turned away and then swung back at her.

"You miserable bitch!" He spat out the words.

"What do you mean?"

"You know. You damn well know."

"No . . . I don't know what the hell you're talking about."

He pointed at the man but still kept his eyes fixed on her. "He told me. The whole world knows what happened. The boy. Escaping up the chimney. He wasn't asleep in the room at all, was he? In fact, he wasn't even *in* the room. And you knew it! All the time. . . ."

"But you see . . . ."

"You diverted my attention. That was your job, wasn't it?"

His dark eyes seemed to bore into her.

"No . . . not a *job;* it wasn't like that at all. . . ."

She tried to explain; he had to understand. There was more to it than that, much more, for God's sake, surely he could see that.

But he didn't listen.

"They are dead because of you! My comrades! To think that I began to trust you. . . ."

"No, you must understand . . . please. . . !"

"Deceitful, lying *cunt!"*

She reached out, trying to touch him to reestablish the contact that had existed between them. But already he was dragging the gun out of his shirt. . . .

*   *   *

A man appeared in the left aisle of the 747. Young, dark, wearing a sport jacket and an open-neck shirt. He carried a machine pistol. He pointed it at the passengers, waving it slowly and deliberately from row to row, like a wizard with a wand. With his free hand, he ripped and tugged the curtains that separated first class from coach. Behind him, men in clerical garb looked back from their seats, their eyes wide with apprehension.

Now a woman appeared in the right aisle. A young, quite beautiful woman. She too carried a pistol.

She spoke in a strong, clear voice. "If any of you makes any attempt to get out of your seat, you will be shot. Is that understood?"

Mrs. Lefler nodded obediently.

Mr. Squires thought the girl resembled a dark Ursula Andress. Remarkable resemblance.

A man raised his hand like a kid at school, wanting to go to the bathroom. "How long are you going to keep us here?"

"Until we let you go," the girl replied.

Snappy dialogue, thought Mr. Squires.

An elderly voice, cracking with emotion: "What are you going to do with the Pope?"

"That is none of your concern."

"It is! How dare you touch him. You are not worthy to touch him!"

"Silence!"

"Devil! Evil devil!"

She raised the pistol with both hands and fired. Once.

A single gasp seemed to burst from the passengers.

Mr. Squires winced. He heard the bullet snapping through the air above his head. It made a neat hole in a utility compartment door.

There was utter silence, broken only by the whistling of the wind and the clatter of the trucks outside. The woman had made her point. She turned and went forward through first class. She gestured. Two stewardesses opened the forward passenger door, admitting a blast of sand-laden wind. A newspaper fluttered like some wounded bird.

Mr. Squires swallowed. It was sobering, having a bullet pass by that closely. He glanced through the side window. Trucks were maneuvering toward the nose of the 747; a bevy of villainous-looking characters hurried about, waving submachine guns.

He tried to make a mental note of everything he saw. It all had to be mentally catalogued and stored away: great stuff for the Carson show. In fact, it was probable that every talk show on TV would be after him to recount his experiences. Actually, the whole thing could turn out to be a very good thing, careerwise. It was indeed an ill wind. . .

*   *   *

Balancing himself on the roof of the truck, the colonel reached out and touched the airplane's metal skin. His fingers closed on the doorway frame. He straightened up. The cabin floor was only a couple of feet above the truck roof: no problem, thank God, to jump aboard the aircraft—or out of it.

In the doorway above him stood the statues. Statues with tense, strained faces. Their eyes were fixed on him. A woman—dark, attractive, but for her grimly determined mouth; a tough-looking young man in a sports jacket; armed, both of them. An

Burly. Angry. But still not quite believing what was happening.

Pistol up and aimed.

Adroitly, the Pope extended his left leg.

The man tripped. Stumbled. Thudded into the wall of the aircraft. At once a pair of commandos were on him, pinning him, helpless.

The colonel scrambled to his feet.

"Thank you very much, sir."

The Pope was unabashed. "I can't deny that it was something of a pleasure."

* * *

Above, in the cockpit, the guard leveled his gun at the crew members, the barrel moving jerkily from man to man.

"Don't move a fucking inch," he snapped, wincing as each shot cracked out on the lower level.

"Seems to be somewhat of a problem down there," Mallory observed.

"Shut your mouth!" He was young—and suddenly very frightened. Everything was going terribly wrong. "Don't move!" he ordered again. Then, trembling like a kid who has done wrong and fears punishment, he hurried aft, into the lounge area. Mallory could see him, peering down the spiral stairway.

More shots. Feet scuffling.

Confused bastard, thought Mallory, he doesn't know what the hell to do.

At that moment Nowakoski got out of his seat. He took the fire extinguisher off the wall and checked its pressure gauge. He accorded it a curt little nod. Then, almost mechanically, he walked out of the cockpit door, carrying the extinguisher with care, as one might carry a large valuable vase.

After a few more careful steps, the engineer said,

"Hey, mister!"

The hijacker turned.

Nowakoski had already swung the extinguisher. It hit the man full in the face. He folded like a rag doll tossed into the corner. The extinguisher fell, struck the floor and burst into life, spraying chemical down the stairway. Nowakoski grabbed it and directed it at the hijacker; stunned, half-drowned, the man could only wave his arms in feeble protest.

Mallory picked the man's gun from the floor. He wondered if there was any trick to firing a machine pistol. Did you just pull the trigger? Or were there any special gadgets to operate first?

"Nice work," he said to Nowakoski.

Nowakoski smiled nervously and looked at the terrorist as if not quite believing what he had done.

* * *

The girl was dead, her companions neutralized. Suddenly there seemed to be no one else to fight.

The colonel glanced into the passenger cabin. No sign of trouble in that direction; just a lot of terrified civilians. And a lot of holes in the airplane.

"Are there more hijackers aboard?" he asked the stewardess.

"What are you talking about?" The girl seemed dazed. "Who the hell are *you?*"

"I'm an Israeli commando."

"Israeli? You don't look . . ."

"Fancy costume," said the colonel. "I assure you we are Israelis. Now, tell me, are there any more hijackers aboard the airplane?"

The girl nodded. "Upstairs, I think, At least one more." Her eyes returned to the body of Fadia. Ugly, bloody. The Pope and another cleric were kneeling beside her.

"Where?"

"Upstairs. The flight deck."

The colonel nodded. He looked up the stairway. Narrow as hell.

"Is there another way up there?"

The girl shook her head.

The colonel beckoned to two of his men. Damned stairway. You were never more vulnerable than when trotting up a thing like this. But he had no choice. Someone had to go.

"Follow me."

Up the steps, darting from side to side, anticipating, almost *feeling,* the hail of bullets. Behind him there was the comforting clatter of his commandos' boots.

But there was to be no shooting.

"Welcome aboard."

A smiling man in airline uniform stood at the top of the stairs.

"Good day," said the colonel.

"We've taken care of this one." The pilot indicated a young man in a sports jacket, slumped against a bulkhead, barely conscious. He was drenched; blood mingled with the extinguisher chemical soaking his head.

In moments, a trio of commandos had secured the prisoner.

"I'm Mallory, the captain. I hope to hell you're Israelis."

"Yes, yes. . . I'm Colonel Gelner, Israeli Army." Relief made him want to laugh; he satisfied himself with a grin. "You did well. Are there any more of those bastards around?"

"Not up here. There was just this one. And he seems to have lost interest in things. Everything all right below? We heard a lot of shooting."

"It's all over," nodded the colonel. "You are safe in Israel. Great work, Captain; you did brilliantly."

"You did all right yourself," said Mallory, smiling. "You sure as hell look the part."

"I almost blew everything," the colonel confessed, fingering his Star of David. "But we were lucky." Then he became aware of the extraordinary locker room scene in the lounge area. He blinked. Naked men were scrambling about, sorting out items of clothing.

"We're Secret Service," one of the men announced. "My name's Cousins. Is the Pope all right?"

"Yes."

"Thank God. Anyone hurt?"

"The girl's dead, I think."

Mallory nodded. "Under the circumstances, I'll bet she's glad she is."

"Who cares whether she's glad or not?" The colonel felt strongly about such things. "She was a dangerous, murdering bitch and the world is a better place without her."

"Yeah, but she had great tits," remarked another man in airline uniform, a stocky fellow whose hands shook and who kept grinning then frowning then grinning again.

"This is Mr. Nowakoski, our flight engineer," said Mallory. "He was responsible for the assault with the fire extinguisher."

"Good work, sir."

The engineer shrugged. "It was nothing."

He seemed to be suffering from a slight case of shock. It was understandable.

They stood aside as commandos dragged the groaning, dripping hijacker down the steps.

The Secret Service men seemed unsure what had happened.

"You're an Israeli officer, right?"

"Correct, sir."

"And we're in Jordan. Is that right?"

"No. We're in Israel. But you'd better ask Captain Mallory about that. He deserves all the credit."

The colonel followed the others down the stairs. He felt good. All in all, it had gone far more smoothly than he had dared hope.

* * *

Mr. Squires peered cautiously over the seat back.

The shooting seemed to have stopped. There was still a lot of movement up in the nose of the airplane, but the guns were silent. So, presumably, someone had won. But who? What was going to happen now? The Pope could be seen near the open door, the wind catching at his white robes. The odd thing was, all the priests and clerics seemed to be grinning. One of them was chatting in what could only be described as a thoroughly friendly way with one of the Palestinians. It looked like a class reunion up there.

Then, astonishingly, one of the Arab soldiers came bounding into the coach compartment. Laughing at the passengers, he ripped off his headgear.

"It's okay," he cried. "I'm Israeli!" He pointed at himself, still laughing. "I'm Israeli!"

"Israeli?" said Mr. Squires. "You're an Israeli?"

"What'd he say?" Mrs. Lefler still crouched on the floor. "What'd he say?"

Another passenger asked the soldier to repeat himself.

For some reason the man seemed to find the request hilarious.

Mr. Squires asked, "Are we in Jordan?"

"No. Not Jordan. Israel."

"Where's Jordan?"

"There." Grinning, the soldier pointed. "Not far. You want to go?"

Mr. Squires shook his head. Through the window he could see the trucks and the tough-looking armed men, apparently ready to machine-gun anyone at the drop of a hat.

He noted too that the storm seemed to be abating. The wind was losing its ferocity; he could see the outlines of ramshackle buildings in the distance.

An elderly male passenger was talking to the soldier in what sounded like Hebrew. Both men laughed. Gleefully.

The old man turned to the other passengers. "A trick!" he announced, his hands spread wide as if to show they were empty. "They tricked the hijackers! We are free!"

Free? What was the old guy babbling about?

Then a stewardess came back from the nose section. Grinning, undeniably grinning.

"Good God," muttered Mr. Squires. Could it be true?

"What's happening? I can't see. For God's sake, what's happening?" Crouched in a self-protective ball on the floor between the seats, Mrs. Lefler squealed her questions up at him, her scarlet mouth opening and closing like that of a baby bird in the nest asking for more. "Why don't you tell me what's happening?"

"Because I don't know!" Mr. Squires looked at the stewardess again. She was still smiling, as she was chatting to passengers. "But, I think . . ."

"What do you think? What? What?"

"I think," said Mr. Squires, "we may be all right."

And at that precise moment the shot rapped out.

The Israeli soldier slumped sideways to the floor, a bullet hole in his forehead.

Across the aisle from Mr. Squires, the drunk had risen. And suddenly he was no longer the wobbly-limbed, slack-jawed idiot. He was alert and vigorous.

He had a gun in his hand. It seemed to have materialized from nowhere; it jutted from his fist, ugly and angular.

Mr. Squires stared.

"Anyone moves, they get it!" the man yelled.

The heads of nearby passengers seemed to sway back from him in concert.

"What's happening now?" Mrs. Lefler shrieked.

The man turned. He could see her, crouched down. Perhaps he thought she was concealing a weapon. He didn't stop to ask. He shot her, twice.

The bullets sliced through the air only inches in front of Mr. Squires.

Mrs. Lefler emitted a tiny croak, then she was silent. Her head rolled forward; her fist opened slowly.

The man ignored her. He thrust his way through first class into the nose section, holding the gun with both hands and swaying it around him. Passengers and cabin crew fell back, terrified anew.

Mr. Squires watched, openmouthed. His eyes flew from the man to Mrs. Lefler, then back again to the man.

He shot her! Deliberately, mercilessly.

He still didn't quite believe it.

He blinked. The man was pointing his gun at the Pope now, yelling orders at the people around him.

Damn the man!

Outrage propelled Mr. Squires to his feet.

The nerve of the bastard! He must have been carrying that gun throughout the flight—and all the time pretending to be drunk!

And now—curse him!—he was wresting victory from the victors, dashing all the newborn hopes of so many brave, innocent people, who had been through so much. . . .

There he was, the eternal bully; having slaughtered a poor,

defenseless woman like Mrs. Lefler, he was now brandishing his gun, manhandling a kindly old guy who had never done anyone any harm. . . .

"You bastard," he said.

He found himself striding, filled with indignation, determined to set things straight.

"You son of a bitch!" he declaimed as he hurtled along the aisle. "How dare you!"

It was curiously reminiscent of many a first entrance on the stage. Heads turned in his direction, eyes lit up with recognition.

The man looked. He knew Mr. Squires.

He didn't hesitate.

Mr. Squires saw the flash in the gun's muzzle.

He was conscious of a *thing* in his chest, but for a strange, stretched moment he felt nothing. But everything had come to a halt. Around him, faces were frozen, arms outstretched.

"You son of a bitch," Mr. Squires wanted to say again. But the words wouldn't form. And then they really didn't matter anymore. There was no reason for words. Softness enveloped him.

He thought how his first wife would chuckle when she heard that he had been shot going to the aid of the *Pope,* of all people! And Mrs. *Lefler!* He couldn't *stand* the woman! Good grief!

The End. He could almost see it, centered, as if on a movie screen.

But, damn it all, he would have liked to have done that Carson show, to have sat down and told the whole story to the entire United States. . . .

* * *

The colonel was on the last step of the stairway when the man fired. An instant later he saw him, grabbing the Pope, thrusting him back against the wall of the aircraft near the open entrance door.

A dozen weapons were leveled at the man. But no one fired, for fear of hitting the Pontiff. The old man was bent back awkwardly, the terrorist's arm around his neck.

"If anyone gets in my way I kill him. Understand?"

He had an American accent. New York City. He was fortyish. A professional revolutionary? A mercenary?

"Don't be a fool," the colonel told him. "You're in Israel. We're not Arabs, we're Israeli commandos."

The man sneered. "And I bet you were goddam pleased with your little trick, weren't you?" He had edged along the wall of the aircraft until he and his hostage were beside the doorway. Fadia's body lay near his feet. He stepped over it. "But you're not going to get the last laugh, after all, asshole!" He threw a glance out the doorway. The weather was clearing rapidly. In the distance there were vehicles and troops lined up along an embankment. The Jordanians had deployed an armored unit along the border, between Ramat Shamon and El Maghreb. The colonel stared, concern growing within him. Was this thing going to erupt into war?

"I'll tell you something else," the man snapped. "I've got enough explosive around my body—taped around my waist—to convert this bucket into strips of aluminum foil. You guys put your guns down on the floor. Nice and easy. That's it. Now get back into the main cabin. Hands high, all of you."

A woman screamed, as if suddenly aware of the new danger.

The man motioned with his gun. "Get back. I told you. Get your asses back into the cabin or your next trip will be to the grave."

He was a burly man with florid cheeks. A powerful-looking individual. He wore a sports jacket, a white shirt and a spotted tie.

"You, you and you." He pointed; the pistol was like a finger. "Come here!"

The colonel started to protest. "Leave the passengers out of it. . . "

The man fired two shots. One disappeared cleanly through the aircraft's skin; the second hit something in the galley and snapped angrily through metal components.

More shrieks.

"Now! Move it!"

Tired, frightened people: two men, two women; they

shuffled uneasily into the nose section. They were forced to form a shield around the hijacker.

He pointed at the colonel.

"Tell your men to get the hell away from this airplane. If they're not moving in one minute flat, I let one of these characters have it."

"They're innocent people. . . ."

"So don't let them die."

It was hopeless. There was no choice. The bastard was clearly capable of killing anyone who got in his way.

"Over there," the hijacker indicated. "Over by the hangar."

The colonel complied. The hangar was completely visible now. The storm had abated totally in the sudden, unpredictable way of the *simoom*. Now the sand merely swirled around the soldiers' feet, playfully, as if trying to demonstrate that it had never meant any real harm.

"Leave one truck. And a driver." Then he turned to Mallory. "Get me a megaphone."

"Megaphone? We don't . . ."

The man's face twisted with anger. "Don't shit me, man! You're not dealing with an amateur. All U.S. airliners carry battery-powered megaphones, for emergencies. You do. So go and get me one of the fuckin' things!"

Mallory nodded at Dee. "Get him one."

The sun had broken through; it sparkled on the 747's broad wings. The entire expanse of the field could be seen. A bleak, windswept place.

The commandos pulled back, their eyes still on the aircraft.

"Faster! Get those bastards moving faster!"

The colonel so ordered.

The man shoved the Pope into the open doorway. "Stand right here and don't move. This way everyone can see you." The barrel of his machine pistol traversed the pale, tense faces. He took the megaphone that was handed to him. "All right, listen, everybody. I'm getting off this airplane in a minute, and I'm taking Jesus Christ here with me. Also these passengers. We're going to get in the truck and then we're going to take off. Now just remember that I've got enough high explosive tied around my body to blow us all to hell; so if anyone decides to take a pot shot at me, that's just what'll happen. Understand? You—" he pointed at the colonel "—you'd better tell your men that in your lingo. Here!"

He tossed the megaphone.

"Talk!"

The colonel hesitated. Rush the man? Gamble everything on a flurry of movements? No; the man had foreseen the possibility; hence the passengers around him. It would be impossible to get him without hitting them and the explosives.

The colonel nodded dumbly. He took the megaphone.

"Keep moving back toward the hangar," he ordered his men. "The hijacker will be leaving the airplane soon. He's got the Pope and claims to have high explosive around his body. He's going to make a dash for the Jordanian border. Make no attempt to stop him unless I give the order. That is all."

The Jordanian border. Hell, it was a short distance. A simple matter to get there in the truck. . . . The colonel's eyes narrowed. With every moment, the border could be seen more sharply. There were definite—and disquieting—signs of movement over there. Men. Vehicles. Armor. A reception committee for the hero and his prize.

Despair was a sickening weight deep down in his guts. He had failed, totally, miserably, just when success had been so goddam close. . . .

It was his fault. He was to blame. He should have reasoned that the hijackers might have a back-up man in the passenger cabin. He should have been prepared. He could have shot the bastard down the moment he made his move. Inexcusable incompetence!

Awkward, fearful, the passengers stumbled out onto the truck roof, blinking in the sudden sunshine, wobbling on the thin metal surface, clutching at one another for support.

The man prodded the Pope with his gun.

"Your turn, Jesus."

"I'm desperately sorry," muttered the colonel.

"Do not blame yourself, my son."

"Move, for chrissake."

The Pope nodded and stepped forward. People on the truck roof helped him to step down.

The hijacker jumped down at the same instant, swinging quickly back to cover the colonel.

Gun your motor! The colonel silently pleaded with the truck driver. A sudden movement would send everyone tumbling off the roof. There might be a chance. . . .

Too late. The forlorn little assembly was already scrambling over the cab, down onto the hood, then to the ground. The passengers were ordered to get into the back of the truck; the Pope and his captor entered the cabin.

The motor clattered. With a groan and a heave, the truck struggled into motion, its wheels slipping on the loose sand.

Then it gathered speed and roared off along the taxiway, leaving a cloudy trail of dust.

A truck detached itself from the hangar and came roaring toward the aircraft.

Now everyone was around the colonel, talking, pointing, praying; some were relieved that the danger for them was over for the moment; a priest was in tears; he kept shaking his head as he watched the truck.

"Son of a bitch," muttered Mallory. "I thought we had them."

"You did well," said the colonel. "We failed you."

"The hell you did. It's my fault; I was told there was at least one more. . . ."

"I think we'd better disembark the passengers as fast as possible. God knows whether that guy left any explosives aboard. Okay with you, Captain?"

"What? Yes, yes, of course." Mallory nodded. "A good idea."

The first truck braked beside the 747. Commandos jumped out, their weapons ready. Most had already discarded the hated Palestinian headgear.

"Orders, sir?"

The colonel bit his lip. He wished he had some to give.

The storm might never have been. The sun beat down from a cloudless sky. It created a sharp shadow around the fleeing truck, a shadow that stretched and shrank as it sped over the undulating sand.

Not only do the terrorists get the Pope, the colonel thought bleakly, but they get their damned truck back as well.

But would they? He stared.

"Who's got field glasses?"

Someone handed him a pair of binoculars.

"The bastard's stuck."

So he was. He had turned off the airport taxiway and had attempted to strike out across the sand, direct to the border.

He had driven into deep sand. The wheels were spinning, sending up explosions of dust and sand.

So near—yet so far! The truck was up to its rear axle in the stuff! The frantic revvings of the motor were serving only to aggravate the situation.

The hijacker flung himself out of the cab. Angrily, he ordered the passengers out of the back. He made them push. But it was hopeless.

The colonel focused the glasses on the border. There were armored vehicles and steel-helmeted men. He swallowed. The Jordanian army! Poised and waiting.

God, it was maddening, being able to do nothing but stand and watch!

"He's going on foot!"

The ceremony was played out on the open sand. The hijacker and the Pope, backing away from the truck; the others moving away from it in the opposite direction, back toward the aircraft.

"I think we could pick him off from here, sir."

The colonel shook his head.

No, the Pope's slender figure was too close; besides, there was that damned *plastique* around the man's middle.

He watched the two figures as they stumbled on across the loose sand. The border looked so damnably close; surely they could reach out and touch it. . . .

"Sir, we can't let the bastard get away with it!"

Anguished, pained voices.

"What the hell do you suggest?"

"Something . . . anything's better than just *watching.*"

Now the figures seemed to submerge as if they were stepping into deep water.

"They're nearly there!"

A few more paces; down the slope to the dry river bed that defined the border. The Wadi Araba. And no doubt industrious cameramen with zoom lenses were diligently recording the moment for all the world to see.

They were out of sight now.

In a way, it was a relief.

It was possible to see the Jordanians on the embankment on the other side of the Wadi, still motionless, still waiting.

The colonel lowered his glasses.

The men still awaited orders. But he had none to give. It was total defeat. In spite of all the effort, all the initiative, all the courage, all the blood. . . .

Damn them.

Damn them, damn them, damn them. . . .

A single shot.

It shattered the suddenly-still air, reverberated across the empty sands, echoed within the ramshackle buildings on the other side of the field.

"What the hell . . ."

Every head turned.

The shot had come from the direction of the border.

"My God," said someone, almost reverently.

Another shot, sharp, incisive.

The Israeli colonel froze. Bastard! He was gawking like a tourist. Beckoning to the nearest commandos, he broke into a sprint toward one of the trucks. He jumped on the running board and pointed the direction to the startled driver.

"Go, man! Now!"

There wasn't time to see if any of the other men reached the truck. Already it was in motion. But the overly eager driver fed it too much power. It slithered on the loose sand, its rear end snaking as if trying to throw the colonel off.

"For God's sake . . ."

"Sorry, sir."

At last the tires found traction. With a final, convulsive slither, the truck accelerated.

"That way! Fast as you can go!"

The colonel pointed at the stalled truck halfway to the Jordanian border. Scattered about it, bewildered, frightened, were the hostages who had been taken from the aircraft. Poor bastards, they didn't know what was happening.

Who the hell did?

He clung to the truck as it left the taxiway and bounced onto the open sand. For a heart-stopping instant, his boot slipped off the running board and hit the speeding ground. A close call; damned close.

Past the hostages, ignoring their pleading looks. No time to worry about them.

Was there more shooting? It was impossible to tell in the rattling of the truck and the roar of the wind in his face.

The truck's pace slowed. The sand robbed the tires of their grip, nullifying their power; at last the truck came to a grinding halt.

And at that moment the figure appeared over a gentle incline.

A weary, elderly man, wearing white robes.

Alone.

The colonel stared. Good God Almighty, had the Pope *shot. . . ?* No; out of the question! Impossible!

He jumped off the running board. Yelling.

"Are you all right, sir?"

He tried to hurry, but the loose shifting surface was his undoing; he stumbled and fell.

"Are you hurt, young man?" There was genuine concern in the thin voice.

The colonel picked himself up and shook his head as he brushed the sand from himself.

"I am fine, sir. How about you?"

"I am unharmed," the Pope replied.

He was hot and pale with fatigue, but there was no sign of any injury.

"Thank God you're all right, sir. We thought . . ."

A commando ran up, stumbling behind the colonel. A fresh-faced boy, sweat pouring from every pore. He pointed.

"Look. Look, sir, what d'you make of that?"

The border was less than a hundred meters away. God only knows how many Jordanian troops were poised, arms at the ready. Half a dozen others were busy stuffing the hijacker's body into a truck.

A Jordanian officer, hand on holstered pistol, stood watching.

He turned toward the colonel and the Pope, snapped to attention and saluted.

The Israeli returned the salute and held it . . . totally bewildered.

Openmouthed, they watched. Truck doors slammed; motors clattered into life. Troops clambered aboard. Tanks and other armored vehicles moved back from their positions. In moments, it was all motion: vehicles wheeling, lining up, shifting position. Dust billowed as if there had been an explosion. The roar of the vehicles was deafening. Mechanical thunder. The desert seemed to tremble beneath the steel and rubber as the Jordanian convoy moved away.

Soon there was nothing but a pall of dust over the area and the dull rumble of engines in the distance.

The colonel shook his head.

"I don't understand. What on earth. . . ?"

The Pope reflected. "I can only presume that the Jordanian government despises this kind of terrorism as much as you Israelis do. My captor was shot dead the moment he set foot on Jordanian soil."

"But the explosive . . ."

"The Jordanian officer was a skilled marksman and caught the man completely off guard. Expecting an ally, he met his executioner. The Jordanian merely raised his pistol and shot the man in the head. I truly think he was dead before he hit the ground. In any event, the officer made sure with a second shot. Upon examination, it was found that the man was indeed carrying explosives." He wiped his brow with a handkerchief and took a deep breath of the arid air. "Tell me, young man, now that it is all over, is there any reason why I may not now continue my journey? Can you tell me how long it will take to travel from here to San Francisco?"

* * *

Tel Aviv was in an uproar. Crowds thronged the streets, cheering the commandos, the passengers and the Trans American crew. It was a day of joy! There was a victory to be celebrated, there were heroes to be féted!

Every news agency in the world clamored for information. How had Black September been outwitted? Who was responsible? Was the Pope harmed in any way? What was the price asked for his release? How many casualties? What was the identity of the actor rumored to be one of the casualties? Who were the hijackers? Was it true that at least one had been involved in the Olympic massacre at Munich?

On the third floor of the Tel Aviv Hilton, a stocky man in a well-cut business suit stood at the window and watched the arrival of the flight crew. He observed the wild enthusiasm of the crowd, the fluttering of hand-held Israeli and American flags, the arms outstretched, the faces wreathed in smiles.

But the man didn't smile.

Below, police formed an avenue through the crowd, through which the crew members made their way into the hotel lobby.

The man took a deep breath. As a representative of the United States State Department, you were handed some lousy assignments from time to time. This was the worst, bar none.

"They're coming straight up here?"

"Yes sir."

"I want to see Captain Mallory in here . . . alone!"

"I know, sir. It's been arranged."

"Thank you."

He sat down and closed his eyes. Only a few moments left. How the hell do you break such news to a man? Especially a man who has just pulled off a totally brilliant effort like this, possibly saving hundreds of lives and probably averting an explosive confrontation in the Middle East. . . .

How would he react?

Would he be angry at the deception, the *lie* that had been transmitted to the aircraft? Would he be outraged? Or would he simply cry?

Didn't it say in the dossier that he lost his wife recently?

How much can a man take?

He heard the footsteps outside, the excited voices, the elation.

Sweat, breaking out around the collar . . .

A wetting of the lips . . .

The door handle turned. The aide's face appeared.

"Captain Mallory to see you, sir."